# KENDRA

# KENDRA

## COE BOOTH

## SCHOLASTIC INC.

NEW YORK  TORONTO  LONDON  AUCKLAND  SYDNEY

MEXICO CITY  NEW DELHI  HONG KONG  BUENOS AIRES

ISBN-13: 978-0-439-92536-5
ISBN-10: 0-439-92536-3

Copyright © 2008 by Coe Booth

All rights reserved. Published by PUSH, an imprint of Scholastic Inc., *Publishers since 1920*. SCHOLASTIC, PUSH, and associated logos are trademarks and/or registered trademarks of Scholastic Inc.

Library of Congress Cataloging-in-Publication Data Available

Printed in the U.S.A.
First printing, October 2008

The text type was set in Electra
Book design by Steve Scott

# ACKNOWLEDGMENTS

Special thanks to: *My family* (Mom, Lisa, Rashid, Mike, Haadiyah, Micayla, Alyssa, Hamza, Hasan, & Halima) — I couldn't do any of this without y'all!; *Samantha* — thanks for your endless help, especially with this one!; *Denise, Tammy, Mark, & Faith* — how did I get so lucky to have you guys in my life?; *Kathryne Alfred, Daphne Grab, Lisa Graff, Lisa Greenwald, Jenny Han, Caroline Hickey, & Siobhan Vivian* — aka The Longstockings — aka the best writing group ever!; *Leslie Margolis*, for our Monday marathon writing sessions (with mocha frappés and mosquito bites, of course); *Everyone at Scholastic*, for being so incredibly supportive of me; *Maja, Hans, & the boys*, for inviting me to Laurenz Haus. I can't thank you enough for all you've done for me; *Marie Brown* — you're the best agent I could ever want. Thanks for being so wise and so funny at the same time; and *David Levithan* — thank you so much for continuing to believe in me. You're the best!!!

where it was before, patting it into place and smiling at her own reflection.

Watching her, I have no doubt she could do this all day if I let her. It's like time stops when she's looking in the mirror. I sigh real loud. "Can we just go already?"

Adonna looks over at me. "What's with the attitude today?"

I shake my head. "Nothing."

"You know, Kendra, every time you see Renée, you start acting different." She bends down and grabs her book bag fast like I'm rushing her or something. "What did she do this time? And where is she, anyway?"

"She didn't come back with us." I try to keep my voice flat and not let her know how upset I am. Because I thought Renée was coming home, too, and it wasn't 'til we got out there that I realized she wasn't planning on going anywhere. I mean, not one thing in her whole apartment was packed. "She's still interviewing for teaching jobs, and, um, she don't wanna pack up and move 'til she knows where she's gonna be working."

"Whatever," Adonna says.

I hate when she does that. Especially because I know what she's thinking, that Renée could have come home in the meantime, while she waited. And she probably could have. But that's none of Adonna's business.

"I gotta stop at the store," she says. "Unless you got a tampon to give me."

I give her a look like, *Don't be stupid.*

"Oh, I forgot. Your grandmother don't want anything up in there!" She starts laughing. "She still threatening to have you checked by the doctor?"

3

I roll my eyes and walk outta my room in front of her. Yeah, I know Adonna's just being herself, but I'm really getting tired of it.

When I pass the kitchen, Nana calls out, "Bye, girls." She's in there washing the breakfast dishes, but that don't stop her from looking over her shoulder and giving me the once-over. "And, Babe, I want you coming home right after play practice."

I try not to look behind me at Adonna. "Yes, Nana," I say as I open the front door.

"That means *straight* home."

"I know, Nana."

This time I can't help but see Adonna covering her mouth with her hand.

We leave the apartment and Adonna busts out laughing even before I can close the door behind me. "Yes, sir, Massa, sir," she says. "I don't know how you put up with that shit."

I move away from the door and whisper, "What am I supposed to do? I still have to live with her." I wanna add, *At least 'til Renée gets a job offer and decides where we're gonna move,* but I don't wanna bring up Renée's name and get Adonna started again.

Not that I can stop her.

I press the button for the elevator and Adonna leans against the wall. "This is what I wanna know," she says. "Renée graduated. She got her fancy Ph.D., and there's no more degrees for her to get, right? So what kinda excuse is she gonna have now for not wanting you to live with her? 'Cause, knowing her, she's gonna come up with something."

I don't wanna hear this. Not from her. Part of me just wants

4

to tell her to mind her own business, but I can't. Because the other part has the same questions she does.

So instead, I just fold my arms in front of me and say, "I'm not gonna talk about this with you."

"Fine. All I'm saying is, if she wanted to be here, she would have brought her ass home. That's all." She throws her hands up in the air. "I'm done now."

"Good."

"Good."

I roll my eyes again. "Fine."

I hate starting the day like this, fighting with Adonna. But I'm not gonna just take her crap. Not with the mood I'm in.

Things were supposed to be different today. At least that's what I thought yesterday when me and Nana took an early morning train from Penn Station out to Princeton just in time for the big graduation. I was all happy, too, at first, sitting there on one of those folding chairs on that big lawn, watching all those people in their black caps and gowns. And Nana was so proud, bragging about Renée to all the people around us.

And then, afterward, there was some kinda reception across campus for all the Ph.D. graduates and their families. Me and Nana stood around eating the hors d'oeuvres while Renée took pictures with her friends. And I stood there watching her, seeing how happy she was and how everybody wanted to be in a picture with her, and I felt like I was just another person caught up in her glow.

Then, while I was standing there watching her, Renée's classmates and professors kept coming over to me, saying stuff like "I know you must be so proud of your sister" and "Will you

be following your big sister to Princeton one day?" And since I didn't know what I was supposed to say and what I wasn't, I just put on a fake smile and kept my mouth closed.

Because it was the first time I knew for sure I didn't exist when Renée was at college. I was just the little secret she kept in the Bronx. And that hurt.

As for Adonna, I know she don't mean to hurt my feelings when she talks bad about Renée. I know she only wants me to be happy and all that, but she don't understand.

For me to be happy, I need to be with Renée.

# TWO

"That boy is too fine for his own self," Adonna says, coming up behind me at lunch and completely cutting the cafeteria line like nobody else is even there.

I know who she's talking about before I even look over. Nashawn Webb. Again.

He's ahead of us in line, at the cash register, buying some potato chips and a Pepsi. And he's smiling at the cashier, probably charming her the way he does every other girl in the school.

And yeah, he's fine. Only problem is, he knows it.

"He ever say anything about me?" Adonna asks, reaching in front of me for a turkey sandwich in plastic wrap.

I sigh. "How many times do I have to tell you? We just have lockers next to each other. We're not friends or anything." I make myself look away from him. "And everybody in the whole school knows he likes you."

Adonna smiles real big. "Yeah, I know. The only thing is, why does he dress like that? God, what kinda guy would come

out his house in jeans that old? And I'm not gonna say anything about them sneakers. Shit, what's his problem?"

She always says the same thing about him, but today it annoys me. "You ever think he don't have money for new clothes and expensive sneakers?"

"Guys can't be dressing any ol' way, you know that. Now girls, we can get away with some cheap ten-dollar-store clothes sometimes, but guys, they just can't be doing that shit. They gotta be fly. If they ever expect to get a girl like me, they do." She shakes her head. "Like I'm gonna be seen with him."

I don't say anything to her because there's nothing I really can say. That's just the way she is. Instead, I'm back to looking at Nashawn but, you know, trying to act like I'm not, just in case he looks over and sees me.

I gotta say, he does have the right combination. Pretty-boy face and strong, kinda athletic body. And there's nothing wrong with his clothes, in my opinion. He always keeps his jeans and T-shirts nice and clean, and I know he don't have all the newest styles or anything, but what he has looks good to me. On *him*, anyway.

Nashawn looks over in our direction and I lower my eyes. I don't want him thinking I'm checking him out or anything. And the thought of making eye contact with him only makes me feel nervous. Personally, I don't know how girls do it, act all friendly and natural around guys. I don't think I could ever get that comfortable around them. Not any time soon, anyway.

When I look back up, Nashawn isn't looking this way anymore. He's too busy handing money to the cashier. I can't help but wonder if he was looking at me just now. But that thought only lasts a second, 'til reality sets back in and I remember who

I'm standing in line next to. Because I know for a fact that when I'm with Adonna, nobody sees me. The spotlight is always on her.

The line moves a little, and I whisper to Adonna, "What are you gonna do if he asks you out?"

"He is fine, isn't he?"

"Yeah," I say, probably a little too fast. "I guess so."

Nashawn gets his change and starts to walk across the cafeteria, and I turn my attention back to Adonna, who's still watching him. No, matter of fact, she's *staring* at him, smiling. And she has that look in her eyes, too. She wants to get him. And, knowing her, she will.

I pick up a yogurt smoothie and a bottled water. "That all you're gonna eat?" Adonna asks me.

"Yeah, I'm not hungry." I try to keep the attitude outta my voice, but it don't really work. "Why?"

She shakes her head. "Nothing. It's just, all of a sudden you're not eating." Then under her breath, she mumbles, "And we both know who's the cause of that, don't we?"

I keep my mouth closed because I'm not looking to get into a fight with her here in front of all the nosy kids they got at this school.

By the time we finish buying our food, Nashawn's sitting at a table with all the other guys on the baseball team. Adonna gives him one last look, then we go over to the table where they got napkins, straws, and all that stuff. When we have everything we need, Adonna starts to walk over to the table she usually sits at, the one with all her sophomore friends. But I don't move. Just looking at all those loud girls, I know I can't do it. Not today.

I mean, Adonna's friends are funny and everything, always

talking about everybody behind their backs, but I'm not in the mood. If I end up sitting there, I'm not gonna be any fun and Adonna's gonna have to work real hard to get me to be part of the conversation. And she shouldn't need to do that.

Sometimes I sit with this girl Mara that I went to middle school with. Me and her have a lot of classes together and both of us are working on the stage crew for the theater showcase this weekend. Only, most of the time, Mara sits with all those other kids we went to middle school with. Whenever I sit with them, it's like I'm going back in time or something, and I don't wanna go back.

"Come sit with us," Adonna says, like she knows what I'm thinking.

"I don't know," I say. "I think I'm gonna go to the theater and work on the set before practice."

Adonna leans her head to the side and gives me that look she been giving me for a while, like she's analyzing me or something. "You sure you're okay?"

"I'm fine," I tell her. "I just have a lot of work to do, and I'm getting all stressed out."

"It's the freshman/sophomore showcase, not Broadway," she says.

"I know, but I still want it to look good."

"That don't mean you have to work through lunch."

I tried telling her a whole bunch of times that I actually like working on the set and being part of the crew, but she don't get it. For her, the only fun thing about being involved with the theater is actually being on the stage in front of the audience like her friend Tanya is gonna be. Adonna just don't get that being behind

the scenes can be fun, too, and that I don't need to get applause to feel good about what I'm doing.

"C'mon, stay for a little while," she says. "Eat with us, then go."

"No, not today, Adonna. I can drink this in the theater." Then when I see she still has that look on her face, I say, "You don't have to worry about me. I'm okay."

She shakes her head. "You know what I hate? I hate the way you let Renée control your emotions."

I wanna say, *You know what I hate? I hate the way you talk about my mother*, but I don't. I just tell her not to wait for me after school.

Maybe it's not the best thing for me to be by myself. Maybe I should stay around other people that can make me laugh and forget everything. But I just don't have the energy to act all happy. I can't do it today. And, anyway, I do have a lot of work to do on that set.

And yeah, I know Adonna's right. I do let Renée control my emotions. But I don't know why Adonna's always blaming Renée for that. It's not Renée's fault. It's mine.

# THREE

I get back to Bronxwood a little after seven. The book I was trying to read on the bus was boring me even though the main characters were just about to do it. I been waiting so long, more than two hundred pages, for the couple to finally get together, but still, my mind was all over the place and I couldn't even get into it.

While I'm walking past the shopping center, I slip the book into the inside pocket of my book bag so Nana don't see it. She thinks these books are nasty, like that's the only reason I read them. The woman would have a fit if she saw this one, because on the cover they got a girl in booty shorts leaning on the hood of some thug's car, and I don't wanna hear Nana's mouth tonight. Like just because I'm reading these books, any second now I'm gonna start doing what the characters are doing. When she should know by now that I'm not even like that.

I walk down the block toward my building, and now that it's getting close to summer, it's like everybody in the whole projects is outside, hanging out in front of their buildings or leaning

up against cars, talking and having fun. I mean, there's still, like, three more weeks of school, but you wouldn't know it from all the kids running around right now thinking they're already free or something.

I pass by Kenny's Kandy truck and lean into the window. Kenny is sitting inside on a stool, scratching off those stupid lottery tickets he's always wasting his money on. And what Adonna told me this morning is true — he did spend last night cleaning the truck and reorganizing the shelves. Now all the candy and cookies are arranged in neat rows, and the potato chips and Doritos and everything are clipped on hanging wires, which frees up more room for everything else. It looks good in there.

"Busy?" I ask him through the window.

He looks up at me and smiles, "Not too busy for my kid." And he gets up, comes to the window, and gives me a kiss on the cheek. "You be coming home later and later every day."

"The showcase is this weekend. We're trying to finish up the set decorations and practice changing everything between scenes."

"Staying out this late, you must be trying to give your grandmother a stroke or something."

"She's gonna have one no matter what I do."

Kenny raises one eyebrow. "Well, what you doing?"

I try to look sophisticated and mysterious. "A lady has to have her secrets."

"Not no daughter of mine!" he says, and we both laugh.

"You're no fun," I tell him. "I'm trying to be a woman of intrigue."

"You be reading too many books, that's what I think."

13

I smile because he knows me too good.

"You wanna come inside and keep me company for a while?" he asks.

I kinda do, but then I'll get upstairs even later and Nana will have more of a fit. I do feel bad for Kenny, though, sitting out here in the truck all day long by himself. But at least he's his own man now.

It's been about six months since he bought the truck and started his own business. Before that, he had all kinda jobs, but none of them lasted too long. He worked at Taco Bell for about a year, then Stop and Shop for a couple of months. The last job he had was working right here at Bronxwood, at the community center, helping out with the after-school program and the summer day camp. He always been real good with kids, so the job kinda made sense. But the only thing was, he was the oldest guy doing that job. Everybody else was, like, nineteen or twenty. And when there were openings for better jobs there, like assistant director, they kept passing him over. I mean, they never even thought about him.

So when Bruce, this guy that used to own the candy truck, decided to retire, Kenny jumped at the chance to be an *entrepreneur*, which is what he calls himself. But now he gotta pay off a big loan on the truck and try to make a living. I'm just hoping this works out for him because he really needs a break. Not only that, but I want him to find out what he's good at soon because he's gonna be thirty next year and still broke, living with his mom and sister. And he can do better than that.

"I can't stay tonight," I tell him. "I better get upstairs."

"Alright," he says. "And, hey, what's up with Renée? I been looking out for her all day."

Something happens to Kenny whenever he talks about Renée. For a split second his eyes get this dark, kinda faraway look, but then, right away, it's gone. Like he don't wanna let himself go there.

I hate having to break the bad news to him, but he has to know. "She didn't come home with us," I say. "She had to drive up to Boston for an interview tomorrow."

"An interview." He nods his head too many times. "That's good. That's real good. I just thought —"

"Yeah. Me, too." Me and him are both quiet for a few seconds. Then I tell him, "She has another interview at City College on Wednesday, and she said she might spend the night. Maybe."

For a few seconds he still looks kinda sad. Then he smiles and says, "You hear that?"

I stop and listen, but I don't hear anything except the cars on the street and some rap music playing outta somebody's apartment window. "What?"

"Them dogs. Your grandmother done sent the K-9 unit out to track you down!"

I smack him on the arm. "C'mon, she's not that bad!"

"Me and Valerie go way back," he says. "*Way* back. And let me tell you, I know that woman, and she don't play!" He starts laughing, and seeing him like that makes me feel nothing but happy myself.

When he's done snapping on Nana, he hands me two Chick-O-Sticks, my favorite. I give him another kiss, then walk down the path to our building. I don't get to laugh about Nana all that much. Most of the time I don't find her all that funny. But maybe Kenny has the right attitude. I mean, maybe I do take her too

serious. But still, it's easy for him to laugh. I'm the one that has to live with her.

When I get upstairs inside my apartment, the only sound I hear is coming from the TV. Nana is in the living room watching one of those Lifetime movies she always gets into. She's sitting there on the couch, leaning forward, with her mouth all open. Like the movie she's watching is all that great. On the other end of the couch, the blankets and sheets she'd took outta the linen closet for Renée are still there folded up. I wasn't the only one expecting Renée to come home.

I stand in the doorway for a minute, quiet. Whenever I stay after school, this is what I come home to. It's almost like all Nana does is go to work, come home, cook, and watch TV. Her life is more depressing than mine. And she's not even fifty yet.

"I'm home," I say.

"Shhh, girl. You see I'm watching the Abuse Channel." On the TV, a man and woman are doing it on the beach with a blanket covering them. And Nana thinks *I'm* into nasty stuff.

"This woman is a fool," she says, not even looking away from the screen. "She don't know she just married the same man that raped her five years ago."

I can tell it's gonna be one of those nights.

I go into the kitchen and drop my book bag on my chair. Dinner is barbecue chicken, mashed potatoes, and corn. The Monday dinner.

I'm about to go into my room when Nana shouts, "Eat something!"

I suck my teeth real loud and fix myself a plate so I don't have to hear her mouth. I take my plate and sit down at the table, then take out my English notebook because I need to work on this

16

critical lens essay I haven't even started yet. I'm supposed to have it done and typed up before second period tomorrow, which means I'm gonna have to get to school early and use the computer lab.

Of course, Adonna has a perfectly good computer I could use, but I know what Nana's gonna say if I ask to go upstairs to her apartment. She's gonna say I don't need to spend any more time with *that girl*. Even though *that girl* is technically my aunt.

Nana comes into the kitchen at the commercial. At first, she don't say anything. She just looks over my shoulder to see what I'm working on. Always minding my business.

"Why you coming home so late?" she asks, and of course she got that tone in her voice. Like she thinks I'm up to something.

"Practice ran long," I say with my voice flat.

"This late? You sure that's all you were doing?"

"Yes, Nana. I'm sure." She don't know that guys never even look at me.

"Why you need to go every day? Thought you were done designing the set."

"I am. But remember I'm on the stage crew? We're doing a lot of the painting and stuff. And I'm gonna help out backstage during the showcase, too." I tell her all this like it's the first time, not the hundredth. "In between scenes, we're gonna move the set around, and change all the decorations and props and stuff. It's fun."

"A lot of boys on this stage crew?"

"Boys and girls, Nana," I say. She don't need to know there are three boys and only two girls, because she's only gonna start imagining all kinda things. "And no, I'm not doing anything with anybody. Trust me."

She don't say anything, but she makes a *humph* sound under her breath just so I know she really don't believe me. For a couple of seconds, I wait for her to ask me more questions, but they don't come, so I try to go back to concentrating on my essay. But it's hard to think because I can feel her still staring at me.

I look up and ask, "What?" The attitude is there in my voice and I don't even try to hide it.

Nana's face goes from suspicious to surprised. "Girl, don't make me have to —"

I always know when Nana's mad, because she don't finish her sentences. Most of the time, when she starts with that, I just tell her I'm sorry and act all good again. Because most of the time, even when she's getting on my nerves, I still feel bad for her, that she's stuck with me.

But today I'm not telling her I'm sorry for the mood I'm in because I got a right to feel this way, in my opinion. Nana was there yesterday. And even though she wasn't around to hear all that "big sister" stuff, she *was* there when we went back to Renée's apartment and found out Renée had no intention of moving back home any time soon.

And Nana had to notice all those pictures Renée had stuck into the frame of the big mirror over her futon. Pictures of everyone, all her friends from home and school, pictures of her and Nana, and even a picture of herself when she was a baby. But not one picture of me anywhere.

I mean, I tried not to let it bother me, but it did, anyway. And if Nana can't understand that, that's her problem. She's just gonna have to put up with me and my attitude for a while because I'm still upset. I can't hide it.

"Renée call?" I ask.

"No, not today," she says. "But you know she spent the whole day driving up to Boston, right? She's probably tired."

"Still. She could call." I fold my arms in front of me. "Don't take that much energy to say hi to somebody."

"Well, why don't *you* call *her*?"

"Never mind," I say. "If she wants to talk to me, she can pick up the phone."

For some reason, Nana don't break on me. She just says, "How long you going to act like this?"

I shrug. "I'm not sure."

All Nana says to that is, "Eat your dinner. Before it gets cold." Then she goes back to the living room, back to her movie just as the commercials are ending. Perfect timing.

I eat because I don't wanna hear her mouth anymore and that's the only reason. It's real hard being back here in this apartment without Renée when I just knew she was coming home right after graduation. I mean, everything around here is exactly the way it's always been, but still, it feels like something's missing now. Even if it's only in my mind.

# FOUR

The computer lab is kinda full when I get there, even so early in the morning. I sit down and rest my book bag on the floor before I even notice that I'm sitting in the same row as Nashawn, with only one empty seat between us. He looks over at me, smiles, and says hi.

"Hi," I say back. Quick. Then I turn back to my screen, log in, and hope he's not still looking at me.

Me and Nashawn never say more than hi and bye to each other when we're both at our lockers at the same time. And I don't really know all that much about him, except that he's a junior and he's only been at our school for a few months, since March. That, and he's on the baseball team. I mean, it's not like we really have a whole lot to talk about or anything.

I look at my watch. Thirty-five minutes 'til homeroom, which should be long enough even though I don't type all that fast. I just don't wanna show up to English without the essay because that teacher, Mr. Simon, likes to go off on kids when they hand in their work late. Just to embarrass them.

I get started typing, but it's not easy trying to focus when I'm

*for mom*

# ONE

There's nothing really different about today. At least that's what I'm sitting here trying to tell myself. Adonna is late, the way she always is, even though I called her twice already to tell her I'm about to leave her if she don't get down here now. Nana's in the kitchen, probably waiting for me to come outta my room so she can make sure I'm dressed decent for school. Like if she left for work before me, the first thing I'd do is change into the skankiest outfit I could find or something.

Like that's even who I am.

Finally, the bell rings. I hear Nana open the door, and all she says is, "Babe's in her room," like she can't even be bothered to say hi.

By the time Adonna gets down the hall, I'm standing up with my book bag on my shoulder and I can't wait to get outta here.

"You ready?" Adonna asks, like it's not obvious.

"I *been* ready."

She drops her book bag on the floor and I see her looking on

1

my desk, at some of the new house plans I sketched. I know she thinks I'm wasting my time doing them, but she don't say anything. Probably because she can see I'm not in the mood today. Instead, she turns to my full-length mirror and stares at herself like she's ever gonna look anything but perfect. I mean, today she's wearing her tight black jeans and a red cami with these cute little triangle cutouts around the neckline. Nana would never let me leave the apartment wearing something like that.

Adonna turns sideways, looks at her butt, then smiles. "So, Kendra, what time did y'all get back last night?"

"Late," I say. "Almost midnight."

"Oh, so that's why Kenny was standing outside all late, trying to act like he was cleaning his truck, not waiting for *Renée*."

Adonna says *Renée* like she's cursing. She never makes it secret how she feels that Renée broke Kenny's heart and that it's Renée's fault the man still can't get over her.

I'm trying not to let anything get to me today. I mean, I know Adonna's only looking out for her brother. My father. Can't blame her for that. Even if it means disrespecting my mother.

"So how was the graduation, anyway?" Adonna asks, fixing her already perfect hair. She got it relaxed real straight at the Dominican place around the corner and it hangs on her shoulders with just a little curl at the end. "Boring as hell?"

I shrug. "No, it was okay." There's no way I'm gonna tell her about Princeton. Not with how she already feels about Renée.

"Any cute guys there?" She moves a piece of hair out from behind her ear, then fusses with it 'til it lays just right.

"Some," I say. "White guys."

"Nothing wrong with that." Now she puts the hair back

2

sitting so close to Nashawn. It's like, I wish I could change seats or something, just so I can relax, but the place is too packed, and how would that look if I just got up and moved? Like I was trying to get away from him. And anyway, he's probably not even paying me any mind.

After I get only a couple of sentences typed, Nashawn leans across the empty chair and whispers, "You know how to make two columns?"

I look over at him and it's hard to concentrate on what he just said, he looks so good.

"Huh?" I say.

He sits back up straight and points to his screen. "Every time I click here, nothing happens."

I just look at him, his profile, and it's hard to talk. His skin is smooth and perfect, the kinda skin a girl would kill for. Yeah, he's a pretty-boy, but he's not all that pretty. I mean, he still looks strong, too.

I take a deep breath. "Um, I think you have to, uh —" For some reason, I can't talk and think at the same time. "Um, first select all, then click on the column button."

He does what I tell him and smiles when it works. "I already knew how to do that," he says. "I just wanted to make sure *you* knew how."

"Yeah, right," I say. And I can't believe I'm actually talking to him like this, like we're friends or something. Then that thought goes through my head again, that maybe I was right yesterday. Maybe he *was* looking at me in the cafeteria.

A second later he asks, "Where's your friend?" And right away any thought I had that he likes me is gone. All I am is a link to Adonna.

"She's outside, um, talking to Tanya."

"That loud girl?" He shakes his head.

"She's nice," I say.

"Nice and ghetto."

I laugh, and it must be way too loud, because Ms. Ballinger, who runs the computer lab, says, "*Shhh.*" And her *shhh* is louder than my laugh. A couple of kids turn around to look at me, like I'm interrupting them or something.

"Sorry," I say and try to get back to typing, because I'm wasting time. But now Nashawn is sitting there laughing at me. "Be quiet," I whisper.

"Shut your mouth, girl," he says. "Don't try to get me in trouble with you." When I look over at him, he has this little smirk on his face like he's so innocent or something. Add to that the fact that he's typing with two fingers, and now I'm giggling at him.

"What's so funny?" he asks, turning to look at me.

"Nothing," I say, still smiling but trying to hide it.

"You laughing at how I type?"

"You call using two fingers *typing*?"

"See, that's what I don't get about you girls," he says. "Y'all always got something to say. Meanwhile, you're not even paying attention."

I duck down behind my computer and whisper, "What am I not paying attention to?"

He leans close to me again. "I'm using my thumbs, too, on the space bar."

"Thumbs don't count," I tell him.

He shakes his head. "That's another thing — y'all be making up your own rules and changing them whenever you want. Thumbs count. Thumbs always count."

22

I laugh again, and this time Ms. Ballinger screams, "You must either be quiet or leave this computer lab. There are other children here and they would like to get their work done."

"I'm sorry," I say again, and try to get serious. I don't want to disturb the other *children*. I look straight ahead at my computer, but none of the words on the screen make any kinda sense anymore. And now I have this weird feeling in my stomach.

Two minutes later, this guy Darnell comes into the lab, and the second he sees me he smiles and grabs the empty seat between me and Nashawn. "Hey, Kendra," he whispers, acting like he hasn't seen me in a while even though we're both on stage crew and we're together practically every day. "You having a hard time keeping up with your homework, too?"

"Yeah," I whisper back. "The showcase is kinda taking up a lot of time, isn't it?"

"I can't believe they got us doing all this, what? Three weeks before finals?"

"Well, it's gonna be over this weekend."

The words are barely outta my mouth when Ms. Ballinger walks over and stops right by my computer. "Kendra Williamson," she says, slow and angry. "This is the third time I've had to talk to you in the last three minutes."

I wanna ask her, *Why are you only yelling at me?* but instead I lower my head and mumble, "I'm sorry, ma'am."

With my head down I can't see him, but I can hear Nashawn laughing at me again. And I really just wanna throw something at him to get him to stop already.

"This is your last warning," she tells me. "Next time, you'll be asked to leave and you'll be restricted from the computer lab for the rest of the week."

"Yes, ma'am. I understand. Sorry."

Nashawn is still laughing and Ms. Ballinger still says nothing to him. It's not even a little bit fair. Guys get away with everything. It's like teachers don't expect any better from them.

When Ms. Ballinger turns to walk back to her desk, Darnell whispers, "I didn't mean to get you in trouble."

I nod and whisper back, "That's okay."

On the other side of him, Nashawn is typing but still smiling like there's something only he thinks is funny. It's so annoying. Personally, I don't get what Adonna sees in him. Yeah, he's cute. But in my opinion, a guy needs to have more than just a handsome face. A lot more.

# FIVE

Nana's on the phone when I get home from school and I can tell who she's talking to by the way she's sitting. She's at the kitchen table with her legs crossed and her head tilted to the side like she's a young girl or something. And she's smiling, making herself look more her age than like the old lady she been turning into lately.

"Yeah, I heard you were looking for me," she says into the phone. "John told me as soon as I got back from lunch. But when I went over to your department, you weren't at your desk."

I know she's talking to Clyde, this guy that works with her at Verizon. They been in the same office for a while, but all of a sudden he been checking her out, like he just noticed she worked there or something.

I met him a couple of weeks ago. He don't live that far from here, and sometimes he calls in the morning and asks her if she wants a ride to work, and he even drives her home whenever he don't do overtime. But they never go out or anything, except maybe to lunch together. At least as far as I know.

The thing about Clyde is that he don't give up. He calls her all the time, and I can tell he's probably asking her out. But she always turns him down. Real nice. Probably so she can stay home and babysit me, like if she turns her back for a second, I'm gonna turn into the biggest ho out here. I swear it's like Nana's okay being alone and miserable just so long as I'm alone and miserable right along with her. And pretty soon Clyde's gonna see that and stop calling, just like the last couple of guys did.

I step into the kitchen, and the first thing I wanna know is if Nana's heard from Renée and if there's any way possible she left Boston right after her interview and is coming home tonight. But I know what Nana's gonna say if I even think about inter- rupting her phone call. So instead, I wave hello to her and she waves back without stopping her conversation.

On the stove are leftovers from last night, and I'm just not feeling it again even though I am kinda hungry. I skipped lunch again and worked in the theater. I spent the whole forty-five minutes painting framed pictures on the back wall of the living room set so the characters in the play would look more like real people with family and stuff. I even made some of the pictures look old-fashioned, like from back in the day. I'm not the best artist in the world, especially when it comes to drawing people. I'm way better designing houses and creating floor plans. But from the audience, I think my hanging pictures are gonna look kinda real. Hopefully.

Since Nana isn't paying me any mind, I just grab some grapes off the table and take them with me down the hall to my room. Give her some privacy and let her talk to the man with- out me hanging around. I don't have too much homework, mostly just stuff to read. And I got a math quiz tomorrow, but algebra isn't all that hard and I can probably do alright even if I don't study.

Renée wouldn't understand that. If she was home she would be like, "Study. Get an A," and all that. Nana told me Renée was like that her whole life, and that one time in fourth or fifth grade, she came home from school crying because she got a 99 on a test, like she couldn't forgive herself for missing that one point. Nana kept telling her that she was proud of her, but it didn't matter, because Renée wasn't proud of herself.

I know Renée's probably not all that proud of me, either. My grades are decent, but every time Nana sends Renée a copy of my report card, Renée never even mentions it when she calls home. She probably thinks I can do better, and I can if I really wanna. Last marking period my average was 83, and it could have been better if my grade wasn't so bad in bio. But I'm passing everything, which is more than Adonna can say. She's probably gonna have to go to summer school for geometry if she don't start studying.

About twenty minutes later, while I'm sitting on my bed picking on the grapes and trying to finish the boring chapter for world history, the phone rings and Nana comes down the hall and opens my door without even knocking. She never knocks, but I don't have the energy to get mad anymore. If I bring it up, all she's gonna say is it's her apartment and she pays the bills. She don't understand why anybody would expect to have privacy in their own home.

"Here," she says, coming over to my bed and handing me the cordless. I know it's Adonna because Nana never says her name and because, really, nobody else ever calls me.

"Thanks," I tell her. I'm holding the phone and I'm waiting for her to leave, but she don't move. So, because I can't just leave Adonna hanging, I put the phone to my ear and say hello.

"Kendra, what happened to you?" Adonna asks me right away. "You never came to lunch."

"Oh, I wasn't all that hungry." I'm staring at Nana, who's looking like she's trying to figure out what we're talking about. "And, um, I wanted to get some work done on the set, you know, so it can be finished before the dress rehearsal on Thursday. Hold on." I cover the mouthpiece with my hand. "What?" I ask Nana.

"Nothing. I just —"

*You just wanna be nosy*, I actually think about saying, but I know that's only gonna set her off.

Nana stands there for another few seconds, then shakes her head and walks outta my room. I get up and close the door behind her fast, before she gets a chance to change her mind.

"I'm back," I tell Adonna and go back over to my bed. I grab the grapes I still got left, push my books over to the wall, and pick up my small hardcover sketchbook. Then I take my pencil and try to get comfortable because, most of the time, Adonna can talk forever, especially when she starts talking about other people. I start sketching a house, starting with the plans for the first floor.

"I'm just saying," she goes on, not missing a beat, "you had me standing around waiting for you and shit. Then that girl Giselle with the moustache, she said she saw you going into the theater. What's up with you, anyway?"

"Nothing." On the page I draw dark lines between what's gonna be the living room and the dining room.

28

"That's all you got to say, 'nothing'?"

"Yeah — I mean, why should I go to lunch when I'm not even hungry? I had breakfast, and I knew as soon as I got home, there was gonna be a big dinner waiting for me. And Kenny gave me some candy last night, so I picked on that at lunch." Really, I don't know why I'm even explaining any of this to Adonna.

"Well, you could have let someone know you weren't coming," Adonna says. "I was standing there, looking all stupid."

"Sorry." I know she probably wants me to say more, but what? I don't even know what I'm apologizing for. For not wanting to go to lunch? For wanting to do something I actually like doing for a change?

"I didn't have anyone to help me jump the line," she says, giggling a little. And I know what she's trying to do, change the subject, keep everything light. "Anyway," she keeps going, "you missed the funniest thing in the cafeteria today. You know that guy with the pleather jacket? Raymond whatshisname. He was wearing these tacky jeans with white piping, and he was walking around and he didn't know that a long piece of white string was hanging outta his fly. Everybody was elbowing everybody else and laughing at him, and by the time he noticed, all the guys were calling him Tampon."

I laugh and shade in the area that's gonna be the back deck.

"Kendra, that shit was so funny. He sat down and tried to pull the string off, but he couldn't, so he got up, got one of those plastic knives, and tried again. It took so long and everybody was laughing, even Ms. Griffin, but she was trying not to let anybody see."

I laugh again. "Okay, you're right. I do always miss the good stuff."

"I know. I try to tell you to stay with me because shit like that always happens when I'm around."

That's definitely true. But I don't think she just happens to be around that kinda thing. I think she actually *attracts* the craziness to her.

"So," she goes on, "did Nashawn say anything about me at the lockers today?"

I drop the pencil on my bed. Most of the time when she asks me this, I just tell her no real fast because he don't ever talk about her, but now I'm not sure what to say. I don't know if I should bring up that me and him were in the computer lab at the same time this morning, because that's just gonna lead to a whole bunch of questions. And, knowing Adonna, it's never gonna end.

"Um, no," I tell her. And it *is* kinda true, too. I didn't even see him at the lockers today. I mean, yeah, when we were in the computer lab, he did ask me where she was, but I don't know if he was really looking for her or anything. It seemed more like he was just surprised me and her weren't together.

"Oh," she says. "I was just wondering. I saw him at lunch and I think he was looking over at my table, but he still never talks to me. You think he's shy?"

"I don't know. Probably." All of a sudden I feel kinda guilty for not telling her, but now it's too late. If I say anything now, it's gonna sound like I was hiding it from her. And I don't want her thinking I'm going after Nashawn. I definitely don't need that kinda drama in my life.

"Kendra, you okay?"

"Yeah, fine," I tell her. "Just trying to study, why?"

"You're acting, I don't know, kinda weird."

30

"Adonna, I don't know what you're talking about."

"You're hardly even saying anything."

"I'm *listening* to you."

"Okay, whatever." She does one of her long sighs.

"What do you want me to say?"

"Nothing. Screw it."

In the background, on her end, I can hear Kenny's voice. He probably just finished parking the truck and bringing all the refrigerated and frozen food back upstairs. It's a whole process every night. He even got a second refrigerator in Grandma's apartment just to keep all that stuff in. The rest of the food stays locked up in the truck, and so far nobody around here broke into it or anything. I hear Kenny saying, "How you gonna drink one of my Sprites when you ain't ask me?"

"Hold on, Kendra," Adonna says. "God, Kenny, it's only one little can."

"Adonna, you better pay up!" Kenny yells.

By then the phone is completely away from Adonna's face and, even though I can't really understand what she's saying, I can hear the attitude in her voice. I pick up my pencil again and draw the parallel lines for the staircase.

The next thing I can make out clearly on the phone is Kenny yelling, "Yo, Ma! You better come talk to your daughter 'cause I'm gonna hurt her if she keeps on touching my stuff!"

I'm really not in the mood for one of their stupid fights.

Finally, Kenny comes on the phone. "Babe?"

"Hi," I say. "What's going on with you two?"

"Look, Babe." He's real mad and not trying to hide it. "Your friend is gonna get her butt kicked, I swear. That girl needs to start showing me some respect, you know what I'm saying?"

31

In the background, Grandma and Adonna are arguing now, their voices getting louder and louder.

"Kenny," I say, "can you just tell Adonna I'll see her in the morning?"

"Alright," he says, but I can tell he's not even thinking about me. His mind is deep in the fight with his sister. Over a stupid can of Sprite.

I click off the phone and lay there for a couple of minutes, finishing the grapes and trying not to let myself think too much about Kenny and Adonna.

I close my sketchbook and go out to the kitchen. The TV in the living room is actually off for a change and Nana is sitting at the kitchen table eating, not putting her plate on a dinner tray to eat in front of some Lifetime movie.

I put the phone back on the base to charge and, without her even telling me to, I make myself a plate.

"Did Renée call?" I ask.

"She called me at work this afternoon and told me her interview went real good. She thinks they're going to make her an offer, but she still got that second interview at City College tomorrow and she *knows* they want her."

I put just enough vegetables on my plate that I won't have to hear Nana's mouth. "Is she coming home tonight?" I ask.

"No, she said the college paid for her to have the hotel room tonight, too, so she's going to take them up on it. And she don't like driving at night."

I sit down next to her. "What did she say about tomorrow? Is she gonna spend the night here?"

"Yeah, she said something about meeting some friends in the city for dinner, and she'll be here after that."

"Oh," I say. I know it don't make sense, but I was kinda hoping Renée was gonna get here tonight instead of tomorrow, just so we could have some extra time together. Because I know she's gonna leave early on Thursday to start driving down to Maryland and I think she said she was gonna stay there all weekend for her friend's graduation party or something.

We eat for a little while, quiet. Then Nana says all proud and everything, "I knew Renée was going to be in high demand. Every college that got any sense is going to want her, a smart girl like that."

"I know. I can't wait to hear what she's gonna decide." It's kinda hard not knowing what's gonna happen next, where Renée is gonna work and where we're gonna live. It's hard having to just wait like this.

"So, Nana," I say when I'm finished eating practically everything on my plate. "Are you gonna invite Clyde over? 'Cause he seems like a real nice guy."

"He is," she says, and there's a tiny little smile on her face that she can't hide. But then she sighs all heavy. "But you know how I feel about having men in and out of here."

"I know, but I'm not all that little anymore."

She looks at me for a few seconds. "I can see that." Her voice sounds more tired than it usually does. "But, Babe, you're at that age now. You need someone looking after you, not thinking about no man."

And there it is again, her big fear. That I'm gonna do what Renée did, go and get pregnant at fourteen. "You don't have to worry about me, Nana," I tell her. "I'm good."

"We'll see," she says, and she looks at me for a split second, but it's not me she's seeing. She never sees me anymore. It's like she's always looking into the future or something, at how she thinks I'm gonna turn out.

I been seeing that look ever since my birthday in December. It was like, all of a sudden, I was in danger or something and I needed her protection. Her *overprotection*. Nothing ever happened to make her think this way. The only thing I did was turn fourteen.

Sometimes I think Nana looks at me like I'm her second chance to get it right. Because I know for a fact she feels like she messed up with Renée. And no matter what, she's not about to let the same thing happen with me.

# SIX

After school the next day, the stage crew gets together for the last time before dress rehearsal tomorrow. It's not an official play practice. It's really just for us to do finishing touches on the set and work out any problems we might have now, before the first show on Friday.

Even though it's a lot of work, the funny thing is, no matter how tired I am from school all day, the second I come into the theater, everything changes and I have energy all of a sudden. It's like I just had three cups of coffee or something. I love being here, smelling the wood and the paint, and hearing the hammering and the drilling. Not that there's all that much hammering and drilling going on now. I mean, the set is just about done and it looks nice, too. And the best part about it is, I'm the one that designed it.

Well, I came up with the sketches, anyway, in my theater design class. My teacher, Mr. Melendez, told us about the showcase and how it's a chance for us to get some experience in the theater. Our school's big musical is in March, but mostly only juniors and seniors get to have anything to do with it. So the school came up with this freshman/sophomore showcase, which is basically six really short plays, no singing or dancing.

All of us in our theater design class had to come up with a set that could work for the showcase, with all six settings. It was one of our class projects that we got a grade on, and Mr. Melendez said he was gonna actually use the most functional set. Everything about theater design is how *functional* it is. Yeah, it has to look good and be creative and everything, but if the actors are gonna break their neck standing on it, or if a beam or something is too low and someone trips and gets hurt, it don't really matter how pretty it is.

So I kept my design simple. Really, I thought it was *too* simple, but Mr. Melendez thought it was good, and he picked it to be the one they used for the play. I mean, all I did was sketch this weird huge triangle kinda merry-go-round thing. Each side has a "floor" that can hold furniture and props and stuff, and there are hooks on the wall that we can hang different backdrops from.

When one side is facing the audience, the other two sides are behind the curtain, and that's when we have to get to work making a three-sided set into six separate settings. Like, we have to change the apartment setting into the subway car setting. And the classroom gets turned into the beach. And the bus stop is the restaurant, too. So behind the scenes, we change all the background art and furniture and props, and then, when the scene is over and the stage is dark, all we have to do is spin the set and lock it into place.

For me, I'm just happy they used my design. After it was picked, my whole class, which is only eight of us, had to work as a team to get this thing done. Mr. Melendez helped a lot with the technical stuff. He had us make sure all the dimensions and measurements were gonna work and all that, and then we had to create the blueprint on the computer with this special program architects use.

Once we had the blueprints, our class work was done. But no way was I gonna stop there. I wanted to help build the set and work on the showcase. So I joined the crew. It was hard work and it took up a lot of time, but I have to admit, it was kinda fun, too, seeing the whole thing go from just an idea in my sketch pad to a realistic-looking set.

But the best part about this is finding out that I really like being on the crew and hanging out with everybody after school. For the first time since I came to this school, I feel like I found the kinda people I like to be around. Not that Adonna's friends aren't fun, because they are, but they're fun in a different way, and whenever I'm around them it's like I have to think if I'm saying the right thing or doing the right thing. Adonna never has to think about those things, probably. She fits in with them perfect. But me, I'd rather be right here.

Today is busier than usual because we're all under pressure to finish, but that don't stop the guys from acting like guys. Like, I'm standing on a ladder painting the top of the set blue and Darnell comes by and holds the ladder for me, which is real nice considering I didn't even ask him to. So I look down real careful and tell him thanks.

He smiles up at me, but before he can even say anything, this other guy on the crew, Trevor, yells out, "He's just checking out your ass, Kendra!"

I swear, I almost fall off the ladder from what he says, like it's something I never thought of. Even though I *am* wearing this smock over my clothes that ties in the back and basically covers everything except my butt.

But I know Darnell's not like that. He's too nice a guy.

"Be quiet, Trevor!" I shout, looking right at him and trying to balance myself at the same time. "That's your own dirty mind talking!"

When I look down at Darnell, he's not saying anything. But he's like that. Kinda quiet. But still, I hope he wasn't actually doing what Trevor said he was.

Me and Mara are the only two girls on the crew, and I kinda like that. It's, like, the first time I'm getting to spend time with guys in a while because Nana never lets me hang out with them at Bronxwood. I mean, when I was real little, it was okay to ride my scooter with boys and hang out in the community center with them. But by the time I was, like, twelve, she started watching me with boys more and more and giving me a hard time when I wanted to be around them. It got to be more of a problem than it was worth.

This is probably why I don't know how to act around guys. Well, the cute ones, anyway.

Not that Darnell, Trevor, and Gregg, the stage manager, aren't cute. They're okay. But we're just friends, all of us on the crew. It's not like any of us is trying to hook up with each other or anything.

I put a coat of paint on the part of the set that faces the audience, and I come down from the ladder, real glad Darnell is there to keep it steady for me. When I get to the ground, Darnell says, "Don't listen to him, Kendra. I wasn't —"

"I know," I say. "Don't worry about it."

He lowers his head a little bit and says, "Okay. Good."

**38**

I hold up my hands, which are splattered with blue paint. "I'll be right back."

As I'm walking to the janitor's closet, I see Mara working on adding more details to the bus stop backdrop. She painted a garbage can and more trash on the ground *near* the can than inside, and she even added some pigeons. "That looks nice," I say, walking up behind her.

She smiles. "You think so?"

"Definitely. You're good with that kinda thing."

"So are you. I saw the pictures you painted on the living room backdrop."

"Yeah, but they're not as good as this. I wish I was a real artist like you."

"You are," she says. "You're just better at seeing the big picture than the little stuff. I see all those houses you're sketching all the time. Those are great."

"Thanks," I say, but I'm not so sure they're great. I mean, they're okay. But it don't make me an artist, not like the real artists here.

The school I go to is called the North Bronx High School for Arts and Communications, so to get in here you have to pick a concentration and you have to get approved. Adonna wanted me to be in advertising and marketing like her, but they always have to make presentations and stuff and I'm not good at that kinda thing.

I wanted to be in the fine arts concentration so I could learn how to paint and sculpt. But Mr. Melendez was one of the teachers looking at our portfolios on the evaluation day, and when he saw that 95 percent of what I was drawing was houses and floor plans, he said he thought I should be in the design concentration instead. He told me, "You don't want to sit around painting bowls of fruit all day, do you?"

And I mumbled "no," because that's what he wanted to hear. And, really, it didn't matter to me which program I got into, as long as I got to go to the same school as Adonna. Because if I didn't get into this school, I would have ended up at the high school near Bronxwood and it's way worse than this school. *And* I would have been all alone.

While I'm washing my hands in the janitor's closet, I'm thinking about what Mara said, that I'm better at seeing the big picture. And it's kinda true, too. In my drawings, I'm always trying to make my houses look nice and pretty. Perfect. But I never even think about the little details that could make them look more realistic. Probably because they're never gonna be real, anyway.

When my hands are dry, I look at my watch and it's almost six o'clock. As much as I like being here with the crew, today is one day I can't wait to get home, because Renée's gonna be there. I mean, I know she's supposed to be going to dinner with some of her friends, but maybe if I'm lucky they ate early or the dinner got canceled or something. Because I need time with her, too. She's only gonna be here one night. And that's really not enough.

# SEVEN

Renée don't get home 'til almost eleven o'clock. And I kinda wanna jump up outta bed as soon as I hear the door open, but I don't want her to know I was waiting up for her. At the same time, I don't want her to just go to sleep right away and not know I'm still awake.

So I wait about two minutes. Then I push aside the book I'm reading, which is really kinda nasty, put my slippers on, and go down the hall.

Renée's in the living room taking off her shoes when I get out there. Even though the hall light is on, the living room is still dark. Before I can say anything, she looks over and sees me, and she jumps a little. "Babe, oh, you scared me."

"Sorry, I was just —"

"What are you still doing up? Don't you have school tomorrow?"

"Yeah. I was reading a book, um, for English."

That gets a smile outta her. "Good." She kicks her shoes aside and starts unbuttoning her blouse. Then she sighs. "Oh, I am *so* exhausted. Today was way too long." She takes off her blouse and throws it over the chair. "I had to drive in from Boston, then go to City for the second round of interviews and a teaching demonstration. The whole thing was grueling."

"Where'd you go after that?"

"Nowhere special," she says. "When I was finally done at City, I met up with some Princeton girls and we all went out to dinner at this Italian place on the Upper West Side. Then we ended up at some club in the meat-packing district." She shakes her head. "It was wall-to-wall people. You know, the after-work crowd. The men were working the most tired pickup lines I've ever heard. They were pitiful!" She's smiling while she talks, so it probably wasn't all that bad. It sounds a lot better than sitting at home with Nana, which is what I did after play practice, while waiting for Renée to get home.

Renée takes off her pants and throws them on the chair with her blouse. "I'm standing at the bar with my friend Jennifer, and this guy comes up and tells her that she's the most beautiful woman he's ever seen and how he just *has* to know her name. Then when Jennifer tells him she has a boyfriend, he turns to me, without missing a beat, and gives me the exact same line of bullshit." She laughs. "I was standing right there the whole time. He didn't think I heard him the first time?"

I laugh, too. "Was he at least cute?"

She flashes me an *oh, please* look. "There were a few decent guys, but as soon as they walked into the club, all the desperate girls would practically pounce on them. As a sociologist, I have to tell you, the whole club scene is fascinating. It's like watching the mating rituals on an alien planet, trying to make sense of everything."

Renée opens her little suitcase and takes out a T-shirt. I stand there and watch her take off her bra and let it fall to the floor, then pull the T-shirt on over her head. Every time I see her change I notice the same thing, that her body is almost, like, the total opposite of mine. She's all curvy and sexy and everything. Me, I can only hope to maybe grow into a body like that one day. But it's not looking good for me. Not any time soon, anyway.

As Renée lays out the sheet and blanket that's been waiting for her on the couch, I lean against the wall, not really knowing what to say to keep her talking. I do know I wanna sit down on the couch with her and talk for a while, but I don't wanna keep her up too long when she just said how tired she is.

The real truth is, I wanna tell her that I wasn't really reading anything for school, that I waited up just to talk to her. But I don't wanna come off sounding all needy. I just wanna say *something*. I mean, it's like I'm looking at the person I been waiting for my whole life. And here she is, right in front of me, and I don't even know how to get to her.

"Do you know where you're gonna work yet?" I ask, slowly going over to where she's sitting on the couch.

"Not yet," she says, moving over to make room for me next to her, "but I think City College will make me an offer real soon. They were talking to me as if I were already part of their faculty. I'll probably get an offer from Boston, too, but I think I'd prefer City. I love it here in New York, and a lot of my friends from college and grad school live here. And Gerard lives in Jersey, not that a woman should choose a job because of a man — don't ever do that, Babe — but it would be great teaching and doing research here in the city, and getting to spend time with Gerard. Because long-distance relationships never work."

43

I swallow hard.

Renée goes on. "Gerard and I have already spent too much time apart with me studying and writing all the time. For once, I actually have time for the man."

I met Gerard a few times, and he was there at the graduation on Sunday, but all I know about him is he's a New Jersey cop and he's even cuter than all of Renée's other boyfriends, who were pretty cute, too. He's tall, dark, and muscular, with a real deep voice and everything. Other than that, I don't know a thing about him.

"Well," I say, "I hope you get the job at City."

"I will."

Something tells me not to get too excited for her because nothing is official yet. It feels weird, too, because whatever decision she makes is gonna change my life, too. If she ends up teaching in Boston, I'm gonna have to move and change schools and friends and everything. But if she chooses City College, maybe she can stay home for a while, at least 'til she saves up enough money to get us our own apartment.

"There are so many great things about being in the city again," she says, and I'm not really sure if she's talking to me or just thinking out loud. "Of course, there are the museums and theaters, but the restaurants and clubs — I missed all of that, by doing this whole school thing for so long. I just want to have some fun for a while, you know?"

"Uh-huh," I say, swallowing again.

I don't know why, but I'm kinda surprised by what she's saying. I mean, Renée is young and I can understand that she wants to have fun, but I don't need her to be going to clubs and everything. I need her to be my mother now.

Me and Renée stay up and talk for a little while longer, 'til she starts yawning and I decide to let her get some sleep. Especially after she tells me she's gonna leave in the morning to drive down to Maryland. Then, before I go, she says she's not even sure if she's coming back here after Maryland or going straight back to Princeton, which she still calls "home."

And to me, it's sad. It's like she just got here and she's already leaving. So fast. I don't know why, but I thought once she graduated, she would be ready to kinda stay in one place. I mean, at least for more than one day.

# EIGHT

It's Luther's voice that wakes me up. The music is coming from the living room, reminding me that Renée is really home, that last night actually happened.

It's only a little before seven, but when I finally get outta bed and down the hall, I see that Renée is already dressed, wearing jeans and a white T-shirt. She's packing and singing loud and off key, *"You are my shinin' star, my guiding light, my love fantasy."*

I lean against the wall watching and can't help but smile because she loves to sing but can't do it to save her life. I mean, she's really, really bad. But she don't hear herself like the rest of us hear her.

The living room is a mess. Renée's suitcase is open on the floor by the coffee table, but most of her clothes are still thrown over the back of the chair. And the blanket and sheets she used are rolled up at the end of the couch, while the pillow is on the floor.

Not that there's anything new about this. The living room

always gets this way when she comes to visit because, really, there isn't any room for her in this apartment anymore. I sleep in her old bedroom, in the same bed she used to sleep in. As a matter of fact, practically everything in that room used to be hers. The dresser, the desk, everything.

Hopefully, when Renée finally gets us a place of our own, I can get some new stuff, kinda like what Adonna got a couple of months ago, a whole new bedroom set. I mean, assuming Renée is gonna make that kinda money at her new job.

The kettle whistles and Renée rushes past me with a quick "Hey, Babe" and goes into the kitchen to turn it off. I follow her in there and see her pouring water into a bowl of oatmeal. I can smell my favorite flavor, apples and cinnamon, and for half a second I think she's making the oatmeal for me, but then she stirs it and licks the spoon, and I know it's hers. She takes the bowl to the table, sits down, and starts eating. When I go over to the counter, all that's left in the variety pack are the plain ones.

I don't say anything to her. I just close the box and put it back in the cabinet. Nana will eat the plain ones because she can't stand to waste anything. I need to get dressed, but Nana's still in the bathroom. So while I'm waiting, I go into the refrigerator and grab a yogurt. I sit down next to Renée and, while I'm still licking the inside of the foil lid, she starts questioning me about my grades. Before I know what's going on, she's lecturing me.

"It's almost the end of the school year, Babe," she tells me, like I don't know that. "You need to put all your energy into bringing your average up. I know you think it doesn't matter, but colleges look at all your grades, even from freshman year. And don't you want to get into a good college?"

Like I'm even thinking about college already.

"My grades are fine," I say.

"Fine isn't good enough." Her face is so serious, too. "Anybody can get fine grades. Don't you want to stand out?"

I shrug. "Yeah, I guess so."

Renée kinda shakes her head, and inside I feel like I'm missing something. Like me and her aren't really talking to each other. Not like we were last night. And I don't know what changed.

By the time I get dressed, Renée is in the living room on her cell phone, laughing with somebody about something that happened last night. Nana is in the kitchen having breakfast. I go in there and pour myself a glass of apple juice, the little Renée left in the container, and remind Nana that I'm gonna be late again today because of dress rehearsal.

"Dress rehearsal?" she asks, and I can't believe it, but she actually looks all confused like she don't know what I'm talking about. Never mind the fact that I told her about this at least ten times already. Sometimes I don't know about her. I kinda think she's too young to have Alzheimer's, so probably she's just forgetting things on purpose.

But it's kinda annoying, especially so early in the morning. "You know," I say real slow, trying to be patient with her. "We're running through the whole show with costumes and set changes and all that. Then we're having a pizza party. Remember?"

She sighs, aggravated. "How much is this going to cost me?"

"Nothing. Kenny gave me the money last week. It was only five dollars, anyway."

I know Nana would like to complain about Kenny more than she already does. But she can't. Everybody knows Kenny don't have a dime to his name, and still, every couple of weeks, there he is at our door with his little envelope for Nana. It's never a whole lot of money, only about thirty or forty dollars at the most, but even she knows it's the best he can do.

"Okay," Nana says. "Just don't be out there to all hours of the night." She drinks a little of her green tea and makes the face she does after every single sip. It's crazy. The only reason she even started drinking the stuff is because Oprah said it's supposed to be good for you. After she heard that, she started making herself drink it twice a day, every day. Morning and night. Funny thing is, she always has a big slice of Entenmann's pecan danish with it, so it's probably not gonna improve her health all that much, in my opinion.

"I'm gonna come home as soon as it's over," I tell her in that goody-goody way that always makes Adonna laugh. "*Straight* home."

Renée comes back into the kitchen to throw something in the garbage, still singing along with Luther.

"I better get going," Nana says, finishing her tea and making the face again. She gets up from the table and puts her dishes in the sink. "Clyde is picking me up and I don't need to have that man out there waiting for me."

Me and Renée glance at each other and then look away fast so we don't bust out laughing. And it's a lot of work, too. Nana rushes outta the kitchen and opens the hall closet. Then, like two seconds later, she has her jacket on and she's flying outta there. "Bye, girls," she says, then don't even wait for us to say bye back.

That's when me and Renée lose it. We're laughing for a good two minutes. Hard, too. "I can't believe that's my mother," she says. "The woman's acting like a teenager, all giddy and shit."

"I know," I say. "It's weird."

"You think she's in love with this guy?"

I shrug. "I don't know. You ever seen her in love before?"

Renée shakes her head. "Never." Then her cell phone rings again and she runs into the living room to get it.

I throw away the apple juice container. Then, while I wait for Adonna, I wash all the dishes so I won't have to hear Nana's mouth when I get home from play practice, talking about how could I leave the sink full of dishes when I know how hard we have it, trying to keep Ms. Grier's roaches to her own apartment?

Nana don't have use for women who keep a nasty house.

Finally, the bell rings, and I dry my hands and go to open the door. Adonna practically runs in. "We have to leave right now," she says, talking all fast. "For real."

"Why? What's going on?"

"Somebody said — and I'm not sure, but I have to be there — somebody said that that girl Broomhilda —"

"*Brunilda*," I say.

"Whatever. Someone said she's gonna get jumped in front of the school today." Adonna's smiling, all excited.

"Why are you so happy? She's only a freshman. What did she ever do to you?"

"Nothing. But you seen her." Adonna starts walking down

the hall shaking her butt like a crazy person. "C'mon, tell me this ain't how she walks."

I know she's just trying to get me to laugh, but I'm not gonna let her. Not about something like this.

"I'm just saying," Adonna says, like she's trying to explain. "You see how she dresses and all that makeup she be wearing. When she first came to our school, I thought she was a tranny or something 'cause she wore so much foundation. Not only that, but she's always in designer this and designer that." She shakes her head. "I'm not jealous or nothing, but you know, what's her problem? Why she gotta be like that?"

I shrug. "Let me get my book bag."

Adonna follows me down the hall to my room. "Hurry up."

I don't wanna go see anybody get jumped. I saw enough of that back in middle school. And no matter how cute Brunilda thinks she is, nobody deserves to have that happen to them. Actually I kinda feel sorry for the girl. She's probably only dressing that way because she thinks it's gonna help her get attention or make friends, only to find that everybody is hating on her behind her back.

It wasn't all that long ago I was walking into that school for the first time myself, and I probably would have made all the same stupid mistakes Brunilda's making if I didn't have Adonna telling me how to dress, who to be friends with, and how to act all the time. Last summer she took one look at me and said, "No way am I gonna let you start high school at *my* school looking like that, not if you're gonna be hanging around *me*."

And yeah, I knew I was a mess, even at the time. According to Adonna, I was too miserable, I had bad clothes, and, maybe worse of all in her opinion, I was too skinny. She said to me,

"Look, you don't have to have a booty like mine or nothing, but you gotta get some meat on you. High school guys like an ass that's gonna make them break their neck checking you out, you know what I mean? And you gotta smile sometime, have fun, and stop dressing like you don't care."

All summer she worked on me, trying to get me excited about high school and guys and dating. Like Nana was ever gonna let me date anybody. Like I was even ready for all that. Me and Adonna shopped together and ate a lot. I guess it was kinda fun, even though I know deep down I'm still the same girl with the same problems. Underneath.

But the good thing is, I'm almost done with freshman year and nobody hates me, so she probably did something right. I mean, I'm not the one about to get my butt kicked in front of the whole school.

I pick up my book bag off the floor. "Alright," I say. "I'm ready." But, of course, Adonna is looking in the mirror, smiling. I clear my throat, and that gets her to turn away from herself.

Unfortunately, she ends up looking at me. "Your grandmother's not here for a change. Why don't you put on something nice? You got so many clothes you never wear."

I got on jeans and a tan Old Navy T-shirt. The kinda stuff I wear every day. "I don't know," I tell her. "I don't wanna get all dressed up when I have stage crew later."

But she's already going through my dresser. She opens the top drawer, which is now empty, and says, "What the fuck?"

I try to act like it's nothing. "Oh, I thought Renée would need a drawer, but —" Right away I feel stupid for bringing up her name.

Adonna shakes her head but don't say anything, which is a good thing. She just opens the next drawer down and goes through my tops. "Ooh, wear this." She holds up my white wrap blouse, the one she practically made me buy when we went shopping together last month. I don't even know why I bought it, because I know for a fact Nana would never let me leave here in something like that.

Actually, I can't wear most of the stuff I got that day. I mean, Adonna even talked me into buying a couple of thongs, but I stuffed them way in the back of my underwear drawer so Nana wouldn't find them. I figured I wouldn't get to wear any of the things I bought 'til I was living with Renée.

But now I pull the blouse on without really thinking about it and tie the strings at the side. Then I look at myself in the mirror. The top is fitted and hugs my body, and the neckline is kinda low, too. Nana would go off if she saw me. She would say I was trying to be grown. Like that's a bad thing.

"I don't know," I say, still looking at myself. "You don't think I look kinda *stank?*"

"Your titties ain't big enough for you to look stank," Adonna says, grabbing my wrist and practically pulling me outta the room. "C'mon — we're gonna be late for the fight."

"Wait," I say, slowing her down a little bit. "Can't I at least cut the price tag off first? God!"

When we go back down the hall, Renée's zipping up her suitcase. "You girls leaving right now?"

I nod. "Yeah, why?"

"I'll walk out with you."

Next to me, Adonna breathes out heavily. "We're kinda in a rush."

"So am I," Renée says, putting on a cute pale blue blazer. Then she turns off the CD player and grabs her suitcase and bag.

In the elevator I'm all uncomfortable. In a way I wish it was just me and Renée in there, but then I feel kinda guilty for wishing that. I mean, I don't wanna push Adonna away every time Renée's around. Adonna's the one that's always been there for me when Renée was too busy, and I can't just forget about that.

So for a few floors, we're quiet, 'til the elevator stops on nine and this lady, Ms. Jenkins, gets on. When she sees Renée, she gives her a big hug like she hasn't seen her in years instead of months. She's looking at Renée all proud, saying stuff like, "Girl, I can't believe it! A Ph.D! See, that's the kind of thing they need to put in the papers instead of all that negative stuff they write about kids from the projects." She goes on and on for the whole rest of the way down. Meanwhile, Adonna has her arms folded in front of her, all attitude, looking as bored as she's ever gonna get.

Outside, there's a line at Kenny's Kandy, working people trying to get their coffee and buttered rolls before they get to the train. But as we get closer to the truck, Kenny leans his head outta the window and yells, "I *know* that ain't Renée!"

She hurries up ahead of us and gets to the truck about a second after Kenny opens the back door and jumps out onto the street. Renée sets her suitcase down and Kenny grabs her up in a big hug, smiling like a crazy man.

"Damn, you look good, girl," he tells her, letting her go just enough to check her out. "Look at you."

Renée laughs. "You're looking alright yourself."

54

Kenny grabs her in another hug. "You don't know," he says. "I been waiting to see you."

Me and Adonna look at each other, and it's like I can read her mind. And she's right. This is embarrassing, at least for Kenny. And all the people that are waiting in line at the truck are watching him make a fool outta himself, like he's some little boy that can't get over his first love.

"Um, Kenny," I say, when we're close enough to him, "don't forget, you have customers waiting."

But he's not listening to me. *At all.* His attention is 100 percent on Renée, and his arms are still around her.

Adonna grabs my wrist. "Let's go, Kendra."

"Okay," I say, and let her lead me away. I wanna say bye to Renée, but I don't wanna interrupt them. I know how much Kenny wanted to see her.

When we get to the corner, I look back and see Renée already walking across the street to her car, looking all sophisticated with her blazer and her suitcase. And then there's Kenny, still standing there in the street.

Watching her.

# NINE

The second we get off the bus, it's obvious the fight is still going on. We can't see what's happening or anything, but about a block away from the school, a whole crowd of kids is standing around cheering and acting wild. I can't help feeling like I been dropped in the middle of a riot or something. The crowd is so big, it spills out into the street, blocking the cars that are trying to get by. And between the screaming kids and the car horns, the whole scene is just crazy.

"I can't see shit," Adonna says, taking ahold of my wrist for the second time. Again I let her pull me where she wants me to go, weaving through little openings in between kids 'til we're close enough to the action to see it all.

And what I see isn't even a little bit right. Two big-boned girls got Brunilda up against the metal gate of the car repair shop on the corner. One girl has Brunilda's long hair wrapped around her fist and she's yanking her head back. Hard. The other girl is punching her everywhere: the head, the chest, the stomach. And Brunilda is just screaming and crying. More than anything else, what gets me is the look on her face. She's more than just scared. She's in shock.

Not one person does anything to help her, either. Most of the kids are laughing, acting like they're watching a TV show, not a real girl getting beat up for no reason. The whole scene is making me sick.

I break away from Adonna's grip, but she don't even notice, she's so wrapped up in what's going on. All I know is I'm getting away from here. I mean, there's no way I can do anything to stop the fight myself with all these kids out here, not if I don't wanna end up like Brunilda. But that don't mean I have to stand around and watch it, either.

A few minutes after I make my way back through the crowd, the police finally get there. But I don't hang around to see what's gonna happen. I just walk away with my head down. I mean, maybe I was just stupid, but I thought a school like this would be different than a lot of other schools around here, like since these kids are artists and stuff, they wouldn't be fighting on the street. But I was wrong.

When I get inside the school, through the metal detectors, the halls are practically empty even though it's ten minutes before homeroom. As I'm passing by the theater, Darnell comes out. And he has dried blue paint all over his hands just like I had yesterday.

"Hey, Kendra," he says, smiling at me. "You look nice today."

I almost forgot what I was wearing. "Oh, thanks," I say. Then, because I don't know what else to say, I ask him why he's still working on the set when we were supposed to be done yesterday.

"I had to add another coat of paint to some of the edges, and I wanted everything to be dry and ready before dress." He looks up and down the hallway. "Where's everybody? Fire drill or something?"

"Fight," I tell him. "Two girls against one."

"That don't sound like a fight to me. More like a crime." He looks as upset about it as me.

I nod. "Yeah, I know. But tell that to half the school. They're out there like there's nothing wrong with it."

Me and Darnell walk down the hall together. When we get close to the boys' bathroom, he tells me he has to get the rest of the paint off of him before homeroom. So we wave bye to each other and I head upstairs.

I get to my locker, open it, and I swear there are now more of Adonna's things in there than mine. She got two pairs of shoes and all kinda magazines over the bottom. It's like she left me just enough room for my own books. Nice of her.

I kneel down and dig around for my stupid history book for first period, probably buried under Adonna's junk. I'm pulling all of her stuff onto the floor when I hear, "You sure one locker is enough for you?"

I look up and it's Nashawn staring down at me with his arms folded like he's a teacher or something.

He clears his throat. "Young lady," he says, "don't you know you're creating a safety hazard in the hallway?" He tries to make his voice all deep and grown-sounding. "Not only that, but you're messing with a very handsome man's ability to get to his own locker."

*"Handsome? Man?"* I ask, looking around. "Where?"

"You trying to be funny?" He smiles down at me. "Good thing my ego is so strong."

"And big," I mumble loud enough for him to hear.

He laughs and goes, "Everything about me is big."

I don't look up, but before I can even think about what I'm doing, I say, "That's not what I heard."

Nashawn don't stop laughing. "Okay, good one. I like that." He steps over the books to get to his locker. "But tell all your friends, that's big, too."

I laugh, but it comes out real nervous-sounding and — I don't know why — I get that weird feeling in my stomach again and just start throwing Adonna's stuff back into my locker. I put the books I need in my bag and all of a sudden I just wanna get away from him fast. Before I can, he asks, "Where's Adonna? Second time this week I'm seeing you without your Siamese twin."

I slam my locker closed. "She's um —" I don't wanna tell him Adonna's out there, probably standing around with her friends still laughing about that girl getting jumped. I mean, he's one of the only kids inside the school, not out there acting stupid, and I don't wanna say something that's gonna make Adonna look bad to him. "Um, I don't know," I tell him. "Probably in her homeroom already."

"Or doing her hair somewhere," he says. "That girl loves to look good."

I don't know what to say to that, so I just go, "Well, bye."

"See ya." He's not even paying any attention to me all of a sudden, probably because he's too busy thinking about Adonna now.

So I head down the hall to my class, still feeling kinda strange. And embarrassed. I can't believe I just said all those things to him. The only good thing is, now at least when Adonna asks me, I can tell her that Nashawn said he likes her hair and that she always looks good. She's gonna love hearing that.

# TEN

At lunch, I'm sitting with Adonna, Tanya, and these two juniors, Malcolm and Craig. And since there are guys around, Adonna isn't losing her mind over Nashawn, at least not out loud.

When me and her were in line to buy our food, I told her what he said about her, and she was all like, "He said that *about my hair*? What about the rest of me?"

"He said you look good, not just your hair," I tell her. Sometimes Adonna gets like that. She don't hear what people are telling her.

"I know I look good," she said. "But why is he telling *you* that and not *me*?"

This wasn't the reaction I was expecting. Probably shouldn't have even said anything to her.

And now Tanya is sitting here talking about how she don't know if she's gonna be able to cry on cue this afternoon during dress rehearsal, but she knows for a fact that she's gonna be able to do it for the real showcase when the audience is there. In all the rehearsals so far, she just been fake crying, and it's really

61

funny, but I know I'm not the only one that's nervous that she's not gonna be able to do it when it counts.

Adonna's isn't even listening to her. She's watching Nashawn and trying to be cool about it. He's all the way on the other side of the cafeteria, so she's doing this thing where she puts her head down like she's looking at her food, but her eyes aren't on her sandwich at all. Then every couple of minutes she says something like "Uh-huh," so it looks like she's paying attention.

I unwrap my Devil Dogs, take one out, and lick the cream that's squeezed out from the sides. Outta the corner of my eye I can see Malcolm and Craig staring at me with their mouths open and everything.

"Adonna, yo, your cousin is wild," Craig says.

"A freak," Malcolm adds, and before I even know what's going on, the two of them are high-fiving each other.

"*What?*" I ask.

Malcolm shakes his head. "Girl, the way you was licking that thing, shit, that was like a porno movie."

Now it's my mouth that's open. "What are you *talking* about?" But a second later I get it. "*Ill.* Y'all are nasty!"

"Word," Craig says, and they're back to high-fiving like two idiots.

I drop the Devil Dog on my tray. Last time I'll eat one of those in front of boys like them. The worst thing is, for a while I have to sit there and hear them laugh some more. At me. Even Tanya's laughing with them.

Then, all late, Adonna finally says something. "She's my niece, not my cousin." I wait for her to say more, anything, but that's it. She's back to watching Nashawn.

"Thanks for your help," I tell her even though she's not hardly listening. "Appreciate it."

For the first time in a while, I look over to the table where Mara and the rest of them from middle school are sitting. And I wish I was over there with them. At least I wouldn't have to put up with these guys. It's too bad the set is finished, because now I can't even use that as an excuse to get away from here.

Then I feel someone tap me on my shoulder and I look up. It's Darnell standing there with his lunch tray in his hands.

"Kendra, you're gonna be there for dress rehearsal, right?" he asks.

"Yeah," I say, a little bit confused because I thought I already told him this when I saw him this morning. "I'm gonna be there." I try to think of something more to say so he's not just standing there, especially with the whole table looking at him, but I can't think of anything.

"Oh, okay," he says. "I'll see you later, then, alright?"

"Yeah, okay."

He stands there for a few more seconds, then walks over to a table in the corner where Gregg and some of the other guys from the stage crew are sitting, eating tacos. *Tacos!* I can't believe it. Those guys are probably gonna have the whole back-stage area *lit up* at dress rehearsal this afternon.

Now Adonna comes to life. She leans over to me and says, "Kendra, I have to know — what's the matter with you?"

"What now?" No matter what I do, Adonna's quick to tell me why it's wrong.

"He wanted to sit with us, stupid."

"No, he didn't."

Adonna sighs. "Look, let me break it down for you, okay?

**63**

He's a guy. You're a girl." She's talking to me like I'm slow or something. "He. Likes. You."

Tanya busts out laughing. "Kendra, he's been checking you out ever since play practice began. The whole cast can see it. You ever notice that every time you need someone to lift something or help you out with something, he's always the first person there?"

"Yeah, but —"

"He's into you," Adonna says.

Malcolm nods. "For real, girl. That boy got it bad."

"*Stupid* bad," Craig says.

I shake my head, but really, I can't be all that sure they're wrong. Maybe he does kinda like me. He *is* always friendly to me and all that. But why can't it just be that he's a nice guy?

Adonna's still looking over at Darnell. "You know, he's not bad-looking," she says. "He could be an okay first boyfriend for you. Short-term, I mean. You don't wanna be stuck with *him* all summer."

"Stop looking at him," I whisper. "He's gonna think we're talking about him."

"We are."

"Still."

But Adonna don't stop looking and I can't do anything to make her, so I just kinda give up. I'm not sure how I feel about Darnell possibly liking me. Only thing I'm hoping is that he didn't see me with that Devil Dog just now and get any ideas. Because that's the last thing I need.

✳    ✳    ✳

64

Of course, all through dress rehearsal I'm feeling weird around Darnell, even though I'm still not even sure if he likes me or not. For the past month, I been hanging out backstage with him, even spending time in the storage room and the tiny little janitor's closet together, and I just never thought anything about it. I mean, I never got any vibes or anything. Not once.

But Adonna's probably not wrong about this. I mean, if there's one thing she's good at, and there's really only one thing she *is* good at, it's guys.

So all during the rehearsal, I try to act real natural around Darnell, like nothing changed. We have so much to do, there's hardly time to think about anything else. In between the short plays, the whole set has to be rotated and the furniture and decorations have to be changed. And everything has to be done fast, and real quiet.

Well, it's *supposed* to be real quiet. But a couple of times, Mr. Melendez has to come backstage to tell us that we're not working quiet enough, that we can be heard from the audience. Not only that, but the crew screws up a few times, like we put the furniture in the wrong place in one play and we forget to change the backdrop for another, which actually turns out really funny because it looks like the characters are having a beach party right in the middle of a classroom.

The actors don't let it stop them, though. I have to give them that. The only time they break character is when this guy Kevin trips over a chair on the set and slides about two feet across the stage. First they check to see if he's okay, and then when they find out he is, they bust out laughing, which is what all of us on the crew are already doing backstage. We can't help it.

The pizza gets delivered right in the middle of the last play, so I set up a table backstage and start laying it out, along with paper plates and napkins for everybody. I'm just about finished when I hear the side door open and see Nashawn poking his head in from the hall.

"Oh, good. It's you," he says when he sees me. He's still in his baseball uniform from practice. "I hear y'all got pizza up in here."

I put my hands on my hips and try to act tough. "You know, we had to *pay* for this."

"C'mon," he says. He looks around like he's making sure nobody else is back there. "You can't spare a couple slices for a hardworking first baseman?"

I just look at him and don't say anything.

He flashes a bit of a smirk. "I made two RBIs."

"Whatever that means."

"C'mon. Hook me up. I'm starving."

For some reason, I can't say no to him, and not only because he's begging. It's hard to explain, really, but before I know it, I'm sneaking two slices of pizza onto a plate for him. Just like that. And when I get close enough to him to hand him the food, I can smell him. He smells like he been playing real hard, all sweaty and musky, and not in a bad way, either.

"Here," I say, and right then from the stage I hear Tanya screaming, "I hate you! I hate you!" It's like she's really into her character now. I just hope she's crying for real this time.

Nashawn's eyes get wider for a second. "What the — ?"

"One of the plays," I tell him.

"Sounds a little crazy to me," he says.

"It is." I hand him a napkin. "Oh, yeah, make sure you

don't tell anybody where you got the pizza from, because nobody else is getting any."

"I hear you," he says, smiling all big. "You know, you're one of the nicest girls at this school."

"Yeah, right."

"For real. I'm serious. Any girl who feeds me like this, man, what can I say?"

"Just say good-bye. Before I get caught."

"I owe you," he says, but he's already looking away, pushing up against the door to get out. And then he's gone. Just like that.

I pull the door closed as quiet as I can and go back to the table to finish getting everything ready before the rehearsal is over. And I don't know why, but now I'm the one that's smiling all big.

# ELEVEN

"I know you didn't leave out this house dressed like that," Nana says in that sharp, angry voice of hers. I only been in the apartment, like, three seconds and that's the first thing she has to say to me.

I look down at my clothes like I don't know what she's talking about.

"What? It's jeans and a blouse." But even as I'm saying it, I can't believe I forgot to take a jacket to school with me, so I could cover myself up before I came home.

Nana's standing in the hall right in front of me, practically blocking me from moving. She's holding a dinner tray with a plate of spaghetti, and she's staring at me hard. "I don't know why you think it's okay to dress like *that girl* upstairs."

"I *don't* think that."

"And don't think I don't know about them thongs you got in your dresser, and who got you to buy them."

"I never even wore them," I say. "And why are you going through my stuff?"

"Don't try to change the subject, because that shit don't work with me, pardon my French. If you think I'm going to watch *that girl* change you into some kind of —"

"That girl has a name, you know." I roll my eyes before I can stop myself.

"Look, you keep on dressing like her and talking back to me, you're really going to have me thinking you're up to something. I'm *this close* to taking you to the doctor and —"

"I know, I know. You're gonna have me checked, right?" I shrug. "Well, go ahead."

"Girl, don't get fresh with me today." She's still looking at me like she *knows* I did something wrong. "Don't forget your place."

"Sorry," I say, looking down at the floor.

"And I don't understand how that school expects you kids to pass your classes when they got you out to all hours. On a school night, too. This shit don't make no kind of sense to me, pardon my French. Like y'all don't got nothing better to do but work like slaves all night."

She heads into the living room, still mumbling to herself. She can have a whole conversation like that. Actually, I'm convinced another person would only get in her way. I stand there near the front door, watching her set the tray on the coffee table and settle into her favorite spot on the couch, right across from the TV. And all I feel is stupid for letting Adonna talk me into wearing this top. Like Nana wasn't gonna find out about it. I mean, it's easy for Adonna to come up with these ideas, but she don't have to be here when Nana's going off on me all the time. It's just not worth it.

The phone rings and I run into the kitchen to get it, since

Nana's too busy flipping channels now. Like she's not just gonna end up watching one of her stupid *women's* movies. I pick up the phone and say hello, hoping it's Renée. And it is.

"Hey, Babe," she says. "Tell Nana I made it here in one piece."

"Okay, I will."

"And tell her — drum roll, please — I was offered the position at City College and I accepted!"

I laugh. "Congratulations!"

"Thanks. It's so weird. Me, a real college professor."

"What are the students gonna call you, Professor Williamson?"

"No way!" She's laughing, too. "They're gonna have to call me *Doctor* Williamson. You know how hard I had to work for that title?"

"I know," I say, because, even though I don't really know how hard it was, I *do* know how long it took. She been away practically my whole life. I barely even remember anything before she went away to school.

"Babe, I have to do this faculty development thing at City next week if I want to start teaching this summer, which I need to do. So I'm coming home on Sunday."

"Oh, that's good," I say, "because Sunday's the last show. It's at five and the tickets are seven dollars. You can buy one at the door, so don't worry about that."

"Okay."

"Good," I say, and try to think of something else to talk to her about.

But by now Nana's in the kitchen, right by my side. "That Renée?" she asks, reaching for the phone.

I try not to get an attitude with her again, but it's kinda hard because I don't know why she can't let me talk to Renée without interrupting us. Still, Renée is coming back home and that's all I care about right now. So I tell Renée to hold on, that Nana wants to talk to her.

"I'll see you Sunday, then," she says.

"Okay, bye." I hand the phone to Nana. "Here."

I stand there and listen to their conversation for a while, but all I'm hearing is, "Yeah . . . well, finally . . . that's a good salary . . . uh-huh, yeah . . . 'bout time you're going to be making some money."

My mind isn't really on what they're talking about, though. All I'm thinking is that Renée is coming home and this time it's for good. I mean, moving to Boston could have been good, to start somewhere new and all that. But there's nothing better than staying right here with Kenny and Adonna and, yeah, even Nana.

Because I know everything is gonna get better once Renée gets back. *Easier.* Like Renée can be the one to tell me what I can wear to school and who I can talk to and what time I have to be home. Nana won't have to do all that. And then maybe, hopefully, things between me and Nana won't have to be so bad anymore.

# TWELVE

"You're in a good mood today," Adonna tells me the next morning on the bus. Then under her breath she adds, "About time."

I just smile a little bit, but I'm not gonna tell her anything about Renée coming back on Sunday. She'll find out for herself in a couple of days.

Me and her are squished together in the only two seats that were free, on the long row in the back. The lady next to me got hips for days, and she's taking up her seat and at least half of mine, probably more. And she's wearing this perfume that wouldn't smell bad if she had on a normal amount, but it's like she washed her clothes in it or something. I have to breathe through my mouth just to keep from choking.

"Well, what's up?" Adonna asks me. "Darnell ask you out or what?"

"Not everybody needs a man to feel good," I say. "I'm just happy about the showcase. That's all."

"I can't wait, either." Adonna shakes her head, smiling. "It's gonna be so funny seeing Tanya up there crying."

"Well, we *all* been waiting for that. But she says she can do it, so keep your fingers crossed."

"Oh, I *know* she can do it," Adonna says, and leans in close to me with her eyes kinda lit up, the way she does when she got something good to tell me. "You should have been there last year, because she was going out with these two guys, right? One at school and one from her building. Stupid, I know. Anyway, one day she got busted by the home boyfriend, coming outta the school, *holding hands* with the other guy. And you should have seen the acting she was doing. Man, she was good, crying and telling both of them she was sorry and wrong and confused and all that. And telling both of them she needed time to think and make a decision and all that kinda bullshit. Her crying looked real, too. And I, like, came over and took her away from the whole scene, and all the way down the street she was still crying like a fucking baby 'til we turned the corner and then, like, in a split second, she was smiling, acting all, like, it wasn't a big deal what just happened. I couldn't believe it." Adonna starts laughing. "Then the next day, she was back with both guys, telling both of them that *he* was the one she picked. It was hilarious!"

Adonna really *does* have the best stories.

The bus makes one of those big, lopsided turns and the big-hipped woman practically lands in my lap. And it hurts. A lot. "Sorry," she says over and over, but she can't really get off me 'til the bus finishes making the turn, and by then my leg is just about numb.

Now not only am I gonna be sore, I'm probably gonna be *smelling* like her all day, too.

After a while, when the bus stops at a red light and I'm not being crushed anymore, Adonna asks me who else I invited to the show tonight.

"Just you guys," I say.

"I still can't believe you got me, my mother, and *Kenny* sitting together."

"I bought all the tickets at the same time. I didn't know you wanted to sit by yourself."

Adonna rolls her eyes at me, but I can tell she's just being stupid. "Well, I'm gonna act like I don't know them," she says. "Especially Kenny."

I ignore what she's saying. "I'm just glad I have someone coming every day. You guys today, Nana tomorrow, and Sunday —" I cut myself off and close my eyes for a second, thinking about how dumb I can be sometimes.

When I open my eyes, Adonna is staring at me, so I look away, outta the window as the bus passes the bank, the Jamaican patty shop, and the sneaker store that just opened up. I know she's gonna start something, but I really don't want me and her to end up in a fight today.

"Don't tell me *Renée*'s coming in to see the show," she says with that attitude of hers.

I shrug. "Maybe."

"She moving back to the Bronx?"

"I didn't say that."

"What does she think, that sitting through your show is gonna make up for missing the last ten years of your life?"

I don't know why, but when she says stuff like that, I feel this weird pain in my chest. I wanna tell Adonna to shut up and mind her business, but I don't. Of course.

I just go back to looking out the window, like none of it bothers me.

The showcase starts at seven that night, and by then Adonna is the last person I'm thinking about. Everything is just happening too fast. All of us on the crew are working hard and staying focused, and we don't have time to think about anything except trying not to screw up. Even the guys are doing what they're supposed to, not joking around like they used to do at rehearsals.

Before I know it, it's all over and all five of us are backstage sitting on the floor drinking water, trying to catch our breath. Darnell is sitting right next to me, both of us leaning up against the wall. We're close, but not that close, and I still can't tell if he likes me or not because he's not really doing anything. I mean, yeah, he did sit next to me when he could have sat anywhere, but I'm not sure if it means anything. So I try not to think about it.

On the stage, Mr. Melendez is on the microphone, calling the actors out for their curtain call, and they're getting a lot of applause. It's like it's never gonna end. Then I hear him say, "The freshman/sophomore showcase is also an opportunity for our design students to show off their talents. And don't you agree, this set is truly remarkable."

More applause. Which feels good for, like, a second.

'Til I hear him say, "So let me introduce our set designers, who have been doing double duty as the stage crew."

"Oh, no," I mumble under my breath.

Mara's eyes open wider, too. "He doesn't want us to —"

I nod and slowly stand up as Mr. Melendez says, "So come on out, set designers!"

As he reads off our names, we go out onto the stage as a group and take a bow. I'm practically shaking because this is definitely *not* where I wanted to be. The whole theater is packed and all those people are staring at us, and I don't know how the actors do it because I'm definitely more comfortable behind the scenes. I mean, I can't get off that stage fast enough!

After everything is over, and we're done cleaning up backstage and putting everything away, I meet up with Grandma, Kenny, and Adonna in the lobby, which is still pretty crowded with people hanging around. It's so good to see Grandma outta Bronxwood because ever since she had hip replacement last year, it's like she hardly ever leaves her apartment, much less the building. Well, except to go to her doctors' appointments and that kinda thing. I mean, I know walking around is hard for her now, but still, it's kinda sad that she's just home all the time. So I'm real glad she came out just to see my set.

"You did good, Babe," she says, giving me a half hug with one thick arm around me and the other holding her cane. "That was one of the best shows I ever seen, and that set was something else."

Over her shoulder I see Adonna roll her eyes up to the ceiling. "I'll be back," she says, and heads over to where Tanya is standing with her mom and little brothers.

When Grandma finally lets go of me, Kenny is the next one to give me a hug. "You got talent," he says. "I knew it. Just remember who bought you your first coloring book. Me."

I laugh. "I'll remember that when I'm rich and famous!"

"You better," he says.

I get to go back to Adonna's apartment after the play because that morning Nana told me she had something to do after work. So I actually have to eat the dinner Grandma made. Not that's it's bad. It's just that Grandma don't understand how to put together a normal meal. Not really. Like, she made lasagna, fried fish, and no kinda vegetable or anything. If Nana was here, she would say eating like this is why Grandma is so fat, which is really, really mean, but probably true.

I *feel* fat after dinner. Me and Adonna practically stumble down the hall to her room, and when we get there, we plop down on her bed like two rocks. We lay next to each other on our backs, giggling about how much we ate.

"I love your room," I say, even though I tell her the same thing every time I'm here.

"Me, too," she says. And she really does, because when I look over at her, she's looking around and smiling like she's seeing everything for the first time.

A couple of months ago, she got a whole new bedroom set, and everything is shiny wood, a full-size bed, a desk, and a big dresser with a gigantic mirror, which Adonna just loves.

But what she *really* loves about her new bedroom set is the fact that her father's the one that bought it for her.

I turn on my side to face her. "Did you talk to him?"

"Yeah," she says. "I talked to him Wednesday and he said he was gonna try and make it here tomorrow, if he had the time. But then he called my mom yesterday and told her to tell me he couldn't make it." She sighs. "I mean, you would think he would wanna see the way my room looks now, you know, after all the money he spent, but —" She shrugs.

"Is he busy with work or something?"

"That's what he says, that he has to work on the weekends. But that don't really explain why he can't come around during the week, like after school. He only lives, what, an hour away? An hour and a half, at the most." She shakes her head. I don't get him."

Most of the time Adonna don't let anybody see this side of her. Nobody except me. Because she can get hurt just as easy as me, but she's just better at hiding it when she needs to. "He'll come by," I say, even though he hasn't been around for almost a year already. "Or maybe you can visit him over the summer, *if* you're not stuck in summer school."

She turns over toward me and pinches me real hard on my arm. "Don't even say that!"

"Ow!" I say, starting to laugh. "You're torturing me!" But I'm too full to get away from her.

But at least she's laughing now, too. "Take it back!" she yells.

"Ow! Okay, okay! I take it back!" Because, really, it *does* hurt, what she's doing to me. "You're not going to summer school! Definitely not!"

She lets me go and we go back to laying there, me rubbing my arm. I mean, the things I have to go through just to cheer her up. The suffering!

But the truth is, sometimes I feel guilty when it comes to her father. I mean, yeah, her father bought her this whole new bedroom set and I know mine could never afford to do that

78

for me, not anytime soon. But at least I get to *see* Kenny all the time.

I can't say the same thing about Renée, though.

A little while later, Adonna changes the subject, which is probably a good thing because she needs to get her mind off her father, and I need to get mine off Renée. "When does Nana want you to come home?" she asks.

"She said to stay here 'til she comes for me."

Adonna's eyes get that look in them. "For real? Are you serious? You know what this means, right?" Before I can even think to open my mouth, she answers her own question. "It means, she's probably downstairs with that dude right now and she don't want you walking in on them, you know, doing the nasty!"

"*Ill!*" I cover my mouth with my hands. "Don't even say that!"

"How much you wanna bet?"

"No, not Nana. No." I'm shaking my head. "Both of them are, like, *old*!" But it does kinda make sense. I have to admit that.

And that's when Adonna comes up with her plan, to sneak downstairs to my apartment to see if anything's going on in there.

"And what are we supposed to say if she catches us?" I ask.

Adonna gets off the bed and pulls me up by the arm. "We'll tell her you came down here to get that book I lent you."

"But I'm still reading it."

"Who cares?" she says, dragging me outta the room with her.

While Adonna heads for the door, I go into the living room to get the key outta my book bag. In the kitchen I hear Kenny say to Grandma, "All I need is a hundred, just 'til next week. C'mon, Ma."

I try not to react, which is hard considering how much Kenny sounds like a little kid. And he's borrowing money from a woman that's living on disability checks, which is hardly any money at all. I shake my head, grab my key, and leave. I'm not gonna think about any of that now, not when me and Adonna are on a mission.

All the way downstairs in the elevator, we're giggling and excited about what we're about to find out. I'm just hoping, if they *are* there doing it, they're not in the living room, because I don't wanna have to open the door and actually *see* them or anything.

When we get to the door we have to get quiet, which takes awhile for us. Finally, I stick the key in the lock, look over at Adonna one last time, and open the door real slow and silent. We tiptoe inside and I don't see them in the living room or the kitchen. Thank God.

"Maybe they're in the bedroom," Adonna says. She don't even notice my disgusted face. "C'mon."

We go down the hall without making a sound. But Nana's bedroom door is open and the room is empty.

"Shit," Adonna says, disappointed.

"I know," I say. "I thought we were gonna see *something*." I shrug. "Oh, well."

We walk back toward the front door, and I'm feeling like our spy mission was a big waste of time. But as we pass the kitchen and take a closer look, I see something. Evidence.

There are *two* mugs in the sink and a jar of instant coffee on the counter.

"You were right," I tell Adonna. "Clyde *was* here."

Adonna giggles. "They probably went back to his place for a little *something something*!"

I head straight for the front door, covering my ears with my hands. "I'm not listening to you," I tell her, then start humming to drown out any other nasty thing she might wanna say.

But, yeah, at the same time I know she's right. I mean, *coffee?* Things are probably getting serious between Nana and Clyde.

*He got Nana to turn her back on Oprah.*

# THIRTEEN

All through the play the next night, I can feel Darnell watching me. We're backstage working together and everything is getting done, but as soon as we get a second to breathe, there he is looking at me again.

At the end of the showcase, after we take our bows and we're finished cleaning up, he comes up behind me and says, "Kendra, I, um . . ."

"Yeah?" I smile a little, trying to let him know it's okay to say what's on his mind.

He looks me in the eye, then looks down. Then he tries again to look me in the eye. "I, I just wanna say, um, you're gonna be here tomorrow, right?"

"Yeah," I say. "Last show. Wouldn't miss it."

"Okay," he says. "I'll see you tomorrow." And he walks away.

I stand there for a second, now knowing that he wanted to ask me out. Definitely. And I'm thinking how hard it must be for guys to always have to do the asking. I mean, look at Adonna. She been checking out Nashawn for months now, and he still hasn't worked up the courage to ask her out. Or even talk to her.

Mara comes over to tell me bye, but I don't want her to leave too fast.

"Come meet my grandmother and her, um, friend," I say to her, thinking it can't hurt for Nana to meet Mara and see that I'm hanging out with a nice girl when I'm at play practice.

Nana and Clyde are still in the theater, sitting down in their seats and talking like they don't even notice that hardly anybody is still there. Yesterday, when she came to pick me up from Adonna's apartment around eleven o'clock, she never said where she was all that time. And I never asked. Because I already knew.

Nana and Clyde get up from their seats when they see me and Mara coming over to them. After I introduce them to Mara, Clyde goes on and on about what a great job we did on the set. "What I mean is, it looked professional," he says, and the way he talks is like every word is important or something. "That's what we kept saying to each other, that it looked like something professionals did. Right, Valerie?"

"It *was* beautiful," she says like she really means it.

"Thanks," I say. "Now you see why it took us so long."

She nods and there's even a little smile on her face. It's like she's being extra nice since she's with Clyde.

"I was telling your grandmother that we should go out to dinner," Clyde says. "And why don't you come with us, Mara?"

Me and Mara look at each other and I nod. "Yeah, please, can you?"

Mara whips out her cell phone. "Let me call my mom, but I'm sure she'll say okay."

An hour later we're all at IHOP and we're actually having a good time.

"Kendra, Mara," Clyde says, turning his attention away from Nana for a second. "You know, you girls could probably go to college for that — what do you call it?"

"Set design," Mara says. "But it was Kendra's design. Mine was rejected." She makes a funny sad face and we all laugh.

"No, but you girls should really think about becoming real set designers, like on Broadway and off-Broadway, because I bet them cats make some decent cash, you know?"

*Cats?*

"My mom wants me to become a teacher," Mara says, "because that's what I wanted to be when I was little, and I still think I'd like it, I guess."

Nana smiles. "When Kendra was little, all she ever talked about was one thing," she says. "She used to walk around talking about, 'When I grow up, I'm going to be a college.' Not a college student or a college professor. No, she wanted to be a college." She laughs, and even her laugh is nicer when Clyde's around. "It was so cute."

"That don't make any sense," I say.

"Well, that's what you wanted to be."

Mara laughs, too. "Weird, Kendra."

The waitress comes over to pour coffee, and after Clyde gets his cup filled, Nana nods at the waitress and gets hers filled, too, and she starts adding cream and sugar like she's really somebody that drinks coffee, which she's not.

Mara leans over and whispers to me, "Come with me to the bathroom."

I nod, and as we get up I see Clyde slip his arm around the

84

back of Nana's chair. I think Mara notices it, too, because we look at each other for a second but don't say anything.

When we get into the bathroom there's only one stall, so Mara goes first, and while she's peeing she asks, "So, is Clyde your grandmother's *boyfriend*?"

"I don't know," I say. "I don't even wanna think about her with a boyfriend. I mean, *I* don't even have a boyfriend yet."

Mara laughs. "Me, neither. But I think she likes him. And he's nice."

"Yeah," I say. "He is."

She flushes the toilet and comes out, and I go in. I'm still kinda embarrassed that I wanted to be a college, whatever that means, but I'm trying not to think about it. Not now.

After we leave IHOP, we drop Mara off at home and make sure she gets into the building safe. Then when we get to Bronxwood, Nana asks Clyde if he wants to come upstairs for another cup of coffee. And, of course, he says yes and parks his car.

Even though this is supposedly Clyde's first time to our apartment, when the elevator reaches our floor, he gets out and already seems to know which way to walk. And then when we're inside and Nana hangs up his jacket, he asks to use the bathroom, and she don't have to tell him where it is.

I'm just watching everything, collecting the evidence. Then I grab the cordless phone off the charger and I'm about to go to my room to call Adonna with all the latest info, not just about Nana and Clyde but about Darnell, too, but the doorbell rings and I have to turn back around to answer the door.

It's Kenny standing there with his envelope.

"How was the play tonight?" he asks, hugging me.

"Good," I say. "Come in."

He walks back into the kitchen with me and, while I put the phone back on the base, I see Kenny hand Nana the envelope.

"Thank you," she tells him, but she don't smile or anything.

Sometimes I wish she would because I know it would make Kenny feel a whole lot better about himself, to know he's kinda helping us out, even a little bit. I mean, right now all I feel is bad for him because he had to borrow money yesterday and now he's trying to act like he can help take care of me when he can't. And at the same time, I really love him for trying. I just wish Nana would show him some love, too.

I walk him out to the elevator.

"When is Renée coming back?" he asks.

I tell him tomorrow, and me and him kinda smile at each other for a while. Then the elevator comes and Kenny gives me another hug. "Good night, Babe."

"Good night."

He gets in the elevator but holds the door open 'til he sees me get back down the hall to my apartment and open the door. Then I wave to him and go inside. I'm kinda worried about him, with the way he still waits for Renée all the time. He's only setting himself up for a big letdown.

Nana and Clyde are still in the kitchen, sitting at the table having coffee and danish. I go in and grab the cordless again, but instead of dialing Adonna, I call Renée's cell phone.

But she don't answer. It goes straight to voice mail. So I leave a message, reminding her when the play starts tomorrow, and telling her that it's the last show. Then I tell Nana and Clyde good night and go to my room so they can spend some time together without me hanging around.

I close the door loud enough so they know they have privacy, and I get undressed in my room. I'm kinda feeling good about everything, the play, hanging out with Mara, even Nana and Clyde. I mean, it's good that she likes him. And soon she won't have to worry about having men in the apartment around me because me and Renée will have our own place. Well, as soon as she saves up the money.

It's not 'til about a half hour later, when I'm already in bed with the light off, that I figure it out. And I don't feel embarrassed anymore because now it makes sense.

When I was little, I wanted to be a college because that's where Renée was all the time.

# FOURTEEN

Sunday. The last show. Backstage, the guys are back to cracking jokes and trying to make me laugh in between scene changes. But I'm too busy waiting for Renée to get there and thinking about the fact that she's still not.

I know I must look like I'm crazy or something, but I really can't help it. Every five minutes I'm checking the audience, peeking out from this spot on the side of the stage and scanning the whole theater, row by row, looking for her face. It's dark, but still, if she was there, I know I would see her.

Then, during the intermission, I'm doing the same thing, like maybe she's there but I didn't see her before. A lot of people are walking around now and it's hard to see everyone. Or maybe she went to the bathroom or she's in the hallway talking on her cell phone or something.

By the time intermission is over, I have to face it. She's not there.

I'm not sure how, but I keep working, just trying to get

through the rest of the showcase. But I can't wait for it to be over now. It's like I'm not even into it anymore.

Then, during the second-to-last play, we're behind the curtain, arranging the furniture and laying out the props for the last play. And, as usual, we're supposed to be doing our jobs real quiet so the audience don't hear us, but then Gregg bumps into the end of the coffee table. Hard. And it makes so much noise, we all bust out laughing and have to run off to the corner by the storage room so the audience won't hear us. We're all covering our mouths but still probably making too much noise, and Gregg's only making us laugh harder by whispering over and over, "It didn't even hurt," because we all know there's no way it didn't hurt.

Then, all of a sudden, Darnell stops laughing and goes, "We still have to finish setting up that scene."

"Oh, shit," Trevor says, and we all take off running back behind the curtain to finish everything before that play is over and the set has to be turned again.

And we do it. Kinda. We put the furniture in place and change the backdrop, then rotate the set right on time. The only thing is, I'm still holding the fake cell phone, which Tanya is gonna need in, like, three minutes.

I'm just staring at it in my hand, frozen, when Darnell comes up behind me, snatches it, and literally slides it across the stage like he's bowling or something. It makes a ton of noise, rattling along the wood 'til it hits the couch and stops. Some people in the audience start laughing, but Tanya and Kevin keep saying their lines like a cell phone comes sliding into their living room all the time, no big deal.

I lean over real close to Darnell and whisper in his ear, "You saved me."

He whispers back, "That's what I'm here for." He smiles, and me and him look at each other in the eyes for, like, a second. Then he looks down at the floor.

It's not 'til the play's over and the actors are taking their curtain calls that I even think about Renée again. Right away I feel that little stab of pain in my chest. It's the same kinda pain I been getting ever since I was a little kid, when Renée would tell me she was gonna come home to see me for my birthday or on Mother's Day or something, then wouldn't show up because she had a paper to write or a test to study for. And I would get all upset. Every time. It's like I would never learn.

Since it's the last show, Mr. Melendez takes extra long with the curtain calls, making sure all of us get to take our bow. I mean, I'm still not all that comfortable in front of the audience, even for the ten seconds I'm out there. The only good thing is being called a set designer for the third day in a row. I could probably get used to that.

After everyone is introduced and the house lights are back up, the cast members practically break their necks running out to the lobby, still in their costumes, just so all their friends and family can congratulate them. Me and the rest of the crew just stand there backstage, shaking our heads. We don't say anything, but it's kinda hard to believe how much attention they need. Like, it's not enough to get people to spend seven dollars to look at you and clap for you, and even give you a standing ovation. No, after all that, they still need more hugs and butt kissing.

Actors.

It takes us about a half hour to put away all the props and clear everything off the set. We don't really *need* to spend that much time, but we're too busy acting stupid, wasting time. Probably everyone is like me, not really wanting it to end. I know I don't wanna go home, if Renée is there or not. I'm not even sure if I want her to be there, not with the mood I'm in now.

Before I leave, I sweep the set while Mara and Trevor put away all the extension cords and stuff. Then, when I bring the broom back to the janitor's closet, Darnell's there and asks me if I'm okay.

"Yeah," I say real fast. "Why?"

"'Cause you look like somebody died or something. And you were kind of, you know, zoned out today."

"No, I'm okay."

"You still coming on Friday, right?"

"Yeah," I say. "You?"

"Yeah."

The crew is getting together after school on Friday to strike the set. Then we're all going to the diner afterward. I already got the okay from Nana, but that's only because she thinks the whole thing's gonna be chaperoned by Mr. Melendez. But it's just gonna be us by ourselves.

"You sure you're alright?" Darnell asks again.

"Yeah." This time I say it kinda quiet because I'm not really sure, now that I think about it. I mean, I don't even know what I'm supposed to think about this. It's getting harder always trying to act like I'm okay when I'm not.

Darnell is looking at me now, like he's worried about me. I give him a weak smile, and after a couple of seconds, he turns around to wash his hands in the big sink. For a second I just stand there watching him, wanting to say something or do something. It's not that I want him to worry about me. I just want him to pay attention to me again.

I stand the broom up in the corner and reach above Darnell to put the dustpan on the shelf over the sink. And I'm not sure why, but when I do, I put my hand on his shoulder to balance myself. My body rubs against his back a little, but he don't even look up. He just keeps washing his hands.

So I leave the janitor's closet without even saying good-bye, and I walk real slow outta the theater. A few people are still hanging around in the lobby, some probably waiting for the actors to finish changing outta their costumes, some looking like they're still there because of the baseball game that was going on in the field.

The game probably just ended, too, because, as I'm walking past the gym, some of the players are coming outta the locker room. And I start walking even slower, trying to see if Nashawn's around. Not that I necessarily wanna run into him or anything. Not really.

A couple of guys come out carrying heavy-looking duffel bags, but no Nashawn. And anyway, I can't walk all that slow without looking like a hard-up girl waiting around to say hi to some guy. What's the point, anyway? It's not like he even really talks to me, well, except when he wants computer help or free pizza. Or when he wants to know where Adonna is.

So I just keep walking toward the front doors, but then, since I'm already miserable, I change my mind and decide to run upstairs to my locker to get my bio book, the one I didn't even bother bringing home on Friday because I knew I wasn't gonna get any work done this weekend.

It's kinda dark upstairs because the only lights that are on are the ones over the exits. I get to my locker and open it, and it looks like Adonna has put even more stuff in there than before. Not only does she have her books and folders and papers, but now she got a denim jacket and an umbrella in there, too. It's crazy how she's just hogging my locker like I'm not gonna mind.

Before I can barely start looking for my bio book, Adonna's hairbrush falls out. As I'm picking it up, I hear footsteps coming down the hall. I look up and see it's Nashawn. He's carrying his duffel bag, looking as fine as always, and he's walking in my direction. I mean, I know he's not coming for me or anything. He's going to his locker. But he is looking right at me.

And, of course, I look away. I can't help it.

I pick up the brush and shove it back in my locker and grab my textbook from inside. When Nashawn gets closer to me, he acts surprised, like he didn't notice me there before. "I can't see in the dark," he says. "But you look like that famous set designer."

I smile. "Famous?"

"I saw that set, man, and it's good. You got talent."

"Thanks."

I close my locker and put the combination lock back on. And I try to act as natural as I can get and not think about the fact that he actually liked my set.

"So, where's your friend today?" he asks me.

I have to admit it to myself: That hurts a little bit. I don't know why, what's going through my head, but I turn to him and ask, "What, do you like Adonna or something?"

"Why you wanna know?"

"Because you keep asking me about her."

He shrugs and digs into his locker for something. Probably looking for some book that's buried so deep he never even used it before. "You and her are always together, that's why."

"Do you think she's pretty or what?" I ask, and, really, I'm not sure if I wanna know for Adonna's sake or my own.

"Of course."

I lean against the lockers. "What about me? Do you think I'm as pretty as her?" The words leave my mouth before I even think about what I'm saying. Or doing. But for some reason, being here in this hall with only a little light, I'm just feeling different. I wanna know what he thinks about me. *If* he thinks about me.

He looks me in the eye with that smirk that just makes him even more adorable. "Let's see." He scans my body, and I'm glad I wore my nicest black jeans with a cute, little black V-neck T-shirt. "You dress real nice," he says, nodding his head. "And your face and body, yeah, it's all good."

I can't believe Nashawn's actually checking me out like this. I mean, the way he's looking at me, it's kinda intense. But I try to relax and stay in the moment, not get nervous and say something stupid and childish. "You're not answering my question," I tell him.

He laughs. "Okay, you got me. Alright. You wanna know if you're as pretty as Adonna?"

"Am I?"

He looks me up and down again and, just like that, my body kinda heats up. I don't know what he's doing to me, but he's doing it. Big-time. Finally, he says, "I'm gonna have to say, yeah, you are. But in a different way."

I shake my head. "C'mon, tell the truth."

"That *is* the truth. You're real hot."

"Then why don't you ever look at me? Why you only check out Adonna?"

"Adonna." He looks like he's thinking of how to say what's on his mind. "Adonna is like a fantasy girl, you know, one of those girls that guys have to look at. But you, you got that nice, quiet kind of pretty."

I roll my eyes and walk away. And without even looking back, I know his eyes are on me. I can feel it. And it feels kinda good.

I pass a few classrooms that are all dark with their doors closed. Then a little farther down the hall is the teachers' lounge, but I can't look inside because they got the little window on the door covered with black construction paper. The door is pulled in, but for the first time since I been coming to this school, it's not closed all the way. And I'm curious what they got in there that they don't ever let us kids see.

I push on the door lightly in case someone's inside. A little light is coming in from a half-open window shade on the other side of the room, but near the door, it's hard to even see what's in there.

Down the hall I hear Nashawn's locker close, and a few seconds later he's standing behind me in the doorway. He don't say anything. He just follows me inside and closes the door behind him. Before I know what's happening, his hands are around my waist, nice and strong, and then a second later he has me up against a wall.

And it's on.

# FIFTEEN

It's weird because, even though I know what's happening, can feel everything, it's like I'm not really there. It's like I'm watching somebody else. Not me.

His hands are on my waist, holding me against the wall as he's kissing me. This isn't the first time I kissed a guy. I did it before, back in sixth and seventh grade when us girls used to play games with the boys from Bronxwood, but feeling how Nashawn is kissing me now, with his tongue all deep in my mouth, I know this is my first *real* kiss.

And I'm kissing him back, too. It don't matter that I don't really know what I'm doing. I'm just going with it.

When his hands start undoing the zipper on my jeans, I just let him. I even help him take them off me. Then, when he pulls my panties down, I step outta them, too. Fast. Without even thinking.

It's like whatever he wants to do, I'm gonna do it, no problem. No resistance, no matter where his hands go or what they do. Like it's something I do every day.

And this goes on for a while, with me and him up against the wall, 'til finally he's leading me over to a big table in the middle of the room. My eyes have adjusted a little bit and I can see him move a couple of chairs outta the way. Then he lifts me up and puts me on the table, facing him.

I wrap my legs around him to keep him as close to me as possible, and we kiss some more. Then I hear him unzip his jeans. And finally I shake my head, trying to wake myself up, and whisper, "I can't. My grandmother, she's gonna, um, have me checked."

I can barely make out his expression even though his face isn't even an inch away from mine. "Checked?"

"You know. By the doctor." His hands are all over me, making it hard to concentrate on what I'm trying to say. "To see if I'm still a, um, virgin."

But that don't stop him for a second. He's breathing heavy in my ear and says, "I need a blow job." And he picks me up off the table.

And, just like that, I do it. I listen to him tell me what to do and how, and all I wanna do is keep him there with me. For as long as I can.

And then he's done. I stand up and wanna say something to make this last a little longer, but I can't think of anything. A few seconds later, his pants are zipped back up and his hands aren't on me anymore. "I left my duffel bag in the hall," he says, talking fast. "I don't want someone to steal it."

And then he's gone. And me, I'm just standing there, in the middle of the teachers' lounge, half dressed, still trying to catch my breath.

I find my panties and jeans in the darkness and put my clothes on, taking my time, not sure that what just happened was real, not a dream. When I get back out in the hallway, it's empty.

I walk to the staircase, slow, listening to the sound of my own footsteps. And as I leave the building, I know for a fact that, for the first time in my life, I have no idea what I'm doing.

# SIXTEEN

Back at Bronxwood, I get off the bus and walk with my head down toward my building. It's getting dark out, but practically every kid in the projects is outside, running around or on bikes or scooters. Screaming and laughing like they lost their minds or something.

It wasn't all that long ago that me, Adonna, and some other girls used to be outside like that, jumping double dutch or roller-skating, or just sitting on a bench waiting for the ice cream truck to come around. And even back then, Adonna used to be snapping on people all the time. Nothing too mean. She would just try to get everyone to laugh, which we did. That's the kinda fun I miss sometimes, because that was the easy kinda fun. Not like now.

I walk fast from the bus stop, hoping to get upstairs without having to talk to anyone. When I pass by Kenny's truck I wave to him, but I don't stop or even slow down. He waves back and smiles, and good thing he has a couple of customers and don't have time to ask me to come over and talk to him. Because I don't think I could talk to him like nothing just happened. I can't even look him in the eye with the way I'm feeling.

In the elevator, as I get closer and closer to the fifteenth floor, there's too much going on in my mind. It's like I'm fighting with myself to not think, but I can't. It's impossible. I mean, I can still feel Nashawn's hands on my body, and it's like every place he touched me isn't only mine anymore. Everything feels different now.

Nana is on the phone when I get into the apartment. "Hold on," she says when she sees me coming through the door. "She just came in." She holds out the phone for me. "Here. It's Renée. She wants to talk to you."

I shake my head and keep walking right past her down the hall. I go straight into the bathroom, then slam and lock the door behind me. The last thing I'm in the mood for is one of Renée's excuses. I don't even wanna hear her voice right now. I can't deal with it.

I can't deal with anything.

I sit on the side of the bathtub, put my head in my hands, and cry hard without making any sound. My chest feels heavy and full, and it's hard to breathe. I feel so stupid and disgusted with myself that I can't keep it inside anymore. I wanna scream.

What's the matter with me? Why would I do something like that? I'm not even like that.

I run the water in the tub, take off my clothes, and make sure not to look in the mirror, because I can't face myself right now. All I wanna do is wash Nashawn off me, fast, before Nana gets a good look at me. Because the truth is, she been waiting for this, and she's gonna know what I been up to. She's gonna

**101**

know that some boy been touching on me. Like, there's probably fingerprints on my body only she can see.

Later, while I'm in the bathtub, sitting in the soapy water, Nana knocks on the door. "You okay, Babe?" she asks.

It takes me a second to answer, to make my voice sound normal. "Um, yeah. I'm fine."

"You sure? You been in there a long time now."

"I'm coming out in a minute."

*She knows*, I tell myself. *She's not stupid. She has to know something's up.*

I hear her trying to turn the doorknob. "Is this door locked?"

"Is it?" I ask. But my voice don't sound right. It's too high. She's gonna know I'm acting weird. I know she is. "Oh, I'm sorry, Nana. I didn't mean to lock it." I stand up and step outta the tub. "Hold on."

I wipe my eyes and wrap a towel around me. Then I look at myself in the mirror, thinking, *Do I look the same? I'm not sure. I can't tell anymore.*

When I open the door, Nana is standing there with her arms folded. Her eyes don't look at me. They look *into* me. Like she's investigating me, analyzing me. At first she don't say anything, but the silence is enough to make me nervous, especially since I can't think of anything to say to her.

So I turn away from her and pick my clothes up off the floor. With my back turned to her, she asks, "Everything okay?"

"Yeah," I say, still not looking at her. "I just needed to take a bath. I felt so —" I almost say *dirty*. "I felt so sweaty from all the cleaning up we had to do after the show."

Nana is quiet, like she's waiting for me to say something else.

**102**

"I feel so much better now," I say, balling up all the clothes and putting them in the hamper.

"Why didn't you want to talk to Renée? She wanted to explain to you what happened."

I shrug. "It don't matter." I try, but I can't keep my voice from cracking a little bit. "It's just a school play."

I walk past her, outta the bathroom and into my room, and she follows behind me.

"She said there was a lot of traffic," Nana says. "You know how those highways get, especially on a Sunday when everyone's coming home from their weekend trips."

"Yeah," I say. "I know."

I search through my drawer for some pajamas to put on.

"How was the last show?" she asks, still staring at me funny. "Anything happen?"

She's not asking about the show. We both know that.

"No, nothing unusual. We got a standing ovation."

"What took you so long to get home?"

"The bus," I say. She's still giving me that look, like she's trying to read me. "Um, can I get dressed for bed now? And I have a lot of homework I didn't do all weekend."

She stands there for a few seconds and I have to look away, it's so uncomfortable. Finally, she says, "Okay. But make sure you come get some dinner."

"I'm not hungry. Um, I got a slice at the pizza shop near the bus stop. I'm full."

More staring. Then, "Well, okay. Get your homework done. Renée's going to be home tonight. I hope she don't get in too late, because she needs to get herself a full night's sleep." She's talking to herself again. "That girl's in the real world now,

**103**

not college. She's a working woman. And when you're working, you can't function on no sleep. You know what I mean?"

"Yes, Nana," I say.

"Well, okay, then," she says and walks outta the room real slow. I close the door behind her, not really sure how I got outta that. I mean, if Nana suspects something about what I did, at least she's keeping it to herself. For now. And that's a good thing.

# SEVENTEEN

I thought I would hear music when I woke up the next morning. And singing. But instead there's nothing. Only the pounding in my own head.

I have the worst headache I ever had. I mean, I could feel the pain in and outta my sleep. It's the kinda pain that you can feel behind your eyes where your whole skull feels like it's gonna break apart or something. I can hardly even pick my head up from the pillow.

So I lay there, trying to relax so the pain will go away, but I can't stop my brain from thinking and thinking about everything. I'm thinking about Renée and how she didn't bother coming to the showcase last night, even when she knew how important it was to me. And, of course, I'm thinking about Nashawn, too. About what almost happened between me and him.

And what *did* happen.

It's too much, what's going on in my head. But if I lay here all day, I'm only gonna drive myself even more crazy, that's for sure. And I have to do something to get rid of this headache. So I get up and go out to the kitchen, where Nana is sitting having breakfast. The green tea is back.

I sit down at the table and rub my forehead, feeling kinda dizzy.

"You okay?" Nana asks me.

"Headache," I say. "It's bad."

She gets up from her chair. "Let me get you something for that."

She leaves the kitchen, and I sit there hoping she don't take too long because I don't know how long I can take this hammering that's going on behind my eyes. She comes back fast with a packet of Goody's Headache Powder. She's kinda old-fashioned when it comes to medicine, and even though I hate the way the powders taste, they *do* work faster than regular aspirin. I pour the powder on my tongue, and Nana hands me a glass of water from the tap to wash it down with. "Let me make you some tea," she says. "It'll help."

I sit still, waiting for the powder to work, trying not to think too much. But I have to ask, "Where's Renée?"

"Oh, she called late last night," Nana says, putting water in the kettle. "She said she wanted to get off the road, so she stopped off at Gerard's apartment in Newark. She's going straight to work from there."

"Oh," I say, not really sure what to feel. I mean, Renée already missed my show. There's nothing more to get upset about now.

"I just hope she gives herself enough time to get to that college this morning," Nana says to herself, "because she don't want to be late on her first day." She puts the kettle back on the stove and turns on the fire.

Then she comes back over to the table to finish eating. And I just sit there trying to relax. To breathe. I'm not sure it's gonna work, though, because I still can't stop *thinking* so much.

Finally, the kettle whistles and Nana gets back up to fix me my green tea. It's not 'til I'm drinking the nasty stuff that I notice the gym bag on the floor by the radiator.

"Is that yours?" I ask.

She turns to see what I'm looking at. "Oh, yeah," she says. "I joined Curves with Rhonda from the office. We're going to work out at lunch hour, three days a week." She laughs. "Well, that's the plan."

"That's good," I say, and go back to drinking. But I'm definitely adding this to the evidence file. Not that I need any more.

After a while, Nana tells me to go get ready for school. "Because you're going to feel better once you get moving," she says, "and you get some fresh air in your lungs. Come on."

Part of me wants to stay home and not have to face Nashawn and deal with what happened yesterday. I mean, the thought of seeing him again, in the daytime, and remembering everything we did, *I* did, is almost too much to deal with. But being home isn't gonna change that. Because all I'll do is lay in bed all day worrying if he's telling everybody about what happened, wondering what he's saying about me.

It takes me a second to stand up, but I do. And I go to the bathroom real slow. I know I have to do this. I can't hide forever.

✵      ✵      ✵

I'm still not dressed when I hear the doorbell ring. I'm still sitting on my bed, putting some lotion on my legs since I decided to wear my denim skirt to school. Before Adonna gets to my room, I take some deep breaths and remind myself to act natural. Because there's no way I can let her find out about me and Nashawn. This is one thing I definitely have to keep from her.

"Hey, girl," she says, coming into my room and sitting next to me on my bed. "Why are you so late today? You're never late."

I don't look at her. I just say, "Headache."

"Well, I still need you to hurry up. I have to talk to Tanya before homeroom."

I stand up and go to my dresser, taking out a plain blue T-shirt and pulling it over my head. It feels like I'm moving in slow motion today.

"Where's Renée?" Adonna asks with that tone in her voice. "She come to the showcase last night?"

"No," I say, not looking at her, tucking the T-shirt into my skirt. "She got stuck in traffic coming home from Maryland."

Adonna sighs real loud.

"Adonna," I say. "Can you please just stop?"

"I didn't even say anything."

I shake my head, which only makes it hurt more.

Nana sticks her head in the door and asks, "Feeling any better?"

I shrug. "Not really."

"You will. Give the medicine some time to work." She looks over what I'm wearing and nods a little bit. The skirt isn't too short and my T-shirt isn't too tight. So I guess I'm just right. "Okay," she says. "Hurry up and don't be late for school."

I hear her walk back down the hallway. And then the front door opens and closes. And right away I pull the T-shirt off and start looking through my dresser for something better. The cute pink top with the square neckline is perfect. I put it on and see Adonna smiling at me outta the corner of my eye.

Between Nana and her, I can't help but feel like everybody's judging me all the time. Like it's up to them to approve of what I'm wearing or doing. And when it comes to Adonna, I always feel like I'm a project to her, something to fix up or make over. And it's not just my clothes, either. With her it's everything. It's *me*.

"Here," Adonna says, reaching into her book bag and pulling out a lip gloss. "Try this. It's called Betrayal."

I take the lip gloss from her and put it on. It's a little darker than the one she's wearing, but it looks good on me. Makes me look a little older.

Adonna leans forward on the bed. "You know that girl Pam, the one with all the teeth and gums?"

"Hmm," I say, because I know Adonna's about to go into one of her stories again.

"Well, let me tell you what happened Saturday when I saw her at the movies in Bay Plaza."

As Adonna goes on and on, I put on my sandals, then stand up to comb my hair back into one of my I-really-need-a-touch-up-*bad* ponytails. My mind is all over the place. I don't know how I'm gonna do it, walk into that school like nothing happened yesterday. And what am I gonna do if I run into Nashawn at our lockers or in the cafeteria? Say hi like we weren't naked together, like, twelve hours ago? I probably won't even be able to look at him.

*And how am I gonna handle it if everybody knows?*

Adonna is still talking. "And when she got up off the floor, girlfriend had popcorn in her hair and butter stains on her ass! It was so funny. You should have been there."

"I was doing the showcase, remember?" I say, so she won't know I missed her whole story. "And I never get to go any-where."

I'm putting in my earrings when Adonna asks, "What's the matter with you?"

"Nothing," I say, not looking at her reflection in the mirror. "Why?"

"'Cause you're acting weird."

"I have a headache," I tell her again. "Remember?" I grab my book bag off the floor. And I even remember to take my jacket this time. "Let's go."

But before I leave, I take one last look at myself in the mirror. I don't really look the same anymore, and it's not just the lip gloss. I kinda look nice. Pretty. And I'm wondering if I always looked this way or if I really changed.

# EIGHTEEN

My head is still hurting at lunch, but Adonna's talking so much she don't even notice that I'm in pain. Or that I'm hardly paying any attention to her. We're sitting at a table together, just the two of us so far, but she's not even looking at me. She's looking — no, *staring* — across the cafeteria at this girl Sade.

At least it's not Nashawn this time.

"Look at her," she says, and the thing about Adonna is that she don't try to hide it when she's looking at somebody. Not even a little bit. "That weave just changed her whole personality. She actually thinks her shit don't stink no more."

I rub my head, but at the same time I'm kinda scanning the cafeteria, looking for him. I don't know what I'm gonna do if I see him, though. Just thinking about that makes my heart race and my head hurt even more. But I'm still looking.

"You see the way she's flipping her hair back all the time?" Adonna says. "Wish that thing would fall right off her head, I swear." She laughs.

Normally, I would laugh with her, at least a little bit, but I can't do it today.

"Her weave *does* look nice, though." Adonna laughs again. "I'm gonna see if I can get my hair done like that for the summer. What d'ya think? Can you see me at the block party with all that fake hair down my back?"

I close my eyes for a second. Why does Adonna have to always sit right in the middle of the cafeteria where she can see everybody and everybody can see her? Especially today, when I'm already feeling all open and exposed. And with Tanya and the guys still in line buying their food, it's like I don't have anybody around to kinda block me out a little.

"You okay?" Adonna finally asks me.

I open my eyes. "I don't know. I just can't get rid of this headache, that's all."

Adonna stares at me for a long while. "That headache named Renée?"

Across the room, some guys at the table where Nashawn always sits, the baseball team guys, bust out laughing. Nashawn isn't there, but still, I can't help but think they're probably laughing about me, about what I did. And, really, it's too much to sit here and have to deal with this.

I look over at that table for a few seconds, but none of those guys look back at me, thank God. They're busy throwing packets of salt and pepper and sugar at each other and ducking and acting wild. Finally, this teacher Mr. Gordon goes over to their table and they start to calm down.

"They are so stupid," Adonna says. "That whole team is made up of one asshole after another. Well, except Nashawn, of course. He shouldn't even play baseball. He really should

**112**

play basketball or something else just so he won't have to hang out with those idiots."

Every ten seconds, I find myself scanning the whole cafeteria, looking for him. I wanna see him, look in his eyes for just a second. Because if I do, I'll know if he been talking about me, telling everybody everything that happened.

"Baseball players aren't even all that hot," Adonna says. "I mean, like one or two, maybe, but basketball players are way hotter with those shorts, and football players with those tight pants that shows off their ass."

He walks into the cafeteria and stands there by the stack of trays. His eyes go straight to our table, to me, but I have to look away because what if his eyes tell me he been talking about me? What do I do then?

"Why does he always do that?" Adonna asks. "Look over here and not come over and say anything to me. It's so annoying."

I can't help it, but I glance up again. Just long enough to see him leave.

And all of a sudden, I can't just sit there anymore. I stand up fast.

"Adonna, um, I'm gonna go see if I can get some aspirin from the nurse's office." I grab my book bag and the apple juice I never even opened.

"Okay," she says. "If you don't come back, I'll meet you after school."

I walk away from her, throw my apple juice in the garbage, and leave the cafeteria. Who am I kidding? The nurse never gives out aspirin, and the stupid headache powder I took this morning didn't help any, anyway. So I just walk down the hall and up the stairs to my locker.

And he's there, waiting for me.

Without saying anything, I open my combination lock and grab the key off the top shelf of my locker. Then I slam the locker closed and walk away, back toward the staircase. I can feel his eyes on me.

"Hey, where you going?"

"Theater," I say.

And again I hear him walking behind me, following me just like yesterday. By the time I get to the first floor, he's walking with me. We don't talk, but we're together. I go straight to the side door of the theater and unlock the door. It's dark and quiet in there, and the set looks kinda dead now. Looking at it makes me feel even sadder because at least I had the play. But not anymore. It's just one more thing that's gone now.

Nashawn follows me inside and pulls the door closed behind him. Then we go backstage to the girls' dressing room, the only one with a lock. As soon as we're inside and the door's closed, Nashawn is pressing me up against the wall and we're kissing real hard and I can't even remember to breathe. It's like yesterday never ended, that we been like this since then. And still I can't get enough.

"You still need to be an um-virgin?" he asks after a couple of minutes, whispering in my ear.

"No," I tell him. "I don't care." I'm feeling kinda dizzy. The way his hands are on me, reaching under my shirt and unhooking my bra, I can't even think straight right now.

Then he's taking off my shirt and my bra and he's saying over and over, "You are so hot. So beautiful." And he's kissing my neck and my shoulders.

What he's doing with his lips and his hands feels so good, it takes me awhile to force myself back to reality. "No, I can't," I say. "My grandmother —"

But that don't stop him for a second. He kisses my ear and says, "We can do it the other way."

"I don't know —" I say, but my voice comes out kinda shaky because I don't even know what he means. Not that it really matters, because no way am I gonna stop now. "The other way?"

"Here." His hands go straight for my butt. "Your grandmother won't know." Then when I don't say anything for a few seconds, he says, "C'mon, girl. I want you so bad it's not even funny. Do I have to beg?"

That gets me to smile, but only a little. "Are you sure? I mean, it's okay like that?"

"Come here." Nashawn takes my hand and leads me over to the couch that's still covered with costumes. He pushes everything to the floor. And then we're sitting down and he's taking off the rest of my clothes and then his own, and he's putting on a condom, and he's kissing me the whole time.

Pretty soon I'm closing my eyes and letting him do whatever he wants. I try not to think about the pain. I just try to relax like he keeps telling me to do. And I focus on how good his hands feel around me and the way his body is connecting to mine. And I don't want it to end. Because right now I know I'm all he's thinking about.

About forty minutes later, right at the beginning of sixth period, I actually make it to the nurse's office. Only I don't want an aspirin. I want permission to leave school early.

I sit on the wooden bench and listen as the nurse talks to Kenny on the phone. "She's going to leave now," she tells him. "Please call the school when she gets home, just to let us know she arrived safely."

I can't believe they're treating me like I'm still in middle school or something.

The nurse hangs up the phone. "Okay, Kendra. Your father says he'll be looking out for you. I hope you feel better."

"Thanks," I say, keeping my head down.

I walk outta the office, then outta the school.

Besides the headache, I'm not feeling anything.

# NINETEEN

When I get back to Bronxwood, I try walking past Kenny's truck again, fast, so I can get to my building without facing him.

Of course, he sees me. He probably been waiting for me, just like he told the nurse he would. Besides, the man never misses a thing.

"Babe," he calls out from one of the windows. "Slow down."

I try to wave at him and keep walking like I did last night, but I know he's not gonna let me get away that easy.

"Girl, come over here and let me make sure you okay," he says. "The school got me all worried about you."

It's hard to ignore him even though all I wanna do is get in the tub, then go to sleep. I stop walking, take a deep breath, and tell myself I can do this. I can talk to him for a few minutes. He won't find out anything.

I walk across the street to the back of the truck and step inside. Right away Kenny's giving me a hug, but I pull away after a few seconds. I just can't take any more touching today. *Any* kinda touching.

"I couldn't believe the school was calling me, telling me you not feeling good and you wanna leave early. What's the matter?"

I can't look at him. I have to keep my eyes away from his. "My head," I whisper. "And my stomach."

"Oh, I got just what you need."

Not only does Kenny sell junk food and soda, he sells those little packets of aspirin and cold medicine, too. He grabs a pack of Alka-Seltzer, then a little tiny bottle of Poland Spring from one of the refrigerators. Before I can say anything, he's opening the packet, breaking up the tablets, and sticking them through the little opening in the bottle. The water bubbles up and almost spills over the top. "Here. Drink fast."

I don't even know why, but I take a sip of the foamy water. Probably because I know he's trying to help. But it tastes so nasty, like salt water, only worse, that I practically gag. "Kenny, I don't need this. It's not that kinda stomachache."

He takes the bottle outta my hand. "Girl problem?"

I nod 'cause I know that's gonna stop the questions.

"Okay . . . alright. Okay. Um, you need anything?"

"No. I just wanna lay down for a little while." I look up at him real quick. "And, you know, sleep."

"Okay," he says again, looking at me, worried. "I'm gonna call you later, make sure my little girl's alright."

I force myself to smile a little bit. "Okay." He gives me another hug, and he don't let me get outta it so fast this time. In his arms, I smell the strong Lever soap he been using forever, and I feel so guilty and stupid and embarrassed, I can't help but start crying. I been holding the tears in for more than an hour, and I can't stop them now.

"Whoa, what's the matter, Babe?"

"Don't call me that," I say, holding on to him tighter. "I'm not a baby anymore."

Kenny breaks away from me and looks me in the eye, and when I try to look away, he puts both hands on the sides of my face and makes me look at him. "What's wrong, Babe? And don't say 'nothing,' 'cause I know it's something."

I stand there crying and crying, not saying anything, and luckily Ms. Lucas from Building D comes up to the truck and asks for a pack of Newport, so Kenny has to let go of me. "Don't move," he tells me, then grabs a pack of cigarettes from one of the shelves. I stand there for a few seconds, listening while he talks to Ms. Lucas and makes change for her, but I know I can't talk to him about anything. I can't do it.

So with Kenny's back turned, I slip outta the back door real quiet. I hate doing it to him, but I have to. I really need to be alone right now.

# TWENTY

"Babe, you awake?" Nana opens the door to my bedroom without knocking, as usual. "Here. Kenny's on the phone."

She comes inside over to the bed and hands me the cordless. I put the phone to my ear, say hi, and wait for Nana to leave, but she just stands there.

"How you feeling?" Kenny asks me. "You better?"

"A little," I say, sitting up. I look over at the alarm clock on my night table, and it's almost seven. "I guess I just needed some sleep, that's all," I tell him.

When I left Kenny's truck, I came upstairs and took a long hot bath, crying practically the whole time, then went straight to bed. I think I just wanted to be out cold so I could forget about everything. At least for a little while.

" 'Cause the way you cut out on me today —"

"I'm sorry, Kenny. I was just feeling sick to my stomach and I wanted to get home."

"You sure that's it? 'Cause the way you was crying, I thought maybe something happened. 'Cause you know if somebody tried something with you, all you gotta do is tell me and I'll take care of him. You know that, right?"

"I know." I glance up at Nana, but this time she's looking at the sketches I have on my desk, the one I did for Theater Design and the houses and the floor plans I do just for myself. "I'm okay. Oh, yeah, did you call the school to tell them I got home?"

"Yeah, they know. But me and you, we still gonna talk, you hear me?"

I tell him okay and try not to give anything away because Nana's looking at me again, outta the corner of her eye.

"Hold on, Babe," Kenny says. "My pinhead sister wanna talk to you." I hear him call Adonna and, while I wait, I cover the mouthpiece and ask Nana if she wants anything.

"I want to know why they called Kenny when you were sick and not me."

"He's my father," I say.

Nana sucks her teeth. "No school ever called him before. Now all of a sudden —"

"They wanted me to call someone who was gonna be home, so they could make sure I got home okay."

"How'd they get his number?"

"I gave it to them."

"Well, I'm going to be calling that school tomorrow and let them people know who to call next time they need to get ahold of somebody."

"Kendra, what happened to you?" Adonna asks me when she gets on the phone. "I was waiting for you in front of the school. Then that girl Tracy with the stretch marks on her neck, she said she saw you in the nurse's office, and you left early. You still got that headache?"

**121**

"Yeah." It feels weird keeping things from Adonna, but I'm not really lying, not about being sick. "And then my stomach started hurting, too."

"Man, you probably got the flu or something."

"No, I think I'm better now." For some reason, Nana finally walks outta my room. Don't know if she heard enough or if I'm just boring her or something. "What are you doing?" I ask Adonna.

"Chem homework. Wait 'til next year when you have to deal with this shit." She lowers her voice a little and says, "Guess who tried to step to me today?" She don't wait for me to guess. "Nashawn Webb."

I stop breathing.

"He walked up to me outside Mr. Pollack's class, and it was so funny 'cause you could tell he had to work up the nerve to talk to me, and he goes, 'Hey, Adonna. Lookin' good like you always do.' And I was like, what happened to him that he's finally saying something to me like we're friends all of a sudden?"

"Did he say, um, anything else?"

"No, not really. We talked for a couple minutes, though. He was asking me why I never come to any of the baseball games, that kinda thing. Nothing serious. I kept thinking he was gonna ask me out 'cause he looked like he was trying to, but he didn't."

"Oh," I say.

"That's all you got to say, 'oh'?" Adonna asks, and I can hear how excited she is, that he finally talked to her after all this time.

But I can't even talk anymore. "No, I just . . . never mind."

"But you should have seen the way he looked at me,

**122**

Kendra." Adonna giggles like a little girl. "Like you could tell what he had on his mind 'cause he couldn't hide it."

I need to get off the phone. Right now. "You know what, Adonna? I gotta go. My stomach's starting to hurt again." And it is. For real. I hit the OFF button on the phone before even saying good-bye, get outta bed, and run down the hall. But I don't make it all the way to the bathroom. The next thing I know, I'm bending over and throwing up on the carpet. And all over my bare feet. I really am sick now.

# TWENTY-ONE

The only reason I wake up is because they're talking about me.

"And can't nobody tell me she ain't into them boys already," I hear Nana say. She's in the kitchen, talking all loud. For some reason my heart starts beating faster. Maybe she does know about me and Nashawn. "You should see her," she says, "walking out here in the morning wearing all kinds of tight jeans and skirts, buying thongs, *thongs*, and acting like *that girl* upstairs. And reading them little ghetto romance novels and hiding them like I don't know everything she does."

That's when I hear Renée laugh.

"Girl," Nana goes on, "I just hope she's not getting no ideas from those books, 'cause I done told that girl I'm going to have her checked if I even suspect anything."

"Are you still threatening her with that?" Renée laughs again. "You tried that with me and you see how well it worked, right?"

I lay there, waiting for Renée to say more, to defend me. To tell Nana that just because I read those books, don't mean I'm a ho. Because I'm not. *I don't think I am.* I wait for Renée to tell her that I'm just like any other normal fourteen-year-old girl. But she don't say anything. Not that anything she says would get Nana off my back, anyway.

I look over at my alarm clock, and it's already after eleven o'clock. I wish I knew what time Renée got home and how long they been talking about me.

I try to sit up in bed, but my stomach twists and I have to lay still because I really don't wanna throw up again. So I wait a few minutes before trying to move again. Then, just as I'm sitting up, I hear Nana say, "So, what's this about an apartment?"

"Yeah, I can't believe how lucky I got. I was telling someone at City about how I need to find a place, and she introduced me to this professor in the foreign languages department who's been looking for someone to sublet her place from now 'til the end of the year. So I stopped by after work and she took me over there to take a look at it."

What she's saying surprises me. She found us a place so fast? And what does this mean? That I'm gonna be moving outta here soon? That me and Renée don't have to wait to live together by ourselves?

"Where is it?" Nana asks.

"Oh, it's a studio apartment in a real nice brownstone in Harlem. It's small but really cute."

I sit perfectly still on the bed, so they won't know I'm awake. But I can't really breathe, not completely. I don't know what she's saying. What does she mean, a studio? Isn't that just like an apartment with one room?

"Brownstone? Harlem?" Nana sounds as confused as me.

"Look, Ma," Renée says. "I know you didn't think I was

moving back here. I mean, I didn't get a Ph.D. so I could live in the projects again."

"And what about Babe?"

I hold my breath and listen for Renée's answer.

"God. I just got out of school. This is my first job!"

"Don't start that with me again."

"I'm just saying I need time, that's all."

"Time for what?"

"Just time," Renée says.

And I sit and wait. I wanna hear everything. I need to hear what Renée's gonna say when she don't know I'm listening. I have to know the truth, now that she don't have school as an excuse anymore.

"Renée." I can hear the frustration in Nana's voice. "We're not going to have this discussion no more, because you're wearing on my last nerve, you understand me? I don't want to hear no more of your high siddity talk tonight, nothing about how you're too good to be in Bronxwood, because we both know that shit ain't gonna fly with me, pardon my French. And we both know that one way or another the time's gonna come when —"

"Please, Ma," Renée whines, the way she always does when things don't look like they're going her way. "I haven't even started working yet. What do you want from me?"

I know what *I* want from her. It's what I *always* want from her.

"I want you to grow up!" Nana shouts. "You expect me to do this forever? When you going to start thinking about somebody other than yourself?"

"I don't know what you're talking about!"

The argument between the two of them goes on and on, and before I even think about it good, I'm laying down again, back under the covers.

When I was little, I used to cry when Nana and Renée had this argument, get in the middle and try to get them to stop. I would tell Renée it was okay she was going back to school and promise Nana I would be good and not get in her way too much. Stuff like that. Just to get them to stop fighting.

But there's no reason to do that anymore. I get it now. Nothing's ever gonna change. Their arguments are always gonna end the same way. With Renée gone and me stuck right here.

# TWENTY-TWO

In the morning, I wanna die, that's how bad I feel. My head and stomach still hurt, and I'm freezing and hot at the same time. Not to mention how much my body hurts from what Nashawn did to me yesterday.

But none of that even comes close to how bad I feel inside when I think about what Renée said last night, how she don't want me. It's like there's this giant hole inside of me now, and it's never gonna close, no matter what.

Nana comes into my room. "How are — ?" She stops talking when she sees me. "Oh, my goodness. You look terrible."

"I feel terrible," I say, but I mumble it into the pillow and I'm sure she can't hear me.

Nana leans over the bed and feels my head. "You're burning up."

"I'm cold," I say.

"Come, let me help you to the bathroom," she says. "And I'll make some tea to warm you up."

Nana helps me up, and it's not easy because I feel weak and

shaky. When we get out into the hall, I hear Luther playing again in the living room, and again Renée is singing. As I walk to the bathroom with Nana's help, I'm trying to figure out how Renée can do that, just sing like she's all happy, like nothing happened last night.

When I'm done in the bathroom, Nana gives me her heavy robe to put on and she walks with me down to the kitchen. As I pass the living room, Renée stops singing and says, "Hey, Babe." She smiles, but I'm not really sure how much of that smile is for me and how much is left over from Luther.

So I don't say anything back. I go into the kitchen with Nana and sit down, waiting for her to make the tea. A few minutes later, Renée comes in and says, "What's going on?"

Nana flashes her a look, and her face is all tight and hard — I can tell she's still mad at Renée from last night. "She's sick," Nana says. "You don't remember I told you she was throwing up yesterday?"

"Yeah, but —"

"She got a fever. The flu."

Renée comes over and puts her hand on my head, but it don't even feel right to me. As far as I know, this is the first time she ever done it. "You are pretty hot," she says.

I don't say anything to that. I mean, she should have been able to take one look at me and see that. A real mother would have.

Her cell phone rings in the living room and she runs to get it, saying, "Oh, I hope that's Gerard."

I pull the robe tighter around me, but it's not helping at all. I'm still shivering. And I'm listening to Renée on her phone, and she's talking and laughing like everything's okay. But she's

**129**

just probably all excited about her *studio* apartment, the one that's just for her.

And I'm thinking, *Wouldn't a real mother be able to tell that I'm not just sick, that I'm in pain, too? Real pain. Why can't she see that?*

If I wasn't sick, I would go in the living room right now and tell Renée I heard everything she said last night. And I would ask her why she don't want me.

But I can't get into that kinda conversation today. Not in this condition.

Nana brings me my tea and I drink it fast, and it does kinda help me get rid of the chills. After the second cup, Nana helps me back to my room and tells me to get some sleep today, that she'll call the school to tell them I'm not coming. She even puts a glass of orange juice and the cordless phone by my bed, and tells me she's gonna call me later to see how I'm doing.

When she leaves the room, I bury myself under the covers and try to get warm. I'm only half asleep when I hear Nana and Renée. It's hard to really make out what they're saying because the music is still playing, but I hear enough to know they're fighting again. And it's all because of me.

". . . a selfish daughter like you."

"Look," Renée says. "I don't need this today, okay?"

"Well, it's the first time you *don't* need something." Nana's voice is loud and sharp, and it cuts right through the music.

"What do I ever ask you for?" Renée shouts back. "What?"

"Girl, don't get me started this early in the morning."

The doorbell stops them, and a few seconds later, I hear Adonna's voice. I should have called her to tell her I wasn't going to school.

I close my eyes and hope she don't come to my room. Because I really don't know how to face her. It was bad enough yesterday, but now, after what me and Nashawn actually *did* in the dressing room, there's no way I can look at her and act natural.

I need time. Time to sleep and time to stop thinking about everything and everyone. What I wish is that I had enough time to forget about what I heard and what I did. But I know that's not gonna happen.

# TWENTY-THREE

"Here. It's a boy, for you."

I open my eyes to see that Nana's in my room, handing me the phone. The door is open and the light coming in from the hallway is burning my eyes.

I been sick and in bed for almost two whole days, feeling just about as bad as a person can. Yesterday, Adonna came by after school, but I acted like I was asleep. Because I still didn't wanna face her, and I definitely didn't wanna hear if her and Nashawn ate lunch together or if he finally asked her out. I was sick enough.

Then late last night, Kenny stopped by after he locked up the truck. He brought up some of those little packets of Comtrex he sells, and he sat with me and told me how he saw Nana and Clyde kissing in the car when Clyde dropped her off after work. "She's into that dude," Kenny said, laughing. "Can't believe, after all this time, Nana done caught her-self a man!"

I was still kinda outta it, so all I remember saying to him

was, "Shh, she's gonna hear you." But Kenny didn't care, and I was too sick to stop him from snapping on her.

Now, with Nana standing over my bed, it takes me a few seconds to catch up to what she just said to me. *A boy? On the phone for me?*

Then, in my next breath, my mind jumps to Nashawn and I'm thinking, *Would he really call me? And why?*

I look up at Nana's angry face and ask, "A boy?"

"That's what I said."

I take the phone from her, dreading the sound of Nashawn's voice, and say, "Hello?"

"Kendra? It's me."

Darnell.

"Oh, hi," I say, my voice coming out kinda breathy, more out of relief than anything else.

"Hey, I'm sorry to bother you, but I haven't seen you around school and I heard you were sick, so I just wanted to see how you're doing."

"I have the flu," I tell him. "But I'm a little better now."

"That's good. Uh, I hope I didn't get you in trouble, calling you, or anything. Because your mom started giving me the third degree just now."

I look up at Nana. She's staring at me with her hands on her hips. Why did Darnell have to call me and get her started? Now I'm gonna be hearing about this for weeks.

"No, it's okay. And that wasn't my mom. It was my grand-mother. I live with her."

"She must not like guys calling you, the way she was questioning me about who am I and what I need to talk to you about."

**133**

"You're right about that," I say. "How did you get my phone number?" I'm asking because, yeah, I wanna know. But, really, because I want Nana to know I'm not the one that gave it to him.

"Oh, I got it off the stage crew contact list. I hope you don't mind, but —"

"No, that's okay. It's fine."

"I missed seeing you around, and now that the showcase is over, it's like I don't get to see you every day anymore."

He stops talking and I can't think of anything to say, either, especially with Nana judging everything that's coming outta my mouth.

"Kendra?" Darnell asks like I went somewhere.

"Yeah?"

"Can I tell you something?"

"What?"

He waits a couple of seconds, then says, "I like you. I mean, a lot. And every time I'm around you I don't know what happens, but —"

"I know." I try to keep my face blank, like he just told me something about the weather, because Nana's real good at figuring out what people are saying on the other end of the telephone. But it's kinda hard not reacting, because I never had a guy tell me he liked me before. I mean, there was Nashawn, but that was different.

The only thing is, I'm not sure if it feels right, because maybe Darnell only *thinks* he likes me. Maybe I'm not the same person he likes anymore.

"You already knew I liked you?" he asks.

"Yeah," I say, and think about telling him it was Adonna

**134**

that told me. But I don't want him thinking we were talking about him behind his back or anything.

Another few seconds go by with nobody saying anything.

"You really knew?"

It's hard not to giggle. "Yeah."

"Well, I wanna talk to you, okay? When are you coming back to school?"

"Tomorrow, probably." Nana is still staring, and I know I have to change the subject before she figures out what we're talking about. "If I'm not back tomorrow, then tell Mr. Melendez that I'll definitely be there for the set striking on Friday. I know I have a responsibility to the stage crew and I'm going to do everything I can to make it. And, um, thanks for calling."

"Got you," he says. "Grandma's breathing down your neck, isn't she?"

"Yes," I say. "I'll be there."

"Bye, Kendra," he says. "See you tomorrow."

I click off the phone and sit up all the way in bed. "That was Darnell from the stage crew," I tell Nana, giving her back the phone. "He just wanted to make sure I was going to be there to help them take the set apart on Friday."

"Hmmph," she says. And I can tell by the way the corners of her mouth turn down and her lips straighten out that she don't believe me all the way.

"Is Renée home yet?" I ask, but as soon as the words are outta my mouth, I don't know why I asked. Because I don't really wanna see her. I mean, I don't think I do. I probably just asked outta habit or something.

"She came home, changed, then left again," Nana says.

"That girl. She needs to stop acting like she's still in college and get serious already."

Part of me can't help feeling all let down. Here I am sick and, in two days, she only came to my room a couple of times. Every time she was on her way somewhere, to work or out to dinner or to sleep.

And for some reason I still haven't said anything to her about what I heard her tell Nana the other night. I don't know, but now that I had a couple of days to think about everything, what's the point of even bringing it up with her? She either wants me to live with her or she don't, right?

I mean, what am I supposed to do to change her mind? What *can* I do?

*Nothing*, that's what. Nothing.

# TWENTY-FOUR

All the way to school the next day, Adonna talks nonstop, trying to fill me in on every single thing that happened since Monday. *Everything.* And even though she's talking my ear off, I'm glad because I don't have to say anything. All I have to do is act like I'm listening.

Of course, I'm still feeling horrible, not just because I still have a little bit of the flu left but because of the way I went behind her back and did it with Nashawn. There's no way to make myself feel better about that. And there never will be. It just wasn't right

Darnell is standing right in front of the school when we get there, and I'm wondering if it's just a coincidence that we're both out there at the same time, or if he was actually waiting for me. Adonna nudges me with her hand and I walk over to him while she goes to stand with Malcolm and Craig and some girls I don't really know.

"Hey, Kendra," Darnell says, smiling but trying to be cool at the same time. "You feeling any better?"

"Yeah," I say. "And I couldn't take it laying in that bed for another day."

"I know what that's like," he says, then stops talking and looks down. He sticks his hands in his pockets and he starts shifting his weight from one foot to the other. I have no idea why he's so nervous all of a sudden.

Then, just to make things even worse, Craig calls out, "Darnell, go get her, man!"

And Malcolm jumps in with, "Yeah, you can do it, man!"

Both of them start laughing. Even Adonna and those girls are looking over at us, trying to hide the fact that they're laughing, too.

I give Adonna a don't-y'all-have-anything-better-to-do look. Then I turn to Darnell and say, "Let's go."

We walk up the steps in front of the school and into the building without saying anything. Then, as we walk down the hall, I say, "Don't let those guys —"

"No, I'm not," he says, opening the door to the staircase and holding it for me.

"Thanks," I say and walk through. And yeah, I'm liking that he has manners and he's treating me like a lady.

The stairs are empty, and as we're walking up to the second floor, he says, "What I said last night on the phone — I want you to know I really meant it."

I smile. "Yeah?"

We get to the top of the stairs and I kinda wait for him to open that door for me, too, but he don't. Instead, he leans over real fast and gives me a kiss on the lips. And I'm kinda surprised because I wasn't expecting it, so it takes me a second to kiss him back, and by then it's just about over. Then he looks me in the eye and says, "Yeah. I meant it."

He opens the door and I walk through, still kinda stunned at what he did.

"See you later," he tells me right there by the staircase, because his locker is in the other direction.

"Okay," I say, still smiling. "Bye."

I walk down the hall to my locker, thinking about that kiss and how different it was from those kisses Nashawn gave me, those ones that practically lasted forever. Kissing Darnell was nothing like that, but it was nice, too. Just in a different way.

"Okay, what do you wanna tell me?" Adonna asks, jumping the lunch line to get ahead of me.

I look behind me and see way too many kids around that could hear us.

"I can't tell you *here*," I whisper. "At least wait 'til we get to the table."

But Adonna barely listens to me. She's already looking around the cafeteria, searching for Nashawn, no doubt.

All morning I been dying to tell Adonna about Darnell kissing me. I passed her in the hall between second and third period and told her I had some news, and she said, "What? What?" And I could tell she thought I was gonna tell her something about *her*. Or Nashawn.

But the hallway was crowded and we only get three minutes to change classes, and I didn't wanna just say "Darnell

**139**

kissed me" without giving her the whole story, so I said I'd tell her at lunch. But I didn't mean now, in line.

When we get to the table with our food, I'm glad the guys aren't there yet. Malcolm was behind us in line and Craig is in the corner talking to this girl Shana. Tanya's the only one at the table, but she's too busy taking a quiz in *Cosmo*, writing her answers on loose-leaf paper, to even care what we're talking about.

Adonna opens her Snapple and leans across the table, closer to me. "So?"

"Okay," I say. "Remember when me and Darnell left you guys this morning? Oh, yeah, why do your friends have to be so stupid? It was embarrassing."

"They're assholes, that's why."

"I know." I shake my head. "Anyway, when me and Darnell went inside, we were talking and we went to the stairs and he opened the door for me, which I thought was really cute, and when we got to the top of the stairs, I was kinda waiting for him to open the door again, but before he did he stopped and —"

"Shit!" Tanya says, kinda loud. She's looking down at the loose-leaf paper with all the numbers she added up to get her score.

"What?" Adonna asks her.

"This fucking quiz is telling me that I'm a boring lover. That's not even right!"

Adonna looks at her like she's crazy. "You're not any kinda lover, stupid. You're a virgin. You had two boyfriends last year and all you did was tease them. I don't even know what you're reading that magazine for."

Tanya actually pouts. "But I'm not *boring*."

140

"Maybe you added wrong," Adonna says. "You know you're as shitty at math as me. Add it again." Then she leans close to me again. "Go on."

"Okay," I start again, not sure how far back in the story I should go. "Okay, when we got to the top of the stairs, I wasn't even thinking of anything and —"

"Can I sit with you?"

Even before I look up, I know it's Darnell, and it takes me a second to answer him because I'm too busy hoping he didn't hear what I was just talking about.

I put on a smile, look up at him standing there with his tray, and say, "Yeah, sit here." I touch the back of the chair next to me. And while he's sitting down, me and Adonna look at each other and it's hard to figure out what she's thinking. I mean, she said Darnell would make a good boyfriend for me, but she don't even know him. Anyway, I don't know why it even matters to me what she thinks of him. But it does.

The second Darnell sits down, he starts eating. He takes big bites outta his cheeseburger and, as soon as he swallows, he starts shoving curly fries in his mouth. Really, it's not all that pretty watching this. But still, at the same time, there's something kinda sweet about him, like even after all those weeks of us working backstage together, all of a sudden he's too nervous to talk to me.

I'm trying to think of something to say to him when I see Nashawn come into the cafeteria. He has on those baggy jeans Adonna hates, but to me he looks as hot as he always does. Maybe even hotter.

Nashawn don't get in line for food or go over to his table. All he does is look over at our table, straight at me. Adonna's back is to him and she's squeezing mayonnaise over her ham sandwich, anyway, but me and him stare at each other for a few seconds and I completely stop breathing, especially when he smiles at me. Then he turns and leaves, and I know what he wants. He wants me to follow him.

I breathe in and out real fast a few times, then start coughing. Adonna looks up. "What?"

I shake my head. "Nothing. I, maybe I'm still a little sick. It's nothing."

Darnell swallows what he's eating. "You okay?"

I nod. "Yeah, um, I'm fine."

He smiles, the second guy to smile at me in the last thirty seconds, and even though it don't make me feel the same way Nashawn's made me feel, I smile back.

Darnell reaches over to my tray and shakes my carton of orange juice and opens it for me. "Here, drink."

"Thanks," I say, putting my straw in it and drinking. I'm kinda liking the attention he's giving me, but part of me is looking for an excuse to get away from the table. To meet Nashawn at our lockers and spend time with him alone again in the theater.

But I can't. I don't even know what's the matter with me. What, am I really thinking about leaving Darnell here and going off with a guy that talks to another girl on the same day me and him hooked up? No, I can't do that. Not to Darnell and not to myself. Not again.

So I don't move. I relax. And pretty soon the table is full of Adonna's friends and everyone's eating and acting stupid, and me and Darnell are having our own conversation about the showcase and some of the funny things that happened back-stage, and about Mr. Melendez and how he's too good a designer to be working at a high school.

Then the next time I look up, Nashawn's back. He's in the doorway again, looking right over at my table. I look away fast and stare down at my tray with the soggy grilled cheese I haven't even touched. It's hard, though, not looking at him. I can't even lie to myself. I wanna get up from this table and be with him. It's like I can already feel his hands on me and I want that again. But, no, I can't. I can't.

About three minutes later, just when I'm starting to forget about him, he comes walking right over to our table with a can of Pepsi in his hand. With his free hand he grabs the chair next to Adonna, spins it around, and sits on it backward. Now me and him are face-to-face, and it's too much for me to act like it's no big deal.

He leans closer to Adonna and grabs some of her chips. "Hey," she says, laughing. "You gotta ask. You didn't ask."

"C'mon, girl. Share," he says. And him and Adonna are looking at each other with these weird smiles, like they're talk-ing to each other without saying anything.

The next thing I know, Nashawn is eating one chip, then feeding the next one to Adonna, and this goes on and on, until the bag is finished. I mean, I can't even figure this out. They haven't even gone out on a date yet. And he's feeding her? Right here in the cafeteria? It don't make sense.

Darnell takes the last bite outta his cheeseburger. "That wasn't bad today," he says, kinda to himself. Then he asks me, "How come you're not eating?"

I'm still staring at Adonna and Nashawn, but I tell Darnell that I'm not hungry, that I'm still not feeling well. "You can eat my lunch if you want," I tell him.

"No, I'm good," he says. "A person shouldn't eat too much school lunch or they might explode from all the toxins."

I laugh a little bit because I know he's trying to be funny and because it's so uncomfortable watching Adonna and Nashawn flirt right in front of us, like they're in their own little world or something. It's like a lot must have happened in the two days I missed school, and for some reason Adonna didn't tell me anything, even with all that talking she did this morning. I mean, the last I heard, he talked to her for a few minutes, but obviously that's old news now.

"Kendra," Darnell says, and I hope he wasn't watching me watch them.

"Huh?" I turn my attention back to him. He looks kinda worried about me, like the way he looked the other night, right before I left him and —

"I think you should try and eat something, you know, before lunch is over."

I nod. "Okay, you're right." He's looking out for me. That's a good thing, right? Maybe he would be a good boyfriend. He's a nice guy and he's cute, too. Just in a different way. I mean, not every guy has to be *all that* fine.

I bite into the soggy sandwich and hear Nashawn tell Adonna, "So I can't be out all night on Saturday 'cause we have a Sunday doubleheader. We have to make up for a game that was rained out last month. So I have to get up early. But next time —"

"How you know there's gonna be a next time?" Adonna

asks, with that sexy smile she used to practice making in her bedroom mirror back when we were both in middle school together.

"Oh, there's gonna be a next time," he says. "Definitely."

It feels like I have a lump in my throat, and it's not 'til I swallow that I remember I was in the middle of eating the grilled cheese. It actually hurts going down and I feel like I'm going to choke. "You okay?" Darnell asks me again.

I nod. "Fine."

He laughs. "Look, if you choke and die, I'm gonna feel real bad for making you eat that thing."

I laugh, too. For real this time. He *is* kinda funny.

"Hey, Kendra." It's Nashawn, leaning across the table toward me. "I forgot to thank you."

My heart stops. Oh, my God. What is he thanking me for? I hope he don't say anything in front of Adonna and Darnell, not to mention everybody else at the table. I feel like I should say something, but I don't know what. So instead, I stare at Nashawn, who has a grin on his face like he's up to something. Which he probably is.

A few seconds go by. Then Adonna asks, "What for?"

"She helped me out with something," he says. Then he pauses and I know he's loving this, making me sweat. "We were in the computer lab," he goes on, "and I couldn't figure out how to make columns, and she helped me. It came out real nice, too. I got a B."

Now it's Adonna who's looking at me funny. "I didn't know you two were in the computer lab together. When was that?"

She's still looking at me, but it's Nashawn that says, "Last week. And she almost got me in trouble, too."

145

Before I know it, I'm saying, "*I* got *you* in trouble? I was the one that kept getting yelled at, all because I was trying to help you."

Nashawn is really smiling now. "Well, you could have helped me without all the talking. I mean, some of us were there to get our work done."

"You were sitting there all lost, like —"

"Lost? Me? Nah."

"You're joking, right?"

He shakes his head. "All I'm saying is, who got in trouble, me or you? You know, those teachers can spot a troublemaker a mile away, and the second you walked in the computer lab, Ms. Ballinger was all over you."

"It was your fault!"

Adonna clears her throat real loud. "Are y'all done? Because I hate to interrupt." She gives me the fastest look with her eyes all squinty, and I can tell she's gonna wanna know why I didn't tell her about this before, especially when she asks me about him practically every day. And yeah, I didn't tell her, but there wasn't anything to tell her. Not really.

I look away from both of them and turn in my seat toward Darnell. He looks as confused as he can get, like he can tell something's going on between me, Adonna, and Nashawn, but he's missing it. "I can't wait for the set striking tomorrow," I tell him. "And it's gonna be fun hanging out with everybody again afterward."

"Yeah," he says, still looking like he's not getting something. "You're coming to the diner, right?" He puts his hand on top of mine.

I nod. "Yeah. Sit next to me, okay?"

"Of course."

Out of the corner of my eye, I can see Nashawn watching us. I wish I could just forget about him and what happened and only think about Darnell, because I know he would treat me right. I mean, I wish I could just stop thinking about Nashawn altogether, but I can't. Not yet.

# TWENTY-FIVE

"I can't believe you're really doing this," I tell Adonna after we get off the bus. It's not even four and I'm home from school on time for the first time since I started working on the showcase. But instead of getting to enjoy the hour and a half I have before Nana gets home, I have to make sure Adonna don't do something stupid. "C'mon," I say, following her to the beauty supply next to the liquor store. "Think about this."

"It's gonna look nice," she says. "And I'm only gonna keep it in for the summer. Something new, that's all."

"But you don't need a weave," I tell her for the umpteenth time. "Your hair is already long."

"I know, but I want it down my back. And then when it gets real hot out, all that hair's gonna look real nice with my off-the-shoulder tops." She flips her imaginary hair and laughs. "And I'm gonna work it, too!"

When we walk into the store, the bells over the door ring and the owner looks up from the floor where she's kneeling, putting some shampoo bottles on the shelf. She don't say anything to us, but she stares at us like we're only there to steal something.

All the hair for weaving and braiding is hanging on the wall in the back. Adonna looks up and starts pointing. "Ooh, that one would look good on me."

"The *red* one?"

"It's not red, it's auburn. Or maybe I'll get brown with blond streaks."

I sigh. "Adonna, this is stupid."

But her eyes are all lit up as she stares up at the wall. "Don't you ever want a change?"

"Yeah, but —"

"Well, so do I. And you know me. I *have* to look good."

I hate when she says stuff like that, like looking good is the only thing that means anything to her. Like she's not anything except somebody that looks good.

Adonna goes up and talks to the woman, and I just stand there looking around. They got all kinda hair relaxers and tex-turizers and straightening combs and flat irons. Then they got a whole row of acrylic nails and glue and rhinestones and stuff. Every time I come in here, I wonder if I'm ever gonna be into all this. Because, to me, all I see is a whole store about trying to be something you're not.

"It's *how* much?" Adonna has her hands on her hips now and she's staring at the owner like she's crazy.

"Twenty-nine dollars for each pack," the woman tells her. "And you're going to need two."

Adonna turns to me. "I don't have that kinda money, Kendra."

I almost say, "Why don't you ask your mother?" But,

knowing her, she would, and then Grandma would end up giving away more money that she don't even have.

"I sell half-packs," the lady says. "You can try a pack and a half, but if you want it to look full, you should get two."

"Forget about it," I tell Adonna. "Your hair is so beautiful."

She smiles and runs her hand through her hair. "I don't know . . ."

"C'mon." I go over, grab her arm, and pull her outta the store before she can find something else to buy.

Outside, it takes Adonna a few seconds to move away from the store. I have to do more convincing, soup her up a little more. "You know most of the girls around here wish they had hair like yours," I tell her. "If you get a weave, all you're gonna do is look like everybody else, and that's not you. You don't copy other girls."

It works. We start walking to our building. The only problem is, now that I'm not trying to talk her outta getting a weave, we're kinda quiet. Even she's not talking, which is definitely weird, and I can't help but think it has something to do with me not telling her about the computer lab. I'm just hoping she don't start asking me questions about that.

So I tell her, "Darnell kissed me." Just like that.

She stops walking. "He did?" Now she's smiling. "That's good!"

"I didn't expect it, but all of a sudden it was just kinda happening!"

Adonna giggles. "Well, did you kiss him back?"

"I don't know," I say. "I mean, yeah, kinda. It happened too fast."

We start walking again. "I told you he likes you," Adonna says, sounding more like her old self. "You really need to start listening to me when it comes to guys."

For some reason, when she says "guys" my mind goes immediately to Nashawn, where it's been on and off all day. After lunch, all through my classes, I kept thinking about him sitting right across from me and talking to me like that. It's weird that me and him did so much together and it's only now I'm starting to get to know him.

"So, when did Nashawn ask you out?" I ask her finally. "You didn't tell me that."

Adonna is smiling. "Oh, I didn't?"

"No," I say. "You know you didn't."

She tries to act like it's nothing. "Oh, he asked me out yesterday. We're just going to the movies in the afternoon. Nothing special."

*Oh, yeah. Like this isn't something you've been waiting for, for like the last three months.*

We get near our building and Adonna grabs my hand and says, "C'mon, I wanna show you what I'm gonna wear on Saturday."

*When she's with Nashawn. On their date.*

As soon as we get close to Kenny's truck, he sticks his head outta the window and calls out to us, "Wait up."

Adonna sighs. "Not another one of these father-daughter moments," she says under her breath. "Like you guys don't see each other every single day."

"Adonna," Kenny says, "I gotta tell you something. Before you go upstairs and find out for yourself."

Adonna folds her arms in front of her. "What?"

151

But we have to wait for Kenny to open the back door and come over to where we're standing. And when he does, he still has the serious look on her face, and it has me kinda scared, like maybe something really is wrong. "Is Grandma okay?" I ask.

"Yeah, she's fine," he says. "It's nothing like that."

"What, then?" Adonna asks.

"It's about your bedroom, all that furniture your father got for you. The bed and dresser and all that. It's gone. Them dudes from Rent-A-Center came a couple hours ago and took all that shit back."

"*What?*" Adonna asks. "What are you talking about? He didn't rent that stuff. He bought it for me."

Kenny walks closer to her. "He lied. All that shit was rented and the asshole didn't keep up with the payments. I ain't surprised, knowing him the way I do."

Adonna has her mouth hung open. Kenny might not be surprised, but she definitely is. "What, what am I gonna do? I need my stuff." And she starts to cry, like, for real. "What am I supposed to sleep on? *The floor?*"

Kenny goes over to her and tries to put his arm around her, but she don't let him. "Stop," she says, pushing him off. "Leave me alone."

Me and Kenny look at each other, and he looks as helpless as I feel. I mean, I don't know what to say or do, either. I know what that furniture meant to her. A lot more than something to sleep on and put her clothes in.

Adonna stands there crying for a little while longer, then this girl Asia that lives in our building comes down the street in our direction, and Adonna wipes her eyes and shrugs. "Forget about it," she says. "I don't give a shit. I don't even want his fucking furniture."

By the time Asia reaches us, Adonna looks more mad than sad. And she's hiding behind her attitude. Asia waves to us and says hi, and we all say hi back, but as soon as she goes by, tears come down Adonna's face again.

She pulls on my arm. "C'mon, Kendra. I'm not gonna stand here all day." I wave bye to Kenny and walk into the building with Adonna, still not knowing what to say to her.

I leave Adonna's apartment and get downstairs to mine about ten minutes before Nana gets home from work. It was hard being with Adonna, because she was so sad, just crying and talking about her father and how he lied to her. And seeing her room practically empty like that was really depressing. I mean, it looks like she got robbed or something.

Nana comes right into the kitchen and starts heating up some leftovers, and even she looks kinda down today. Extra tired.

"You feeling okay, Nana?" I ask, thinking that maybe she got the flu from me or something.

"Yeah," she says, sighing heavy. "I'm fine."

"Is Renée coming home tonight?"

"No, she don't have to work on Fridays, so she went to Gerard's place. Then tomorrow, they're going to Princeton to pack up that apartment. Because she's moving into her new place on Saturday."

It's really happening. She's moving out on her own.

Me and Nana don't say anything for a while. I drink some more orange juice and take another Comtrex, and I sit at the table while she cooks. It's weird, because the apartment is so quiet and it's like Renée is missing even though she was only here for a few days, and even then she was hardly ever here. But when she's here, it's like the place is more alive or something. There's always music playing and singing and the cell phone is always ringing. And now there's nothing.

When dinner is ready, Nana puts her plate on the dinner tray and goes into the living room to watch Lifetime. She hasn't been watching it these last couple of days, ever since Clyde started coming around. But now she's back again. And I don't know if this means something.

At the commercial, I sit next to her on the couch and ask, "Is everything okay, um, between you and Clyde?"

"Yeah, I suppose so," she says. "He wanted to take me to a jazz club tomorrow night where a friend of his is going to be playing, but I told him I can't go."

"Why not?"

"His friend don't start playing 'til ten o'clock. And I can't leave you here alone, especially late at night."

"But I'm going to be at the set striking, remember? And then we're all going out to dinner."

She looks at me and shakes her head. "I don't want you coming home to an empty apartment."

"I can spend the night with Adonna," I say but then I remember about her bedroom set and I'm not really sure that's gonna work actually.

"No, it's fine. Don't worry about it." The commercial is ending. And as the show comes back on, she says to me,

"I invited Clyde over for dinner on Saturday, so everything's okay."

Then she turns her attention back to the screen. Away from me.

I sit there next to her, feeling really bad for her. And guilty. I mean, I'm still the reason she can't live her life the way she wants.

And it's not fair. Renée was supposed to take me with her. And Nana was supposed to finally be free.

# TWENTY-SIX

"In the theater community, the striking of the set is considered a ceremony. A ritual. It is a celebration of what has been created and a way to honorably deconstruct it, to return the stage to its original state — an empty space — one that awaits becoming another world."

Sitting there on the stage, with my feet hanging over the edge, all I can think is, Mr. Melendez can really get corny sometimes. *Seriously.*

"But first," he says, pacing back and forth in front of the stage, "we must pay respects to the one who had the initial vision." He nods his head in my direction. "And to those who took those early sketches and transformed them into blueprints." The whole group of us from his class smile. "And to all of you who took those blueprints and built this beautiful set." Now we all have to clap for ourselves, for all the hard work we put into everything. "So today, the striking of the set is a way to pay homage to our work and respectfully let it go."

I like Mr. Melendez, even when he's this theatrical.

"Before we begin, I want to tell you all about a production I'm going to be involved with this summer at a small theater on the Lower East Side. I'm managing a production of a play written by an up-and-coming playwright from the Dominican Republic. I've already designed the set, but it will need to be built during the month of July. I say all of this because I'd like to invite all of you, anyone who is not working or going away for the summer, to work with me on this production, mostly in the shop — building, painting, and assembling. I can provide you with MetroCards for transportation and a small stipend for meals and snacks, but otherwise it's a volunteer gig. You will learn a lot, work with professionals, and have some fun this summer. Let me know if you're interested and I'll give you the information." He stops pacing, finally. "Okay, guys, it's time to strike the set!"

Everybody jumps up like they're anxious to get started, but for me it's kinda sad that the whole thing is really over. My first play. I never thought I was gonna like it this much.

As a matter of fact, if it wasn't for Mr. Melendez, I would have been happy just sketching house plans for myself. I never thought about why, really, but maybe I thought one day me and Renée would actually get to build our own house and we'd use one of my plans or something. Like that was ever gonna really happen.

Before I can even stand up, the guys rush straight for the tools in the back of the room, the hammers and saws and everything. They look so excited, too. Mara comes over, grabs my hands, and helps me up. "Look at them," she says.

I laugh. "We better save what we can from the set. Fast!"

And we do. We push the table and chairs and cardboard

television set off to the side for their own protection. Then we run back for the bookcase with the fake books and the big plastic vase with all the paper flowers. Not even two seconds later, the guys attack the set.

"Boys, boys, boys," Mr. Melendez yells. "This is a dismantling, not a demolition. You're theater production people, not a wrecking crew."

"Oh, man," Gregg says. "That ain't right."

Darnell pushes his protective glasses up onto his forehead. "C'mon, Mr. Melendez. This is supposed to be fun."

"Fun," Mr. Melendez says. "*Safe* fun."

Me and Mara push one of the chairs toward the storage room in the back, away from the noise and possible flying wood. "Thanks for taking me out to dinner the other night," she says.

"You already thanked me," I say. "And anyway, Clyde paid for everything."

"So, did you find out anymore info? Is he really her boyfriend?"

"I think so. I mean, she invited him to come over for dinner tomorrow night. And she even joined Curves!"

We both laugh.

"I don't know how I'd feel if my grandmother had a boyfriend," Mara says, shaking her head. "But she's *sixty* something. And that's just plain nasty."

"Mine just turned forty-nine."

"That's weird," she says. "My *mom* is forty-five."

I don't wanna tell her that my mother is only twenty-eight. Not everybody has to know that she had me so young. I mean, not that it's all that embarrassing or anything. It's just that it's not everybody else's business.

When we get to the storage room, Mara whispers to me, "So what's up with you and Darnell?"

"What do you mean?" I try to act all innocent, but I can't help smiling.

"C'mon, I'm not blind. Y'all are staring at each other, and he makes these faces whenever you're around — you know, like *love* faces."

"Love faces?"

"Or maybe *lust* faces, but you know what I mean. He really likes you."

I look at the door to make sure nobody's around, then I tell her about the phone call and how he kissed me yesterday.

"I knew it!" she says. "He's in love!"

"Stop it," I say. "He didn't say anything about love. He said he likes me. That's it." I look around again. "Anyway, with my grandmother on my back all the time, I shouldn't even be thinking about guys. She's never gonna let me have a boyfriend."

"Well, she doesn't have to know everything!"

As the guys tear the set apart, me and Mara spend about forty-five minutes putting everything that can be saved into the storage room, especially any wood that can be used again. The storage room is real small, so while Mara's out collecting more stuff, I get up on the stepladder and try to make room for some of the small decorations on one of the shelves.

My back is turned when I hear the door close. And when I turn around to look, Nashawn is standing there wearing track shorts and a sweaty black T-shirt.

"Can you get outta this?" he asks.

"Um," I say, staring at him, trying not to fall off the ladder,

159

and trying not to let myself get all caught up in him again. "What are you doing here?"

"I went for a run out on the track." He looks at his watch. "I'm gonna take a shower and come back for you in twenty minutes. Meet me at the side door."

I nod, not knowing what to say. Then he opens the door and he's gone, and my heart is beating fast. He's coming back for me. What does that even mean? Is he taking me somewhere? Where? I feel like my body is shaking from the inside.

Mara comes back in the storage room with the curtains from the apartment set. "Look what still survived." She stops and looks at me. "Everything okay?"

I shake my head, slow. "I don't know. I feel . . ." I wish I could tell Mara some of what's going on. I don't think she would tell anybody. But I can't say any of this out loud, because I know it won't make sense to anybody else. *I* don't even get it. "Um, I don't know," I say. "I kinda feel sick again."

"You want to sit down for a while in the auditorium?" she asks. "Maybe all the dust in here is getting to you."

"Yeah, maybe," I say, like that's what it is.

I pass Darnell on the stage. He looks like he's having fun, carrying one of the set walls with Gregg. He smiles when he sees me and I smile back, but I don't know what to feel.

I sit down in the front row and watch everybody work for a few minutes, still not sure what to do. I mean, I can't leave now. I already told Darnell I'd sit next to him at the diner, and maybe he was planning on kissing me again. How wrong would it be for me to just leave like that?

But then there's Nashawn, and I don't want him waiting for me, either. Can I just leave him out there and not show up?

That wouldn't be right, either. And what does he mean, he's coming back for me? Why? What does he want?

I'm going back and forth in my head for a while, then, before I can stand to think about it anymore, and before I even know what I'm doing, I'm walking over to Mr. Melendez, who's ripping nails out of a big piece of plywood with the back of a hammer, and I'm saying, "Mr. Melendez, can I talk to you for a minute?"

He looks up at me and takes his glasses off. "You okay, Kendra?"

"No, not really." I take a deep breath. "I'm, um, not feeling that good anymore. I think I'm getting sick again. Maybe. Is it okay if I leave now?"

He looks around, and even though the stage is still a big mess, he says, "I think we have everything under control here. Sure, go home and get some rest."

I nod.

"You did a great job here, Kendra."

I smile, weak, feeling horrible now. I should be here to finish this.

Instead, I walk real slow back to the storage room and tell Mara I'm gonna leave early.

"That's not right," she says, giving me a hug. "You're gonna leave me with all these guys?"

"You love it," I tell her. "Look how much attention you're gonna get."

I grab my book bag from off a chair and wave good-bye to her. I'm on my way to the side door when I run into Darnell. "You leaving?" he asks. And he's not hiding how upset he is.

"I'm sorry," I say right away, and I really am, too. "I'm starting to feel sick again and I don't wanna, you know —"

"Yeah, I know," he says, and the way he says he knows makes me think he's talking about Nashawn, that he knows something about us. But he's not. He's really just worried about me. "Feel better. And I'm gonna call you over the weekend, even if I have to put up with another interrogation from your grandmother."

I smile. "Okay."

He waves bye to me, then I open the side door.

Nashawn's already standing there in the hall waiting for me. Right out in the open.

"Good," he says to me. "You're ready."

I look back over my shoulder, hoping Darnell isn't still standing there. But he is. He's staring past me, right at Nashawn. Hard.

"Um," I say to Darnell, trying to think of some kinda explanation, but his eyes look different now, angry and cold. Hurt. "Darnell, I —"

Nashawn takes my hand and says, "C'mon."

It feels good, his hand on mine. And while I wanna figure out something to say to Darnell, really, there's nothing I *can* say. So I turn away from him and walk out into the hall with Nashawn. And the heavy door closes loud behind me.

# TWENTY-SEVEN

There's so much I didn't know about Nashawn. He has a car. I mean, yeah, it's an old beat-up-looking blue car with one darker blue door and lots of rust, but it runs good. I didn't know that he drives fast and listens to the sports station on the radio. And that he lives in a house, not an apartment. Definitely not in the projects like me.

When he pulls the car up in front of house, all I can say is, "This is where you live?"

"Yeah," he says. "Me and my mom moved in with her boy-friend a couple months ago."

"That's why you transferred to our school?"

"Yeah, we used to live in Hempstead before that, you know, out on Long Island."

We get outta the car and I follow him up to the front door. All of the houses are small and attached together, but still, it must be kinda nice having your own place.

There are kids riding up and down the block on scooters. "Hey, Nashawn," one kid says as he gets closer to us, moving at, like, fifty miles per hour. He's about eight or nine and is smiling real big with the buckest teeth I ever saw. "Watch this," he yells, flying past us, holding both hands out. He looks good for a few seconds, then starts wobbling and has to hold on again.

Nashawn laughs and yells, "Cool, Brian. But come back and let me show you the trick."

"Is he your little brother?" I ask, even though the two of them look nothing alike.

He shakes his head. "He lives two doors down. I don't have any brothers or sisters."

Another thing I didn't know about him.

"Me, neither," I say, even though I'm not sure why.

I stand at the gate and watch for a few minutes while Nashawn tries to demonstrate to Brian how to balance on the scooter with no hands. It gives me an excuse to look at him, at his back and legs and butt. Everything about him is perfect, and the way he moves on that scooter, so easy and confident. And his face, when he rides the scooter back in my direction, he's smiling and having so much fun playing with that little kid, I'm glad I'm getting to see him like this, away from school.

After Brian takes a few turns on the scooter, getting only a little better each time, Nashawn comes back over to the gate and puts his arm around my waist. "Sorry about that."

I open my mouth to say something, but I don't know what. It's not like me and him had plans or anything, or that we ever actually spent any time together before. Not really. Just a few minutes in dark rooms. I'm still not even sure why I'm here, at his house.

"C'mon." Me and him walk to the front door and he unlocks it. Inside, the house is small and messy. Not disgusting, but

Nana wouldn't approve of anybody living like this, especially with the empty beer bottles on the coffee table and the dirty ashtray. No, she definitely wouldn't like that somebody smokes. Straight ahead is the kitchen, and I can see from the door that the sink is full of dishes.

"My mom's outta town," Nashawn says, closing the door. "And now me and her boyfriend think we're bachelors."

I try to smile a little, but it's hard. I don't get how anybody, even fake bachelors, could treat their place like this. Especially when they're lucky enough to have their own house.

"We were thinking about cleaning up this weekend, but we're both gonna be busy. He has to do some overtime and me, I got — I got that doubleheader against South Bronx on Sunday."

*Right after your date with Adonna on Saturday.*

All of a sudden I start to feel uncomfortable. "Why am I here, Nashawn? Why did you bring me here?"

Nashawn puts his hands on my waist again. "C'mon, girl, I brought you here so I could spend more time with you. And not like before." He kisses me on the side of my face three or four times real slow, and I close my eyes and try to relax. "I wanna slow things down," he whispers. "Take my time with you."

He's so close to me now and I feel my heart racing and my breathing getting heavier. I can't help it. He knows how to get me right where he wants me.

"Do you know how sweet you are?" he says, kissing my neck and shoulder. "You are so sweet."

A little part of me wishes we could stop, at least for a while and maybe talk or something first. That's what my head is telling me. But my body is already gone and it's hard to think of

165

anything else. After a while, he takes my hand. "Let me show you my room."

Nashawn leads me downstairs to the basement. "It's like my own apartment," he says. "Only, the washing machine's down here, so I gotta put up with my mom being here all the time."

The basement is actually cleaner than upstairs. His bed isn't made and there are some clothes thrown on the floor, but there's nothing nasty.

"Sit down," he says. "I'm gonna go up and get us something to drink."

I smile and sit down on the only thing there is to sit on, his bed. While he's gone, I look around. He has a TV with a stack of DVDs on the side, mostly action movies from what I can tell, lots of Spider-Man and stuff. He has a lot of books, too, and not the kind they make us read at school, either. He likes to read. Something else I didn't know about him.

Nashawn comes back with two bottles of beer. He opens a bottle and hands it to me. "You like beer, right?"

I shrug.

He laughs. "You never took a sip of beer in your whole life?"

I laugh a little, too.

"I would say you're a real good girl," he says, coming over and sitting next to me. "But I know what you been up to."

I look down, embarrassed, not really knowing what to say to that. There actually is nothing to say to that.

"C'mon, try it."

I take a small sip and it's kinda bad, but I don't care. I can deal with it. Maybe it'll make me more relaxed.

"You like it?"

"It's okay." I take another sip, which is worse, but I take a third, anyway. Then I ask him, "Do you drink a lot?"

"Nah, not too much. More since my mom been away. But I'm an athlete." He pulls up his shirt a little bit and pats his stomach. "Can't be getting all flabby."

I check out his stomach, which is nice and hard. It's the first time I'm seeing that part of his body in the light. God, there's nothing not hot about him. I look away real fast and take another sip of the nasty beer.

Before I know it, Nashawn's got his shirt all the way off, and he moves even closer to me on the bed. He takes the beer bottle outta my hand and puts it on the nightstand next to his. "This is gonna be good," he says, kissing me on the lips. "We don't have to rush now."

I wish I was strong enough to stop him or slow him down. But his lips and his tongue feel so good. I'm weak, I know it. Maybe I do wish we could have talked and spent time getting to know each other and all that, but the truth is, I know why he brought me here. And this is what I want, too. It is.

Soon his hands are everywhere, touching me, taking off my clothes, and the rest of his. And when he whispers, "Um-virgin?" I nod, not really sure why I care anymore. I close my eyes, and a few seconds later I hear him opening a condom wrapper.

Then, when we're doing it, for the first time on a bed, it's the closeness that I'm feeling. We're together. Our two bodies feel more like one and he's whispering in my ear and we're moving together, my back pressed against his chest and him pushing himself into me. It feels different this time. It means something. And not just to me, but to him, too. That's how connected we are.

Later, me and him are sitting on the bed together finishing our beer. It's almost night now and the room is darker since Nashawn never bothered turning on the lights. And I sit there wishing he would talk to me, say something, but he don't.

So instead, I ask him what time his mom's boyfriend will get back from work.

"He won't get home 'til, like, eleven or eleven thirty. He's the night manager at Home Depot, the one up in New Rochelle."

"I went there once with my father and I almost got run over by some kinda truck, inside the store!"

He laughs. "Yeah, they got those things speeding around there carrying wood and stuff. You gotta keep your head up in those kinda stores."

At least we're talking now.

"Do you get along with him, your mom's boyfriend?"

"He's alright. She could do a lot worse than him. She *has* done a lot worse. He's okay. As long as she's happy with him."

I wanna ask him where his mom went, and when she's coming back, but I don't wanna be nosy. And he probably would have told me if he wanted me to know. But he hasn't told me a whole lot of anything, really.

I finish my beer and put the bottle back on the nightstand. Then I move closer to him. He puts his arm around me and it feels nice, just being with him like this. But then, a few minutes later, he's kissing me again and touching me.

And everything is happening all over again. Like it's all we ever do. And I'm not sure what it means.

\* \* \*

It's his cell phone that wakes us up. The room is pitch-black and I have no idea what time it is or how long I been there. Nashawn jumps up and looks for his phone, and he finds it on his nightstand.

I sit up in bed and can see it from there. Glowing from his phone is the name of the caller: ADONNA.

He looks at the phone ringing there in his hand and, meanwhile, I can't breathe, waiting to see if he's gonna answer it or not. Because if he does, I don't know what I'm gonna do.

But he don't flip it open. He stops it from ringing, then puts it back on the nightstand, mumbling under his breath, "This is hard."

And that's it. I get it now.

I jump up outta bed and try to find my clothes in the dark room.

"What?" he says to me.

"I gotta go. My grandmother is —"

"Slow down."

I find my bra and my shirt on the floor and start putting them on. "She's gonna kill me. What time is it?"

"Calm down."

I button my shirt. "I gotta get outta here." I bend down and try to find my panties, but I can't. So I pull on my jeans without them, rushing so fast I almost trip and fall down.

"Kendra. Hold up. I'll take you —"

I find my sneakers and put them on without my socks. My book bag is on the floor by the bed. I grab it and head for the stairs.

"Wait," Nashawn says, and I see him stepping into his jeans. "C'mon. Slow down."

But I don't. I run up the stairs and outta the house as fast as I can, leaving the door open behind me. I practically run full speed down the block and don't stop 'til I'm around the corner, where he can't see me and try to come after me. Because I don't wanna see him right now. I can't even face him.

I walk two blocks without even knowing where I'm going or where I am. Or how I'm gonna get home from here. I look at my watch and it's 9:24. By the time I get home, Nana's gonna kill me and I'm gonna have to hear her mouth all weekend. And for what?

My head is jumping from one thought to the other so fast I can't keep up. What just happened? Why would I do that with him again, especially when I know Adonna and him are going out tomorrow? What is Nana gonna do to me? What is Darnell thinking of me? Or is he even thinking about me at all? Why did I leave with Nashawn in the first place? Why would I go and hurt Darnell like that?

And why do I keep hurting myself? Why do I keep letting Nashawn do this to me? It's not real. It can't be because it's not me he wants. It's Adonna. Why can't I just stop letting him use me? Because it's me that's the problem, not him. I mean, I could always just say no.

I'm crying. Walking fast and crying and not caring who sees me because it's not my neighborhood, anyway. All I know is, none of this is worth it. I mean, what do I have now? Nothing.

Nothing and no one.

I don't even have Renée.

I could have just asked her why she don't want me even after all the time I been waiting for her. I could have opened my mouth and asked her. But I didn't.

Even with Nashawn, it's the same thing. Why didn't I just ask him who he likes, me or Adonna? Why do I keep doing it with him when I don't even know what he thinks about me?

I get to the corner and finally see a bus stop. The number 31. I can take that and transfer at Gun Hill Road.

Standing there, waiting for the bus, I can't stop the questions. The only thing is, everything I wanna know I could have found out in a second if I would have just talked to Nashawn. And Renée. Just looked at them and asked them. And I don't know why I didn't.

All I know is, I'm scared.

What if both of them told me the same thing? That they don't want me? What do I do then? Because, the truth is, I don't think I can handle hearing that.

I mean, I *know* I can't handle that.

# TWENTY-EIGHT

I'm forced to spend most of Saturday with Nana, and I'm really not in the mood for her today. Especially after I got home late last night and she wouldn't even believe me when I told her how the diner was crowded and me and the rest of the crew had to wait for more than an hour for a table big enough for all of us. And how long it took for the waitress to serve us.

She wasn't even listening. She kept asking me about Darnell and if me and him were together. The boy called me one time and that's all it takes to get her imagination going.

"Yeah," I told her, "he was there, but so was everybody else. *And* Mr. Melendez, remember?"

She didn't yell and scream at me like I thought she was gonna, but she kept looking at me like she knew what I was up to, and it was hard facing her because I knew what I was up to, too. And the truth was probably worse than what she was thinking.

Then because she was probably more tired than me, she finally said, "We have to get to the hairdresser early in the morning. But we're gonna talk about this some more, you can be sure of that." And she let me go to my room, which was good.

But today, while I'm getting my hair relaxed and she's in the chair by the sink getting hers washed, every time I look in the mirror, I catch her checking me out, sizing me up. It's like now she's collecting evidence against me, instead of the other way around, and right when I let my guard down, she's gonna make her case against me and prove that I been doing it with somebody. Only she got the wrong boy in mind.

Leesa, the hairdresser, combs the cream into the hair at the back of my head. "Look at your kitchen," she says. "Why you wait so long to come in and get a touch-up?"

"I was too busy," I tell her. "I was doing a play at school."

"Well, your hair is starting to break, and don't you want your hair to grow?"

I sigh. "Yeah."

She works the cream into my whole head for so long, and even though it's starting to burn, I don't say anything because I don't wanna have to sit that close to Nana, right at the next sink, and feel her eyes on me.

"It ain't burning yet?" Leesa asks me, using her large hands to smooth my hair back and, man, does it sting now.

I make a face. "A little."

"Girl, why you ain't tell me?" Leesa laughs. "C'mon before you have more straight hair in the sink than on your head!"

As I pass Nana's chair, she gives me that look, and this time I give her a look right back. It kinda makes me mad that she don't believe me. I mean, what did I ever do to make her not trust me? It's not fair.

Nana is done before me, and she tells Leesa to just blow-dry my hair and not worry about styling it because we gotta go. I don't say anything, because I know she's just trying to get to me, or punish me for coming home late last night, but that's okay. Fine. Anyway, I don't need to get it styled all fancy when Nana don't like me to wear my hair out for school because she says it makes me look too grown. Like wearing my hair back in a pony-tail for the rest of my life is gonna keep me from growing up.

When we get outside in front of the shop, Nana says, "Hurry up, we have to stop by the store, and you know how crowded it gets on Saturday."

"Why are we rushing?" I ask even though I don't really wanna talk to her.

"I told you, Clyde is coming over for dinner. And we have a lot of cleaning to do. Can't have that man coming into that pigsty."

I sigh loud. "Do I have to go shopping with you? I don't want anything."

"You want to eat, don't you? When you open that refrigerator and don't see your special kind of yogurt, you're the first person to whine about it. Well, where do you think the yogurt comes from? "

"God," I say under my breath. Like she can't just buy my yogurt for me. Like it's too heavy for her to carry or something.

I'm actually glad when we get home and start cleaning

because at least I can stay outta Nana's way. While she's in the kitchen, I start cleaning the living room. And when I find one of Renée's T-shirts behind the couch, everything starts to come down on me again. It's just like last night, only now everything feels even more real. Because it's that day. The day Renée's moving into her new little apartment in Harlem. The day Nashawn and Adonna are going out on their big date.

I turn the vacuum cleaner on real fast so Nana won't hear me crying, and I keep my back to the kitchen so she can't see my face and start asking questions again. It's so hard, thinking about everything. Being here in this apartment with Nana and knowing nothing's gonna change. It hurts. And it hurts that I was so stupid and desperate with Nashawn and now there's no way to go back and change anything. I did what I did. I can't hit the undo button.

At around six o'clock, I ask Nana if I can go downstairs and see Kenny. The whole place is clean and Nana's busy making lasagna, which I know won't taste nearly as good as Grandma's, but Clyde won't know the difference. He's probably all in love and won't care.

"I don't want you sitting in that truck all night," she says, looking at the clock on the microwave. "And after what time you got home last night —"

"It's not all night. I just wanna say hi to my father."

"Your father." She shakes her head. "I'm giving you an hour, and don't let me look out that window and see you doing something you're not supposed to be doing."

**175**

"Yes, Nana." Sometimes, I think she just carries on because she can't think of anything else to say to me. It don't matter to her how ridiculous she sounds, either.

A few minutes later, I'm sitting on a stool inside Kenny's truck. It's hot in there even though he has the a/c on, because he has to keep sliding the window open every time somebody comes to buy something, and that's, like, every minute.

"I can't even keep these sodas cold, people are buying them so fast," Kenny says, using a box cutter to open up another case of sodas and sticking them in the freezer. "Hope they get cold fast in there, 'cause people ain't gonna buy no warm soda."

"What time did Adonna leave?" I ask him, trying to sound like my question is no big deal.

"You mean with that knucklehead little boy she was with?"

"Nashawn was here? At Bronxwood?"

"Nashawn, huh? That's his name?" He laughs. "Yeah, he was here. He picked her up about two, two thirty. Something like that. She didn't even introduce me to the boy, though. She had on some short shorts, and she walked with that boy to his broke-down hooptie like she was showing off a new dog or something."

He laughs again. But all I can think is that Nashawn was here. Not that I expected him to visit me or anything, but still. It's weird that at the same time I was cleaning up and thinking about him, he was probably right upstairs, or out here on the street.

And how many people saw them together? Were Adonna and Nashawn walking around holding hands or something? I mean, it's like she's getting the part of him I want, the guy that

**176**

shows up at your apartment to pick you up and take you out on a date. And what did I get? Definitely not that guy.

And now I'm sitting here wondering what he was wearing and how he looked and smelled and what him and Adonna are doing now. Right this minute. It's like I can't turn my brain off all of a sudden.

"What's Renée up to?" Kenny asks. "Got her nose in a book?"

"Huh?" I have to shake away what I was thinking about and focus on Kenny. "Um, no, she's not here. She's moving into her new apartment today, some small studio in Harlem, not too far from City College." Tears fill my eyes so fast I can't stop them. "She don't want me to live with her. Because if she did, she wouldn't have picked such a small place."

Kenny drops the box cutter. "Damn. You crying?"

"No, I'm okay." I wipe my eyes. "Nothing to cry about. Nothing changed. I'm still where I was before, right?"

Kenny comes over and puts his hands on my waist and stands me up. Next thing I know, he's hugging me tight.

"You talk to her about this, about how you feeling?"

"No," I say, burying my head into his chest and breathing in his soapy smell. "She told Nana she wasn't ready for me." I start crying harder now. "She don't want me."

"C'mon, Babe. Calm down. It's just for a while, 'til she gets herself settled down probably. It's hard being a college professor, even for someone smart like Renée. Just give her a little time."

I don't say anything else, but it's hard hearing about how Renée needs time. I can't even remember how long I been hearing that. She needs time, just give her time, on and on.

The only thing about time is, I'm running out of it. Did anyone ever think about that?

I stand like that, wrapped in Kenny's arms for a little while longer, trying to let go of everything and just be comforted by him. And it's kinda working, too, until outta the corner of my eye, I see them, Adonna and Nashawn, walking together toward our building, across the street from Kenny's truck. Adonna's talking and Nashawn's smiling, and it's too much for me to see. All of a sudden my mouth gets real dry and I can't hardly breathe anymore.

For some reason, I have to know what they're talking about. What is she saying to him that's so funny? I mean, it's killing me how he can walk down the street with a different girl and act like everything is just so normal, like he wasn't with me yesterday.

"What's the matter?" Kenny asks, looking outta the truck at what I'm seeing. "Oh, look who's back."

My tears are streaming down my face now and I don't even try to control them. It's hopeless. Why fight it?

Kenny's staring at me. "Babe, what's up?"

But I'm still watching them, seeing how close Adonna's legs are to Nashawn's and how she's almost touching him while they walk.

"Babe, what, you like that dude or something?" And he grabs my hand and tries to pull me back, away from the window.

But I don't let him. "Kenny, I'll see you later, okay?" I wipe my face as best I can and walk outta the back door, down onto the street.

Nashawn and Adonna have stopped walking now and she's leaning against the fence and they're talking. I wanna stop and

**178**

ask them what movie they went to see, and why they're back so early. But I can't, not crying like this. I don't want Nashawn to see me this way. And what would I tell Adonna? How would I explain it to her?

So I walk as fast as I can down the path to our building, hoping they won't see me and I can get into the lobby without having to face them.

"Kendra!" Adonna yells from across the street. "Slow down."

But I act like I don't even hear her and walk faster than before.

"Babe." It's Kenny this time. "Hey, what's the matter?"

I'm almost at the lobby door now, and, of course, this guy from the third floor is inside leaning against the door like he's the only one that lives in the building. He's talking on his cell phone, and through the open window I hear him saying something about how his girl isn't treating him right and he's gonna have to find someone new. And he's laughing about it, like none of it matters.

I kick the door with my foot and he still takes his time moving away and letting me in. When he does, I fly past him to the elevators and don't even turn to see if Adonna and Nashawn are coming after me or if Kenny is.

All I wanna do is get in that elevator and not deal with any of this or any of them. I just wanna get inside my apartment and forget about this whole day. Because today is as bad as it gets.

# TWENTY-NINE

About fifteen minutes later, my doorbell rings and I know for a fact it's Adonna. The second I open the door, she's like, "What's your problem? I know you heard us calling you out there."

Only thing is, by now I'm not in the mood for her, so I just fold my arms in front of me.

"You gonna let me in or what?"

I suck my teeth and step aside so she can come in, still not saying anything to her.

"What's up with you today?" She looks around — probably for Nana, who's in the shower, getting ready for her man. "Why you acting so weird — I mean, even weirder than usual?"

I shrug. I'm getting real tired of having to explain everything to her, and her thinking she's my mother or something. I don't even have to talk to her if I don't wanna.

"Oh, I get it," she says. "You got an attitude today."

*Like she's the only one that can get an attitude.*

"Well, fuck you, then," she says.

"Fuck you, too," I say finally. "Or is it too late? Did you already get fucked today?"

I watch Adonna's face get kinda shocked. "Oh, so that's it. You're jealous of me and Nashawn. Me and him went out on one fucking date, and, what, just 'cause you can't get a man, I'm supposed to babysit you all day and not have any fun on my own?"

There's something about the way she's looking at me, like I'm some kinda child, makes me wanna tell her about me and Nashawn and what we were doing when she called him last night. Just to see her lose some of that superior attitude because, really, it's making me sick today.

"You keep on having fun with Nashawn," I tell her. "Just as long as you don't think you're the only one he's having fun with."

She puts her hands on her hips and stares at me for a while. "You got something to tell me, then just say it."

I keep my voice cool and confident. "I'm just saying, maybe you don't know *your man* the way you think you do."

"You keeping another secret, Kendra?" she asks. And I think it's working. I'm starting to get to her. She's not only mad now, but she's kinda worried, too. "Like the one about you and Nashawn hanging out together in the computer lab that day?"

"Whatever." I just shrug, really liking watching her this way, with no control over me.

"I can't believe you're being such a bitch," she says, her voice getting louder. "I hope Darnell knows what kinda girl he's getting. *If* he still wants your ass."

I turn around to make sure the bathroom door is still closed. Because that's the last thing I need right now, Adonna yelling out Darnell's name when Nana's already convinced I was with him last night.

I lower my voice a little bit. "Leave Darnell outta this. It's not about Darnell."

"Then why don't you keep Darnell and stay outta me and Nashawn's business?"

I wanna say, *Nashawn* is *my business*. But I don't. I can't.

"Just go, Adonna. It's not like I asked you to come here or anything."

Adonna shakes her head while she looks at me. "You are such a baby. All that time I spent trying to get you to grow the fuck up and, look, you're right back to where you were before, even after all the work I did."

"The work *you* did?" I'm screaming now.

"Yeah, you don't remember the way you used to look and dress? And *act*? Like a fucking retard. *I* didn't even wanna be around you then. You embarrassed the shit outta me."

"And what, you wanted to help me? Just so long as I didn't end up looking as good as you, right?"

Adonna makes a short laugh, and she starts doing her neck. "You could never look as good —"

"That's not what your *man* thinks." Then I put my hand over my mouth. "Oops, that's another secret." I'm smiling now. "Your man probably didn't tell you who was with him last night when you called him, did he?" I shake my head. "I am *so* bad at keeping secrets. I really need to work on this."

As good as she is, trying to act like I'm not getting to her, she can't do it. For a couple of seconds, it looks like she don't even know what to say or do. But her eyes give her away. She's mad as hell and she's hurt. She can't cover it up fast enough. I mean, maybe her friends at school wouldn't be able to tell, but I can.

"Where were y'all?" she asks. "Still at school? 'Cause I know he wanted to work out and you had that thing with the set."

That last part is more to herself than me, and I don't answer one way or another. Let her think what she wants. Whatever makes her happy.

"Oh, you're not talking now?" she asks.

"If you really wanna know where we were, I'll tell you, but you're not gonna be happy, believe me." When she don't say anything one way or another, I just let it out. "I was at his house when you called."

Adonna's mouth flies open for a second before she catches herself and tries to act all cool again. "What are you talking about?"

But I'm not finished yet. "We were in his room. In his bed."

She moves closer to me and, for a second, I think she's gonna grab me or hit me or something. But she don't. She just gets in my face and says, "You're a ho now? Is that what you're saying?" She's practically spitting in my face, she's so close.

I step back and say, "Why don't you take your skanky ass outta here?"

"Look who's talking!" she screams, moving closer to me again. "You wanna be a ho, fine. But least you could find your own man."

That's when the bathroom door opens and Nana practically flies out. She's in a towel with a shower cap on her head, and she's barefoot and still all wet.

"What is going on out here?" she yells, coming down the

**183**

hall. "Babe, Adonna — what's all this screaming and carrying on about?"

Adonna puts her hands on her hips again. "Ask *her*!"

"Shut up," I say, giving her a dirty look, warning her not to open her big mouth about anything in front of Nana.

Lucky for me, Nana don't give her a chance to say anything. She goes straight for the front door and opens it, not even caring that she's standing in front of the door with hardly any clothes on.

"Adonna, it's time for you to go," she says.

Adonna glares at me for another couple of seconds, then says to Nana, "You better talk to her. 'Cause the way she's going, there's gonna be another baby up in here." And she turns and walks through the door like she's all that.

Me, I just stand there. Heated. My heart is racing and I'm breathing hard. I'm scrambling, trying to figure out what just happened and why. Why did I tell Adonna all of that? What's the matter with me?

I can't sort things out fast enough, because Nana closes and locks the door. Then, just like I knew she would, she starts in on me. "What was that about?" Her voice is still raised. "I could hear you girls yelling and screaming from in the shower. Probably half the building heard y'all. Is this how I raised you? To act like *that girl*, whose own mother couldn't raise a chicken with any kind of home training. And what the fuck does she mean, another baby? And don't tell me 'nothing' or I swear to Christ I will go upside —"

My heart is still pumping and I can't catch my breath. I look down at the floor for a few seconds, trying to find the right words to calm her down. But I can't. It's over.

So I just look up, stare her right in the eyes, and say, "Nothing."

And she's on me in half a second, using both hands to slap and punch me in the head and the face and, when I turn away, the back. "Tell me," she keeps saying over and over. "You better tell me or I'm —" Her towel falls off, but that don't even slow her down a little.

I'm crying, but I don't know why, really. I mean, yeah, her punches are hurting, but it's not like I didn't expect this to happen. I knew I was gonna get it sooner or later. I had to with everything I been up to. Better to get it over with now.

But she don't stop, and pretty soon I'm crying so hard I'm gasping for breath. I finally break away from her to go over to the couch and try to get some air. I'm panting so fast my chest hurts, but it's still not working. And I'm waiting to see if she's gonna come over and attack me again.

But she don't. She takes her time wrapping the towel back around her and tucking it in on the side, her eyes on me the whole time. We're staring at each other and I'm waiting for her to make her move. Tears are coming down my face so fast, it takes me a while to notice that she got them in her eyes, too.

Nana is crying.

I never saw that before. And while we stare at each other, I can swear she's not looking all that mad anymore. She's just looking at me. Finally, she says, "Why are you doing this? Why? I been doing so good with you, and now . . ." She shakes her head. "What did I do wrong this time?"

I put my head down in my lap and cry. I don't know what to tell her. Why *did* I do this? I don't know. All I know is, right now I feel like everything is over. Done. I messed everything up and now I have nobody. Nothing. I'm empty.

"I put my whole life into raising you right," she says, her voice a little softer. "I thought — I thought you were gonna turn out . . . different. I tried to —" She sighs loud, and when I look up at her, she just shakes her head again like she's already giving up on me.

Tears and snot are running down my face like a baby, and I can't help feeling like if I don't stop crying now, I'm never gonna be able to. It just hurts so much.

Nana stands there staring at me for a couple more minutes and I can't take the way she's looking at me. Finally, she says, "Babe, go in my room and get my suitcase down from the top shelf in my closet. Then pack your clothes and school stuff, and make sure you take enough to last you 'til the end of the school year. You can get the rest of your things later."

I look up at her, my heart feeling like it's stopped beating.

"You're throwing me out?" I say. I can't believe what I'm hearing. "I make one mistake, a couple of mistakes, and you're just gonna —"

"You're going to live with Renée," Nana says, still looking at me with the saddest face I've ever seen on her. She takes a deep, heavy breath and says, "You need your mother now." And her voice cracks a little bit when she says it.

"But —"

"Go pack while I call Renée."

I get up from the couch and walk down the hall to Nana's bedroom. I'm too tired to argue, and I don't have anything left to say. Anyway, there's no use trying to get Nana to change her mind. It's already made up. I'm outta here.

# THIRTY

Not even an hour later, I'm standing on the curb waiting for the cab to get here. The dispatcher called and said it was downstairs, but, of course, it's not here yet. They always do that, just so they won't have to wait for people, especially in the projects, where there's always a broken elevator or something. But still, I'm not in the mood to wait, and I feel stupid just standing here like this.

It takes a while for Kenny to see me because a whole group of ten-year-olds is crowded around the truck, buying candy and drinks.

The cab pulls up a second before I hear Kenny call out, "Babe, wait up! Hold on!"

Hearing his voice, it hits me that I'm leaving here, leaving him. But I don't cry or anything. I'm too exhausted. I'm practically numb.

The cabdriver pops the trunk but don't even get out to help me with my suitcase. I start to lift the bag when Kenny runs over and helps me.

"What's going on?" he asks. "Why you — where you —?"

I reach up and hug him tight. He holds me, but only for a couple of seconds. Then he pulls away and looks me in the eyes. "Where you going?"

I shake my head. "I'm going to Renée."

His mouth is hung open, but I don't feel like explaining. I mean, how can I talk about something I hardly understand myself?

"Let me take you," he says. "We can get rid of the cab and —"

"No," I say. "I wanna be alone right now. I'll call you tomorrow, alright?"

I open the door and slide into the backseat before he can say anything else. He closes the door for me and I reach in my pocket and take out the little piece of paper that Nana gave me, the one with Renée's address on it. Convent Avenue. I never even heard of it before.

Before the cab pulls off, I see Clyde getting outta his car, carrying something in his hands. Looks like a bottle of wine probably. And he's smiling. All of a sudden, I can't stand him. I mean, he don't know it, but all of this is his fault. Because if it wasn't for him, Nana wouldn't have been so quick to throw me outta my house. She wouldn't have had someone else to turn her attention to.

As we drive away from Bronxwood, I feel like I'm in some weird kinda zone. Not like I'm dreaming or anything, but like I'm in one of those movies Nana watches on the Abuse Channel. And this is the part where the sad, helpless girl is sent away from the only home she ever knew and has to face life on her own.

Of course, in those movies, right after the commercial break, the poor girl either gets raped, falls in love with a man that beats her, or ends up in a coma after some kinda stupid suicide attempt. And all the other choices are just as bad.

A couple of weeks ago, this was all I wanted, to be on my way to Renée's new place, to be going to live with my mother. There wouldn't have been all this drama. And I would have been happy about this.

I wanted Renée to want me to live with her and to want to be like a real mother to me, but now she's just being forced to take me. Like, really, how's that supposed to make me feel?

I lean my head back on the seat and try to close my eyes while the cab speeds across the Bronx. I don't wanna look outta the window and get all sad as I see my neighborhood fly by. Even though I know the girl in the Lifetime movie would do that.

With my eyes closed, all I can think about is how much everything changed in the last two weeks, ever since Renée's graduation. It's like I was a different person or something. But the biggest change I can see is that I really don't even need Renée anymore. Not like I used to.

It's too late.

When the cab pulls up in front of the brownstone, I'm kinda surprised by how nice it looks, how the block looks, with all these four-story brownstones connected together, and all the steps on the outside. The whole neighborhood is clean and quiet. No wonder Renée wanted to get away from Bronxwood and move here.

The cabdriver turns around and says, "That's twenty-six dollars."

"Huh?" I say, and it's right then I realize that I don't have any money on me. "Um, I . . . I need to . . ."

I start looking in my book bag, like some money is gonna magically be there. I keep my head down because I'm so embarrassed and scared, but I try to look calmer than I really am.

After two minutes of me pretending to look for my wallet, I pick my head up, trying to think of what to say to the cabdriver. But I don't have to, because standing there at the top of the steps is Renée. She's wearing a T-shirt, cutoff shorts, and flip-flops. She comes down the steps to the cab, hands the driver some money, and waits for her change.

Meanwhile, I sit there watching Renée's face, trying to figure out how she feels that I'm here. But I can't tell. Her face isn't giving anything away. So I get outta the car and knock on the trunk to remind the driver to pop it open for me. Then I have to get the suitcase out by myself because Renée don't help at all. Matter of fact, by the time I get the suitcase out and close the trunk, Renée is back upstairs already.

I carry the suitcase onto the curb, wheel it the rest of the way, then make my way up the steps real slow. And when I get near the top, Renée holds the door open for me and I follow her up another flight of stairs and down the hall to what I guess is our apartment now.

When I step inside and look around, I can't keep myself from saying out loud, "It's tiny."

"Told you," Renée says, closing the door behind me.

Why did I even have to open my mouth? "No, I'm just saying . . ." I shake my head. "Forget it."

The apartment is really all just one room, and not a very big one either. Renée brought all the furniture from her apartment in Princeton — the futon, the TV, the little wooden crates she painted and made into coffee tables. Her small white bookcases are here, too, but there aren't any books in them yet. And there are boxes stacked up all over the place and lots of mess from the move.

Off in one corner is the kitchen, which is kinda separate from the rest of the room, but just as little. There's a small table in there with only two chairs, and there are already two plates set out for us and a couple of cartons of Chinese food.

I walk farther into the room and put my book bag down on the floor. Right then, the bathroom door opens up and Gerard comes out. He smiles when he sees me.

"Kendra," he says. "How's it going?"

"Okay," I answer, like getting thrown outta my house by my own grandmother is just great. "And you?"

"Good. Good." He looks around the room. "Lot of work getting all this stuff in here, up all those stairs." He laughs a little. Then he turns to Renée and asks, "You want me to set up the Aerobed before I go?"

"Can you?"

"That's what I'm here for."

I watch him find the box marked AEROBED, PUMP, TOWELS and lift it onto the floor. The one thing about Renée is that all of her boyfriends are fine. She definitely knows how to pick them. Gerard is tall, dark-skinned, and so muscular it's not even funny. His arms are huge, and I can see the six-pack through his T-shirt.

Gerard has to move the futon over to make room for the Aerobed on the floor. As he starts to inflate it, I stand there thinking, *Is that gonna be where I sleep from now on? I don't even get a real bed?*

But, really, there's no room for a real bed in here.

There's no room for me.

I don't know what to do with myself. Renée hasn't even looked at me, I don't think. And every time I look at her, her face is blank. I don't know if she really don't have any feeling for me being there, or if she's holding it all in because Gerard is there.

When the bed is inflated, Gerard grabs his duffel bag off the floor and zips it up. "Well, I'd better get going," he says, slinging it over his back.

And for the first time, I can see something in Renée's face. Her eyes kinda get duller, sadder, and her voice comes out a little softer. "You sure you don't want to eat something before you go?" she asks him, and then bites on her bottom lip a little bit.

"I'm okay," Gerard says. "I'll come by tomorrow and help you some more." He goes over to her and puts his arm around her. "You alright?"

She nods.

He leans closer to her and whispers a little too loud, "You can do this."

She nods again.

Then he kisses her on the lips. I look away and walk over to the other side of the room 'til I hear Gerard say, "Take care, Kendra."

I turn back around and tell him bye, and it's not 'til he's gone that I get it. He was gonna spend the night with Renée. And I'm the one that messed up their plans.

I stand there, not knowing what to say to Renée. She's my mother and I don't know how to talk to her. I'm not comfortable around her. Even in this tiny apartment, we're on opposite sides of the room.

Finally, she looks at me, and now I see it, her anger. She folds her arms in front of her and her eyes narrow in on me.

"Are you going explain this to me?" she asks. "Because I don't understand any of it."

"I don't know," I say, shrugging, not sure what's left to explain. "What did Nana tell you on the phone?"

"She said, 'I'm putting Babe in a cab. I hope you have money to pay the man.'"

"And I'm here," I say.

"I see that." She keeps staring at me, and the look on her face is like she's asking me, *Who are you?*

But after today, I'm asking myself the same question. About myself. Because I don't really know that girl back at Bronxwood, the one that acted like that with Adonna and Nana.

Renée throws her hands up in the air. "Well, I don't know what my mother expects me to do with you."

*I'm* your *daughter*, I wanna say — but, as usual, I don't. Not because I'm scared but because I know if I say that, she's just gonna get madder than she already is. And even though I don't need her anymore, not in that way, I wanna try to make this work because I'm running outta places to go.

So I do the only thing I can think to do. I tell her I have to go to the bathroom, and fly outta the room at top speed. In the bathroom, I take a whole bunch of deep breaths and try to calm myself down. When I woke up this morning, no way could I ever think that I would be here tonight. It's too much.

I mean what's it gonna be like now, both of us living here? Two strangers.

# THIRTY-ONE

I wake up hearing Renée on the phone, and by what she's saying, I know she's talking to Nana about me.

"And you really think that was the best way to deal with her behavior?" Renée asks. "To put her in a cab and send her over here? Because there were a whole lot of better options, if you ask me."

I don't need to have the phone to my ear to know what Nana says next. *Well, nobody asked you.*

"I know you didn't," Renée says, her voice getting a little whiny. "But what am I supposed to do with her here? I don't have enough room. Where is she supposed to sleep?"

I turn onto my other side, facing the wall. I don't wanna hear this, especially not this early in the morning. Couldn't they at least wait 'til the afternoon to talk about how much both of them don't want me?

"She's better off with you," Renée says. "What does she have here? And what about her friends? How's she going to see Adonna and —"

Renée is cut off and quiet for a while, and I know Nana is telling her about my fight with Adonna. I turn back over and see Renée's face as she sits there at the kitchen table. I can tell by the surprised look that Nana is telling her about everything else. Renée really didn't know anything last night. She's finding out all about me right now.

I wish I could jump up and snatch the phone away before Nana can tell her too much. Because it's not fair. It's my business. And if Renée has to know, I should be the one to tell her.

But something tells me I'm already too late. Nana could tell her the whole story in one sentence, knowing her. *Your daughter is nasty, just like you were at her age.*

While Nana is talking, Renée glances across the room at me, and our eyes kinda lock on each other. And even though Renée's looking at me like there's something wrong with me, I don't move, because at least she's looking at me.

Then, all of a sudden, her face gets kinda tired and she looks away from me. Finally, she says, "Okay, okay," like she wants to get off the phone already. "I'll take her tomorrow. Okay?"

I lay there wondering where she's gonna take me and why. Or am I gonna be the last one to know, as usual?

A few minutes later, Renée gets off the phone. I sit up on the Aerobed, waiting for her to say something to me, thinking of how I can explain all of this to her. I mean, Nana might think she knows what happened, but she don't know anything except for what I told her, which wasn't anything hardly. Only I can try to make Renée understand why I did it, what I was feeling.

But Renée never says anything to me. She sighs real hard and heavy, then gets up from the kitchen table and goes straight into the bathroom without even looking at me again. A minute later, I hear the shower running, so I lay back down. Part of me feels relieved that I didn't have to explain anything to her. The other part wants to know what it takes to get her to say something to me. Not that I did everything just to get her attention. I'm not that stupid.

After awhile, I get up and go into the kitchen. I'm starving, but the refrigerator's completely empty except for the leftover Chinese food. And there's nothing in the cabinets either.

"I'm going shopping later," Renée says when she comes outta the bathroom in a short, sleeveless terry cloth robe. "I was going to go last night, but . . ."

"That's okay," I say.

"Eat the rest of the lo mein," she says. "There's still some in there."

I take the white carton outta the refrigerator and open it up. And I try to think of something to say to her, but now that she knows everything that happened, I still think she's gonna say something to me first.

"I'm going to brunch with some of my friends," she says, putting her suitcase on the futon and opening it up. "We made these plans days ago."

"Um, okay," I say, shrugging. Whatever.

"And when I get back, we're going to have a talk, because you're going to have to make some serious changes, from what I hear."

"Oh, you're actually gonna talk to me?" I mumble under my breath, but I don't think she hears me, because she's too busy trying to find something to wear so she can get outta here as fast as possible.

I scoop some of the shrimp lo mein onto a paper plate and put it in the microwave. Nana would have a fit if she saw what Renée was feeding me for breakfast. I mean, there's so much oil in this food, it's soaking right through the plate.

I eat while Renée gets dressed. Before she goes out, she tells me not to leave the apartment because I don't have a key. First Nana, now Renée. No matter where I live, I guess I'm always gonna be locked up like some kinda prisoner. Like I did something *so* wrong.

After I finish eating, I get dressed in the bathroom. I look in the mirror and can't believe the way I look. I have a bruise on the side of my face and one on my shoulder from where Nana hit me. And I have a whole bunch of red scratches on my face and neck. That's why Renée didn't want me going anywhere. So people won't think she's abusing me or something.

Staring at myself all messed up and everything, I can't help but start thinking about everything that happened, about the fight between me and Nana, and how she attacked me and then just threw me out like that. Like everything was fine when I was doing exactly what she wanted, but the second I made some decisions for myself, she just turned her back on me.

She probably wants me to call her up and beg her to come back, just so she can tell me no, but I'm not gonna do that. I don't even wanna go back now and have to listen to her getting on my case all the time. It's not gonna happen.

An hour later, I'm in shorts and a tee, and I'm walking around the tiny apartment bored outta my mind. I open the windows and it's nice and sunny and hot outside, and I can't believe I'm stuck in here like this. I lean out and look down at the street. Harlem. I don't know, but I can't believe I'm here, living here. It's so different.

I mean, a few doors down, there's an old lady actually sweeping the sidewalk, and across the street, this guy is painting the railing outside of his brownstone, making it shinier than it already is. You would never see any of this at Bronxwood, that's for sure. They can't even get people to clean up after their own dogs up there.

I turn away from the window and look around the apartment. I can't even unpack, because there's no place to put anything. There are only suitcases and boxes and books. All the boxes are labeled. CDS & DVDS. KITCHEN. SHOES. BATHROOM.

One box says PHOTOS ETC. and it takes some heavy lifting, but I do get it out from under some other boxes and bring it over to the futon. If Renée wants to leave me here alone, she should be prepared for me to go through all her stuff. She has a folder on top of the box with all kinda certificates in there, starting all the way back in high school. Everything. Science achievement, winner of some kinda math competition, perfect attendance for tenth, eleventh, and twelfth grades. She was probably too busy having me for perfect attendance in ninth.

There are certificates in frames, too. National Honor Society and a Regents scholarship. Then I dig down in the box and pull out a photo album. I kinda don't even wanna open it, because I know I'm only gonna see a lot more of what I saw when I was at her apartment at Princeton. Pictures of everyone else except me.

But when I start flipping, I'm kinda surprised because the photo album goes way back, to pictures of Renée when she was real little, her and Nana in front of our building, dressed up like it's Easter. Renée's wearing a pretty yellow dress with white tights and shiny black patent leather shoes, the same kind Nana bought for me when I was little. Nana has on a funny pink hat with a big giant bow. It's hilarious.

And there are pictures of Renée and Kenny, too, all young and acting stupid, sitting on cars in the parking lot behind our building, eating ice cream, sitting on a couch in Grandma's apartment with their arms around each other, all happy.

I don't show up in the album 'til near the end. There aren't any pictures of Renée pregnant, but all of a sudden, there I am. I smile when I see myself. I mean, Nana has some pictures of me at home, but the fact that Renée has pictures of me, too, it means a lot more. There's a picture of me on the couch crying my eyes out. And there's one of Nana holding me in the kitchen. But the only picture I see of me and Renée is one in Nana's bedroom. Renée is sitting on Nana's bed and I'm just a little newborn right there on the bed next to her. Renée's looking up at the camera, but she's half smiling, half bored. Like she don't really want her picture taken.

Behind her, right in the corner of the room, is my crib. It's light brown wood with white trim, and there's a cute mobile of baby animals hanging over it. And the weird thing is, even though I'm staring at the picture, it takes me a while to really get it.

*My crib was in Nana's room.*

I look at Renée again as she sits there on the bed, and her face, it's so young. She's only my age. And she already has a baby.

I shake my head and just sit there for a while thinking what I would do if it was me. And thinking how it could have been me, how close I came to almost being in that situation. When I really think about it, it's so hard to know what I would do if I did end up like Renée. Just the thought of it makes it hard to breathe.

I close the photo album and put it back in the box. Then I get up and go to the phone in the kitchen and call Kenny because I did promise I'd call him, and there's nothing else for me to do. While I wait for him to pick up, I sit there at the table, thinking about telling him about the pictures and asking him what it was like back then when I was a baby, and how it felt to be a father when he was only fifteen.

But Kenny don't give me a chance to ask anything. He starts talking, telling me all the stuff he been hearing about me from Adonna, who was probably going off on me last night. Like our fight was all my fault or something. "So is it true?" Kenny wants to know. It kinda sounds like he's all disappointed in me, and that's not something I'm used to hearing.

It's hard to answer him. Because it's a lot more complicated than he thinks. I can't just answer yes or no.

"You having sex now?" Kenny asks. "You having sex with the boy Adonna likes?"

"No," I say finally. "You don't know the whole story. And I'm not having sex."

"I don't like this, Babe. I don't know what you doing."

Tears spring into my eyes so fast they actually sting. And I'm surprised because I didn't even think I had any more tears left in me after yesterday. "You don't understand," I say, and my voice comes out scratchy and thin. "You're not letting me explain and —"

"Explain, then," he says. "Go on."

I wish I could see his face, because I'm having a hard time figuring out what he's feeling, what he's thinking about me. And that's making this conversation even harder because I feel so off balance all of a sudden. I don't know what to say and how to say it. "Um, Adonna don't understand," I start, and right away I know there's no way I'm gonna be able to tell him what happened and why. First of all, he's my father and he don't need to know everything, and another thing, he's Adonna's brother, and how am I supposed to be honest about her when he's gonna try to be fair to both of us? Well, there's no way to be fair in this situation. And I don't wanna tell him the whole story only to have him decide that I'm the one that's wrong. "Kenny," I say, "can I call you back? I, um, I can't talk about this now."

The tears feel like they're gonna drown me from the inside, and my chest hurts real bad. I mumble bye to Kenny and hang up. Then I sit there wishing I had someone I could really talk to, about everything. But I can't think of anybody. And nobody's here.

# THIRTY-TWO

Renée is still not back by two thirty, not that I'm watching the clock or anything. I mean, she can come home whenever she wants, but I just happen to see the time and wonder what kinda brunch lasts this long. And how long she expects me to stay trapped here waiting for her.

A little while later, the doorbell rings and I actually have to find where the intercom is before I can ask who it is.

"Kendra, it's me, Mr. Mover and Fixer." It's Gerard.

I buzz him in, then open the door and wait for him to come up the stairs. He really is handsome. I mean, if you like the tall, strong, and sexy type. When he comes into the apartment, I feel kinda weird being there alone with him, especially since I don't hardly know him. And with the way I'm dressed. No way would Nana think this was okay.

Gerard drops a book he's carrying on the futon and looks around. "Damn, there's a lot of work to do here. And I see Renée hasn't done a thing since I left. Where is she, anyway?"

"Brunch," I say, closing the door behind him.

He looks at his watch. "I thought she'd be back a long time ago. Oh, well. I'd better get started here. You girls need a nice place to live."

He picks up one of the boxes and carries it into the kitchen. While he's in there putting things away, I glance down at the book he left on the futon and see it's one of those study guides that Kenny used to have, for all those tests for city jobs he never got. This one is for the Police Sergeant Exam.

"You wanna be a sergeant?" I ask Gerard.

"I don't know," he says, holding a curtain rod in his hand. He looks up at the window. "Come here and help me put this up."

I go into the kitchen, and for the next ten minutes, me and Gerard put up the rods and hang the curtains. Then we do the same thing for the curtains on the other side of the room.

Meanwhile, he's telling me some funny things he sees as a cop on the streets of Newark. "And there was this woman, right?" he says, helping me down from a couple of boxes, after I put up the last curtain. "She called nine-one-one, panicked, whispering, 'Oh, my God! He's in here. Help me. Help me.' Three squad cars respond, you know, with lights and sirens, the whole nine. And when we get in there, this lady is standing on her kitchen table pointing to a hole near her stove where a mouse had got in. And she's looking at us, with our guns drawn and everything, and she's screaming, 'Do something! Get him! Get him!'" He laughs and shakes his head. "It was insane."

I laugh with him. "You probably won't have to do that kinda thing if you get to be a sergeant, right?"

"No, not really. I won't be so hands-on, but I don't know. I like what I'm doing now. You know, when I don't have to deal with crazy ladies on kitchen tables." He laughs again, but then his face gets kinda serious. "Most of our calls are for real problems, and you know Newark can be a tough place. When I show up at somebody's house and they're a victim of a crime, I like that I can help them out. And the kids in the street, I like being a role model, you know, someone they can see doing the right thing, someone who looks like them. And being a sergeant and sitting behind a desk a lot of the time — I don't know if that's what I got into this for."

"Then why are you taking the test?" Even as I ask this question, I already know the answer.

"Renée wants me to take the test, you know, to get a better job, move up the line and all that." He opens another box, the one with the photo albums, and says, "I better put that bookcase back together so we have a place for all this stuff."

He goes to the other corner of the apartment and behind some other boxes are the wood slats and the frame for one of the white bookcases. She had, like, a million books on it in Princeton, all kinda boring sociology books and stuff. But I don't remember seeing the photo albums on it. Unless she didn't want any of her Princeton friends to see those pictures.

I sit down on the futon and try not to think about it. But it's hard. It's like she really didn't wanna have to think about me when she was at school. So I end up asking Gerard, "When did Renée tell you about me? I mean, how long were you dating?" I don't look at him when I ask this, because I don't want him to know how much his answer means to me.

"Oh, I don't know," Gerard says. "Probably after a month or two."

I sigh. That's a long time. What was she waiting for? For

him to fall in love with her? So he wouldn't wanna leave her once he found out she was already a mother?

"You know what I thought?" Gerard goes on. "I thought she had, like, a baby or a three-year-old. You know, a little kid. Then when she told me her daughter was, I think you were thirteen then, I couldn't believe it." He laughs again. "Your mother is really special. I hope you know that."

I turn to look at him and he's already staring at me. "I know," I say, but I'm not really sure I get what he's talking about.

"Not a lot of girls could have a baby in ninth grade and then turn their life around so much."

I nod. I know she could have been like a lot of girls at Bronxwood that have babies and then never even finish high school. Some of them even end up with two or three kids back to back. So I know what Gerard's talking about. I get it. But it's not that simple. He's not seeing everything.

When Renée comes home, she's all happy that we been doing work, getting her apartment together. Not only are the curtains up and the bookcase put back together, but the TV is hooked up to the cable and her little CD player and speakers are set up, too.

She gives Gerard a big hug and then a kiss, and I decide it's time for me to go outside and get some air. I don't ask Renée if I can go, because I never asked her if I could do anything before. And she's not paying me any mind, anyway. But probably as soon as I leave, she's gonna tell Gerard everything Nana said about me, and the next time he sees me, he's gonna think bad about me.

When I get to the first floor, there's a lady going into her apartment. She's probably about Nana's age or a little older. She's a lot heavier, too, but not as heavy as Grandma. She smiles when she sees me, and I say hi.

"You must be Renée's sister," she says in a real friendly way. "You favor her."

I wonder if she's just guessing I'm Renée's sister or if Renée told her she had a sister. Because it wouldn't be the first time.

"No," I say. "I'm her daughter."

The lady's head kinda snaps back. "Oh, I didn't know." She shakes her head. "I thought she was — " She gives a short kinda half laugh. "You never know these days, right?"

I don't say anything to that. I just walk past her to the door, my feet sounding kinda heavy on the wood floors. Outside, I walk down the steps and look up and down the block, not knowing where to go. I mean, I could just walk around and try to get comfortable in the neighborhood, but something tells me not to get too settled, because who knows how long I'm even gonna be here? Maybe Renée will convince Nana to take me back. Not that I really wanna go back or anything.

So I pick a direction and start walking, past the brownstones that all look alike. Probably when I get back, I won't even know which one Renée lives in — which one *I* live in. I walk around for a little while, and it feels like I'm in a place that's been here a real long time, like I'm in a history book or something.

And I'm looking at the design of the brownstones, the wide steps leading up to the doorways with fancy arches. The huge windows with flower boxes. And I can't help but wonder if I could ever design something so beautiful one day.

At first I don't go on any of the streets with the stores or a lot of people hanging around, because I'm out here in booty shorts. Nana never let me leave the house in shorts like this. I could wear them around the apartment, yeah, but she would have a fit if she saw me out here like this, trying to show myself off, as she would say.

But she's not here to see me. So forget her, then.


I walk around for about a half hour, going nowhere special. The neighborhood is really okay, nice and quiet. There's a church on the corner that must be real good, because there are cars double-parked out front and I can hear the music from the street. It's the middle of the afternoon and it don't seem like this church service is gonna be over anytime soon. Probably one of those churches that you go to in the morning and leave at night. I'm glad nobody in my family ever went to a church like that, even if the music is alright.

When I get back to the apartment, Renée and Gerard are sitting at the kitchen table working outta that study guide. She's leaning over, pointing something out to him. And she don't even see that he's barely paying attention.

I sit on the futon, feeling kinda bad for Gerard, and wondering why he can't just tell Renée that he don't really wanna be a sergeant. He's a nice guy. Just like Kenny. Too bad both of them aren't good enough for Renée the way they are.

Gerard leaves about five o'clock, and when he tells me bye,

he don't look at me different, so maybe Renée didn't tell him anything. I hope not, anyway. I go into the kitchen and open the refrigerator, and that's when I remember there's no food.

I sigh real loud. "Can we go shopping already?"

Renée comes back into the kitchen and pulls out a chair, the one Gerard was sitting in. "Sit down, Babe," she says.

"But I'm hungry."

"You're not going to starve." She sits down in the other chair and waits for me.

I roll my eyes, wait awhile, then go and sit down across from her. "What?" I ask, crossing my legs.

"We have to talk."

I fold my arms in front of me and stare up at the ceiling. This is gonna be so stupid, I can tell.

"Nana tells me you're sexually active now. Is that true?" When I don't answer, she says, "Well, is it?"

I shrug and don't look at her.

"Okay," she says, like she's just as bored with this conversation as me. I know she's only asking it because Nana is probably making her talk to me. "Okay, I'll talk and you listen."

And she talks and talks and talks. About everything. About how sex is serious and that if I'm gonna do it, I need to think about it, make sure it's something I really wanna do, and all that. I need to be careful and protect myself. And, of course, I need to make sure it's with the right guy, whatever that means. The whole time she's talking, I'm sitting there thinking, who is *she* to tell me any of this? By the time she was finishing ninth grade, she already had a kid.

The other thing that gets me is the *way* she's talking to me. She don't sound like a mother or even like a big sister. Her voice is all flat and calm and she's telling me the facts like she's my health teacher from seventh grade. Then she says something about how a lot of kids my age have sex when they really only want a connection to somebody and all that. And now I can tell she's talking to me like a sociologist. I'm not her daughter right now. I'm one of her students. Either way, she don't sound like somebody that cares about me, really. It's just that she's *supposed* to tell me this stuff. And when this talk is over, that'll be it. She'll be done.

Finally, there's a break in the conversation and I'm about to get up when she says, "You're not going to school tomorrow. I'm taking you to the women's clinic near City College."

I can feel the shock in my chest first. "Women's clinic? What for?"

"It's time for you to see a gynecologist." She says it in a kinda singing way, like she's talking to a child. "You need to get a checkup to make sure you don't have any STDs, and then you and the doctor can decide on a form of birth control. Being sexually active requires a lot of responsibility, doesn't it?"

"You should know," I say, half under my breath but loud enough for her to hear.

"Exactly," she says. And for a few seconds, we both stare at each other.

"What if I don't wanna go?" I say. "I don't even need to go. I never had sex, not like that. Not like the way you can get pregnant." Suddenly, I'm so embarrassed talking about this. "I don't wanna go to a gynecologist. I'm still just, like, a kid."

Renée leans close to me and says, "You *are* a kid. But your body, inside, is a woman. Trust me, I know. That body is capable of producing a baby. Is that what you want?"

I shake my head.

"Then you have to be smart, smarter than I was, and protect yourself."

I don't say anything.

Renée gets up from her chair and grabs her bag from off the counter. "C'mon, Babe. Let's get to the supermarket before they close."

# THIRTY-THREE

In the morning I spend, like, fifteen minutes going through my clothes in the suitcase, because how am I supposed to know what to wear to a gynecologist? I can't even believe Renée is making me go, and it's like she don't even care how scared I am. I mean, it's not even fair. I'm a virgin and she's making me go to the women's clinic, anyway. It's so embarrassing and it's not even something I need to do. I mean, it's not like me and Nashawn are ever gonna do anything again.

But Renée's not even listening when I start complaining. She gets that from Nana. When her mind is made up, that's it.

I put on a pair of jeans and a cute little blue top, one of the shirts Adonna made me buy when we went shopping together. It looks good on me, but it reminds me of Adonna and that just gets me thinking about her and wondering what she's gonna say about me in school today, and if she's gonna go up to Nashawn and ask him about me and him. Is she gonna tell the whole school that I tried to steal her man or something?

The one thing I do know is, no matter what she says about me, no way is she gonna blame Nashawn for any of it. That's the way she is. Her boyfriend from last year used to disrespect her all the time, but she just took it. And she would still be with him now if he hadn't dumped her first. Knowing Adonna, she's gonna tell herself that no matter what happened between me and Nashawn, it all happened before their first date so it's not like he cheated on her or anything.

The only good thing about going to the gynecologist is that I don't have to be in school today to see the two of them together again. I know Adonna will be all over him, too, trying to make me feel jealous because she got him and I didn't. That he's her *man* and all that.

"C'mon," Renée says, already at the door. "It's first come, first serve at that clinic."

"I'm okay with waiting," I say, but Renée only laughs. And I know she's laughing at me.

When we get there, there are only a couple of people ahead of me, and both of them are much older, like in their twenties. I'm the only teenager. Me and Renée go up to the receptionist, and when she asks Renée about my insurance, Renée gets a look I've never seen on her face before, like she has no idea about something. "I'm not exactly sure," she says to the receptionist, and then she turns to me and asks me if I know.

I shrug and the receptionist says to Renée, "Oh, I'm sorry. I thought you were her mother."

Renée says, "I am," at the exact same time I say, "She is." And the woman just shakes her head like she don't understand why Renée wouldn't know something like that.

Then Renée pulls out her cell phone and gets all the information she needs from Nana, and I can tell she's embarrassed because she really should know all this stuff.

While we wait, Renée flips through an *Essence* magazine and I sit there bored, wishing I had brought my book with me, because they don't have any magazines I wanna read here. I'm starting to get real nervous and I wish Renée would talk to me or something to take my mind off this whole thing, but I can tell she's not happy to be here, either. So I get up and grab a little pamphlet called "Your First Gynecological Examination: What to Expect" from the rack and start reading it. But, really, it's not helping at all to make me feel better about this.

About an hour later when they call my name, I find out Renée's not even coming in with me. "You're a big girl," she tells me. "I'll be here when you're done." And she goes back to reading her magazine.

I have no choice but to follow the receptionist down the hall to an office that has DR. MATHYS on the door. And that's when I see the doctor sitting there. And he's a man. A *man*. Dr. Mathys is a black guy that's not even all that old and he's a gynecologist. It's weird.

I stand there in the doorway hoping and praying that I'm in the wrong room or *he's* in the wrong room. But I'm not that lucky. Before I can turn around and run away, the doctor looks up from his paperwork and says, "Kendra Williamson?"

I nod, trapped. There's no way outta this. I step into the room real slow and he asks me to sit down in the chair next to his desk. Then, after I sit down, he starts talking and I know he's trying to relax me, but it's not working at all. I'm answering his questions about what grade I'm in and what classes I like, but all I'm thinking is, I really *really* don't want this man seeing me *down there*.

There's an examination room right next door to the office, and I'm eyeing the table and the equipment and my heart is pounding.

"How did you get those scratches and bruises on your face and neck?" Dr. Mathys asks me, looking at me like he's ready to file a report to the Child Abuse Hotline or something.

So I say the first lie that comes to my mind. "I got into a fight with a girl."

He nods at me. "Over a boy, I'm guessing."

"Something like that," I say. And I think about Adonna even though we didn't actually *fight* fight over Nashawn, but still. I look down at the floor, thinking how stupid I was because our whole argument didn't even have to happen if I would have just kept my mouth closed instead of telling her. Now that I think about it, I can't even figure out why I did that. Because if I hadn't told her, I could have just gone back to school today and acted like nothing ever happened. But now the whole school probably knows and they probably all think I'm the kinda person that would go behind her best friend's back and try to steal her boyfriend, when it wasn't even like that. The whole thing is a mess.

A female nurse comes into the room, and that's when the doctor starts asking me questions about my so-called sexual history. Like it's so long. I don't look at him, but I tell him about me and Nashawn and what we did, and it's one of the most embarrassing things I ever had to do, tell this man all my personal business. When I finally look up at him, he don't look all that surprised or anything. He probably heard it all by now.

"When was your last period?" he asks.

I shrug. "I don't know." Nana keeps track of it for me on the calendar in her bedroom. Then when it's about time for it, she asks me if I need money for pads. The funny thing is, sitting here now is the first time I get it. She wasn't doing that to help me. She just wanted to make sure I wasn't pregnant.

"I want you to take a pregnancy test," Dr. Mathys says, even though I already told him I never had real sex with Nashawn. It's like he's not even paying me any mind. But I don't argue with him. What's the point?

Of course, the test comes out negative, but I could have told him that myself. Then we go in the room for the examination, and it's just as bad as I knew it was gonna be. The nurse stays in the room the whole time, so I don't have to be alone with this guy, but still.

When it's finally done and I'm dressed again, I go back into the office with him. Right away he starts talking about birth control.

"I don't need it," I tell him. "I don't have a boyfriend or anything, and I'm not gonna do anything with anybody anymore."

But he don't listen to me. Again. He starts telling me about different kinds of birth control, and how I have to protect myself from diseases and stuff even if I'm on birth control. When he asks me if I have any questions, of course I don't, and when he tells me that he thinks the pill is the easiest and the one most girls my age like, I say okay and he gives me a prescription and a whole little bag full of condoms. All I want is to get outta there already.

Renée is no better when it comes to listening to me, because as soon as we get outta the clinic, she heads straight for the drugstore so we can fill the prescription.

"But I don't want it," I say, walking next to her down the street. "I don't need it."

"I don't have time to argue with you, Babe," she tells me. "I want to have this prescription filled and get you back home so I can get to City and try to get a little work done today."

"It's the summer," I say.

"I know, but I'm going to teach a class that begins in July. And I have to get my syllabus together."

A few minutes later, me and Renée are sitting in a Dunkin' Donuts down the street, killing time 'til the prescription is ready. This whole day has got me feeling mad. Not only for having to go through that whole examination, but also for not being listened to. I can't believe Renée wants me to take the pill for no reason.

So when she gets her coffee and I get my smoothie and donut, I try again. "I know you think you know everything about me," I say, "but I'm trying to tell you that I never had sex and I'm never gonna do anything like that."

Renée opens a pack of sugar and pours it in her coffee. "I don't think I know everything about you. But I was your age not that long ago, and nobody was going to stop me from being with Kenny, not even Nana and her threats. I know what it's like, and it's hard to stop having sex once you get started."

She's still not listening.

"And I studied teenage sexuality in school and I know all the statistics. You have to protect yourself from diseases. And it's better to be safe now than sorry nine months later. Believe me, Babe. I know what I'm talking about."

Renée's cell phone rings and even though we're in the middle of a conversation, she pulls it outta her bag and starts talking. And I just sit there waiting for her to get off, but I can tell it's gonna be awhile because it sounds like she's talking to someone from City College about some kinda project. She's talking all professional and everything.

I stir my smoothie with the straw, too angry to eat or drink anymore. I hate the way she said that, about how sorry she was nine months later, when I was born. I mean, I'm not stupid. I know she never really planned to have me. Nobody plans to have a baby at fourteen. But I never thought having me was such a big huge mistake, and that the day I was born, all she felt was sorry. I mean, how's that supposed to make me feel?

As she talks on the phone, I look over at her, wondering if she could do it all over again, would she even have me? Would I even exist? It's a crazy thought, but I wanna know the answer, even though I'm scared to hear the truth.

So when Renée flips her phone closed a few minutes later, I don't even think about it, because I don't wanna talk myself outta anything. I look her right in the eye and I ask her, "If you were fourteen again, and you just found out you were pregnant, would you do the same thing you did before? Would I even be here now?"

I can tell Renée is kinda surprised by my questions, because she was just about to take a sip of her coffee and she freezes for a few seconds. Then she puts her cup down and says, "No, you probably wouldn't be here."

It's hard to describe the way those words feel inside my body. It's like a fast, hot, stabbing pain in my heart. That's how much it hurts.

Renée leans closer to me and whispers, "I'm sorry, Babe. I am. But when I was fourteen, I thought my whole life would be with Kenny. I was in love with him and it felt so real, you know?"

I nod, but it's hard to see through all my tears.

"When I took that test and found out I was pregnant, I was so scared, but I felt like I was going to be with Kenny forever, anyway, so what difference did it make if we had a baby so young?" She shakes her head like she can't believe how stupid she was. "But Kenny and I didn't even last a year after you were born. We were two kids. And look at him now. There's no way I could have stayed with him. He's in the exact same place I left him — and that never would have worked for me. Never."

"So I was just a big mistake, then." It's half question, half statement.

But Renée don't even say anything, because we both know it's true.

I take a deep breath. Then I ask her what I been wanting to ask her for a while. "Why don't you want me? I'm talking about now. Why? I been waiting for you my whole life and you stayed away for as long as you could. And then when you're finally finished with school and you're back here and you're grown up and you have a job and everything, you still don't want me. You never even thought about wanting me." I'm crying hard now

**219**

and hoping nobody else in the Dunkin' Donuts is noticing, because I really can't control it. I feel like I'm falling apart.

Renée looks at me like she feels sorry for me, but I can tell she don't know what to say. Like there's nothing she *can* say.

But there's still more I wanna say to her. "How do you think that makes me feel?" I ask, my hand on my heart now. "My own mother, you're supposed to want me no matter what. But for you, everything and everybody else is more important than me. Well, I need somebody, too. And when I tell you that I'm trying to change, you don't even believe me. I mean, that doctor don't know me, but you, you're supposed to be on my side. You're supposed to get me. And you don't. You don't know me at all." It feels like there's a waterfall inside of me, and nothing can stop it. Not for a while, anyway.

Renée still don't know what to say to me. And for a while, me and her just sit there quiet, with nothing but the sounds of the people ordering donuts and talking at the tables around us.

But after a long time, she puts her hand on top of mine and says, "C'mon, Babe. Let's go back to the drugstore." I sigh, but then she says real fast, "Let's go back so we can cancel that prescription, okay?"

And I nod through my tears. "Okay."

# THIRTY-FOUR

I knew there wasn't any way to get outta it, but still, on Tuesday as I walk up the steps to school, I really wish I could have stayed home one more day. At least. Yesterday was so long and draining that I could use another day just to sit and think and try to deal with everything that's happened. But it's the week before Regents exams and finals, and I know all the teachers are gonna be reviewing, and I need that. Because there's a ton of stuff I barely learned the first time around, and now that I'm with Renée, I can just see her face if I bring home a bad report card.

Plus I need to put my mind on something else besides myself and how I messed everything up. Even thinking about schoolwork is better than that.

When I get into the building, I head straight for the staircase. I'm here extra early, which wasn't easy coming all the way from Harlem, but it's worth it if I can avoid as many people as possible, especially Adonna, Nashawn, and Darnell.

The hall on the second floor is pretty empty, and the few

kids that are up there aren't anybody I know, so I'm able to get to my locker and get all my stuff without running into anybody. Then I walk down the hall, and when I pass the teachers' lounge, I feel this weird tingling feeling in my stomach and I can't tell if it's a good feeling or not. It makes me think of Nashawn and that first time and how hot and confusing it was. I walk faster, turn the corner, and see Brunilda at her locker, putting her long hair back in a ponytail. She's at school early, too, another girl that wants to get to homeroom before the halls get packed with other kids.

As I walk by her, she looks up at me, and I smile but don't say anything. I mean, I don't really know her that good even though we got English and bio together. She missed a couple of days after the so-called fight, and since then, she been more quiet than usual. And she's not dressing like she's all that anymore. She's blending in with everyone else better.

And at this school, you do a whole lot better when you don't stand out that much.

I turn the next corner by my homeroom, and just as I'm about to reach the classroom, I see Darnell coming down the hall, carrying a big poster board with some kinda math formulas on it. He's heading in my direction, right toward me.

I try to read his face, but it's too hard to look at him after what I did. I mean, I know I hurt him and I know he probably hates me, but at the same time, it's not really his place to judge me and it's too early in the morning to be judged, anyway.

So I try to ignore him, but just as I'm about to turn the doorknob, Darnell steps in front of me and says in a real quiet voice, "You're at school early."

"You, too," I say. "The showcase is over, you know."

"I know," he says. He stops talking and looks down at the floor for a while.

And, man, it's not easy seeing him like this, because it looks like he been kicked or something. Like the wind is knocked outta him.

Finally, he looks up at me and says, "Your cousin been saying some —"

"She's my aunt."

"Well, whatever she is, she been going around saying you and Nashawn —"

"It's all true," I say, and swallow real hard. "Everything."

He shakes his head and it takes awhile for him to say anything, but finally he says, "I don't get it. I thought you were, like, I don't know, different from a lot of girls around here."

"I guess you were wrong," I tell him. His eyes look so sad, it's hard to do this to him. But he needs to know the truth. Even if it hurts. "Sorry."

I mumble that last part and push past him and go into my homeroom. I feel bad but, really, it was stupid of me to try to like him that way. Just because he liked me first.

It wasn't fair to him.

I sit at my desk in the empty classroom and try not to feel guilty, but it's too hard after what just happened.

When other kids start coming in, I can feel them looking at me. It's not my imagination, either. And I know it's not the marks on my face they're staring at, because I wore some of Renée's pressed powder to cover them up. It's all because of what Adonna been saying about me.

Actually, all morning I feel like people are staring at me and talking about me, in class and in the hall. It's just so not fair. This is between me and Adonna. Not me, Adonna, and the whole school.

Even while I'm walking past the theater on my way to Mr. Melendez's class fourth period, I still feel like I'm exposed or something. Like everybody knows all my secrets. I can't get away from what I did. And then to make things even worse, Darnell is in this class and I have to deal with looks from him for the next fifty minutes.

But he don't show up. He's cutting class so he won't have to look at me.

Great.

After our class, I sit there in my seat and try to finish the sketch I was making while I wasn't paying attention. It's a one-family brownstone and the whole basement is an office with floor-to-ceiling shelves for Renée's books. And there are large windows so she'll have lots of light to read by. I'm working on a circular staircase leading up to the first floor when Mr. Melendez leans over so he can see what I'm working on.

"Beautiful," he says. "But remember to keep it functional."

"Huh?" I look at what I'm doing, trying to see what's not functional.

He points to my staircase. "If you keep going that way, look where the railing will end up, dissecting the arch to the living room."

I nod, getting it. The circular staircase won't work that way. I'll have to move it. Or change my whole vision.

"I'll recommend you for Ms. Myers's Introduction to Architecture class next year if you'd like. She prefers juniors and seniors, but I think you would do well."

I smile. "I don't know," I say. "My grandmother's, um,

boyfriend came to the show last week and he said I should think about set design — like, you know, for a job. But I don't know."

I look up at Mr. Melendez's face to see what he'll say to that, like does he even think I have enough talent? And his first reaction is to nod. "He's right," he says. "It's a great field, and you know what I think about the job you did on the set for the showcase." He takes a seat in the chair next to me. "When you applied for the design concentration and I looked at your portfolio, I definitely wanted you in the program. But I did notice that you were mostly drawing homes. So why don't you keep your options open and take architecture and interior design and figure out what you like? You have a lot of time."

"I know, but I wanna . . . I just wish I knew what I wanted."

He laughs all hard and deep, like I just said the funniest thing he ever heard.

"What?" I ask.

He shakes his head. "I'm sorry. But what are you? Fourteen, fifteen?"

"Fourteen."

He laughs again.

"What?" I ask again, but I laugh, too, because I can tell he thinks I'm too young to know what I want. I'm being crazy.

He stands up. "I don't want you to be late for your next class," he says. "And I have to get to lunch."

I have lunch, too, but there's no way I wanna walk into that cafeteria today. I know Adonna's gonna be there telling everybody at our table what I did or what kinda person I am. And Mara wasn't at homeroom or in English, so she's probably absent today. There's no way I'm gonna go to lunch and not

**225**

even have a table to sit at. "Do you still have that book you showed us before, Mr. Melendez? The one with all those famous set designs from Broadway and London?"

"Yeah, sure. But I don't like it to leave this room."

"Can I stay here next period and look at it? I'll be careful."

"What do you have next period?"

I tell him lunch, and he looks at me for a while and then says, "Okay." He reaches into his bottom desk drawer and pulls out the gigantic coffee-table-size book. "Here you go," he says, handing it to me. "Put it back when you're done, and if you leave, pull the door closed behind you. It's locked."

I nod. "Okay, I will." But I think me and him both know I'm not going anywhere. "Thanks, Mr. Melendez."

I sit there all through lunch looking at the beautiful pictures and reading about all the famous set designers and how they came up with their ideas. It would be nice flying around the world and working with all those directors and winning awards. Maybe it would be more realistic than building homes for me and Renée.

The rest of the day isn't as bad as I thought it was gonna be. I get through it without running into Adonna or Nashawn, even though after lunch, I see the two of them walking down the hall together. They don't see me, though, and that's a good thing. Only three more days of school to go 'til finals. Then I won't have to deal with any of this all summer.

When school's over, I walk outta the building and down the steps. Just as I hit the last step, I see her, Adonna, standing there. And she's mad.

She don't say anything to me, and everything happens so fast. The next thing I know, she's grabbing me by my shirt and

226

slamming me, hard, against the fence. I close my eyes as the pain shoots across my back, and when I open my eyes again, I see a whole bunch of kids around us now. And there's Adonna right in my face, and all I know is, I can't believe what's going on. I'm about to get jumped in front of the school, in front of all these people.

# THIRTY-FIVE

It's weird, but for a few minutes I can see Adonna screaming at me, but I can't make out what she's saying. And I can see her hitting me, but I can't feel anything. It's all happening so fast but in slow motion at the same time, and I'm numb and can't figure anything out. I mean, Adonna. My best friend, *my aunt*, is attacking me.

*Adonna.*

Then I feel it, a punch, right across the jaw, and, man, it hurts. Like hell.

I start to hear the crowd, too. I hear "Oooh, shit" and "Damn, girl" and I know they're cheering. *For Adonna.*

I hear Adonna, too. "Fuckin' backstabbing ho," she calls me a second before she slams me against the fence again.

It stings. It hurts. But I'm not about to cry in front of all these kids. And I'm not gonna let her beat me down without fighting back. I mean, I grew up in Bronxwood, too. She's not the only one.

That's when I notice it — Adonna's weave. She actually went out and got a weave. And I don't care. I'm going for it.

She's just about to punch me again and I move fast for all that fake hair. I grab it and wrap it around my fist and pull as hard as I can. And that weave must have been sewed in real good, because I can feel her hair rip away from her scalp as she screams. I pull again and I'm not gonna stop, either. She screams again and tries to grab my hand to stop me.

Now the crowd is laughing. At Adonna.

Two seconds later, a whole bunch of school security guards come outta the building and break up the fight. One piece of Adonna's weave is hanging off on the side and she's trying to hold it in place so nobody can see, even though more than enough kids got camera phones and everything, and they probably got the whole fight on video.

"You're such a fucking bitch, Kendra," she yells as two guards pull her away from me.

"Keep trying to cover your fucking bald spot!" I yell back.

She's trying to get away from them so she can come after me again, but the guards got a good grip on her and they take her up the stairs to the school with hardly any problem.

I stand there looking at all the kids from my school. They're starting to walk away, some smiling, some laughing, some looking like they got cheated outta what should have been a better fight. And I can't believe it. I can't believe any of this happened.

Then, before I can even figure out what I'm gonna do, a female security guard grabs me by the arm. "Come on," she says, pulling me back to the stairs.

"I didn't do anything!" I yell at her.

"The dean will be the judge of that."

The *dean*. This is so unfair. Why do I have to go to the dean when I was minding my own business and got attacked for no reason? It's not right.

The security guard manhandles me up the stairs and back into the school. Adonna is up the hall ahead of us, and her weave is really torn off. I can't help but smile. She's so *sad*, running out to get a weave just to try to hold on to Nashawn. I mean, I don't even know who she's competing with. She already got him. And what kinda girl attacks her own niece over a boy, anyway?

Both me and Adonna end up in the dean's office. Well, she has to go inside and talk to the dean and I'm left on the long wooden bench next to his secretary's desk. The woman is sitting at her computer typing away at, like, two hundred words a minute or something, and it don't look like she's planning on leaving anytime soon. I always thought the people in the office got to leave here five minutes after we do, but I guess they still have work to do.

She starts printing out something, and when she gets up to go to the printer, Dean Frey comes outta his office looking like he really has better things to deal with besides this. He looks at me like he's sizing me up and whispers something to the secretary. Then he goes back into his office without even saying anything to me or getting my side of the story.

The secretary sits back down and says to me, "Sweetheart, Dean Frey wants me to call your parent or guardian to —"

"*What?*" I can't believe this. "Why am I getting in trouble when she's the one that —?"

"You're not in trouble. The dean knows it's not your fault.

We just want someone to know what happened to you. Maybe you should go to the doctor or —"

"The doctor? For what?"

The secretary leans closer to me and says, "It's a legal thing, sweetheart. We don't want anyone suing the board of education because they weren't informed about what happened to their kid. What's the phone number?"

I sit there for a while thinking who I should call. My first thought is Nana. She got mad last time when she wasn't the one the school called. But she threw me out, so she don't get to be mad anymore. I could call Renée, but she's still at work and I don't wanna bother her. So I tell the secretary to call my father because at least I know he's gonna be there.

Turns out, Adonna had the dean call Kenny, too, because he comes to the school for both of us. "This shit don't make no kinda sense, Babe," he says when he sees me. Then he goes straight into the dean's office, and I can hear him and Adonna arguing in there.

I sit there on that hard wood, getting more and more mad myself. Adonna didn't have any right to call Kenny to come and get her. I mean, yeah, he's her brother, but he's not her father. She should have called Grandma and left Kenny for me.

A few minutes later, the door opens up and Kenny, Adonna, and Dean Frey come out into the waiting area. Adonna has her arms folded in front of her and her face is all puffy like she been crying, probably because I messed up her perfect hair.

"Ms. Williamson," Mr. Frey says, "are you okay?"

I nod.

"The nurse is gone for the day," he says, like it didn't matter that I just told him I was okay.

"I don't need a nurse," I say.

"You know fighting goes against the school's policy, the one you agreed to abide by when you entered this school in September."

I'm pretty sure this man is a robot because I have no idea why he's telling this to me, unless he's programmed to say this to every student no matter who did the fighting and who did the defending.

"I know," I say. "Tell that to her."

Me and Adonna's eyes lock on each other and she tries to give me her tough-girl look, but I'm not buying it and I'm not gonna be the first to look away, either. For the first time, I'm not backing down.

"It was *after* school," Adonna says, finally looking away, making me feel like I won, even if it's kinda childish. "I don't know why I'm being suspended for something I did after school on my own time."

"You can't be that stupid," I say. Then I think about it and say, "But you are."

"Why don't you go back to spreading your legs, Kendra?"

"Why don't you figure out how to keep your man satisfied, Adonna?"

Kenny clears his throat real loud. "I don't believe what I'm seeing or hearing," he says. "Look at the two of you. Please don't tell me y'all are fighting over some boy."

Both me and Adonna suck our teeth and turn away from each other.

"Say something!" Kenny yells, but I don't know who he's talking to, me or her.

232

Adonna does one of her bored sighs. "Can we go home already, Kenny?"

I stand up and turn back around. "I thought you were here to take *me* home." I stare at Kenny, who looks from me to Adonna and back to me again, like he really don't know what he should do. Like I'm not his daughter.

Kenny shakes his head and says, "I'm not taking you both together and having y'all tear up my truck, that's what I do know."

Adonna rolls her eyes and tells Kenny, "I know you're gonna choose her over me, so go ahead."

"I'm so tired of you being jealous of me and Kenny," I say. "He's my father, you know."

"Take him, then."

"Fine."

Kenny grabs Adonna and starts pulling her outta the office. "I'm gonna take this one home first," he says to Dean Frey and the secretary. "I'll be back in fifteen minutes for that one. And, Babe, don't you leave this office. I swear. I'm not playing."

Sitting there on that bench, when they leave, I'm so pissed off I can't even think straight. The dean goes back in his office and the secretary takes out a Nora Roberts novel and starts reading, and all I wanna do is get up and leave. I mean, why do I have to wait for him, anyway? Why do I need him to take me home? He made his decision, right? He picked Adonna.

Then, outta the corner of my eye I see Nashawn in the doorway, trying to get my attention. "Come here," he mouths.

I look over to the secretary, who hasn't looked up from her book. "I can't," I mouth back, shaking my head.

He tries again and holds up a finger. "One minute."

I shake my head again. I'm not gonna fall for that. One minute. Yeah, right. I know what he wants. It's all he ever wants from me. And if I leave this office, I'll probably end up somewhere with him again and now there's no excuse, because I know he's only using me. He wants to be with Adonna, and I was just being stupid all this time.

But I look over at him again and now he has his hands pressed together, like he's begging me or something. And part of me wouldn't mind hooking up with him again, just to feel something except mad. Just to be with him again. That would be nice. And I do have fifteen minutes before Kenny gets back.

But no, I can't. I'm not gonna do it. Yeah, it would be good for a few minutes, but then what will I have? Nothing. And how's it gonna feel to see him and Adonna together after that?

I shake my head at Nashawn one last time and then look away so I won't be tempted by him again. I'm gonna sit here and wait for Kenny, and I'm gonna be strong now. Especially when it comes to Nashawn.

# THIRTY-SIX

"I can't believe this," Kenny says for probably the hundredth time since we got into the truck. "I can't believe y'all are fighting."

And the way he says *fighting* feels like I'm getting punched all over again, because now he's disappointed in me for the second time this week and nothing I say is gonna make him understand. I'm probably too far down in his eyes.

I look outta the window as we cross a bridge, over the Harlem River. I'm almost back home, whatever that means. Kids are walking across the bridge, coming home from school, laughing and having fun with each other, and that only makes me feel even more friendless.

We stop kinda short at a red light and I hear some cans in the back of the truck start to roll around. Kenny's not paying attention to the road. He's too busy not believing what happened between me and Adonna.

"Y'all was best friends," he says, like I don't know that. "And y'all are fighting over a boy. Two beautiful, smart girls fighting over some idiot boy."

I stay looking outta the window, but I do feel the need to defend myself. "We weren't fighting over a boy," I say. "You're making me seem like some desperate girl that's gonna fight somebody for a boy when I'm not even like that. She's the one that tried to beat me up in front of the whole school just because her boyfriend, or whatever he is to her, just because him and me . . ." I don't even know how to finish that sentence. And I don't have to. He already knows everything.

He starts driving again. "So you trying to tell me you didn't do nothing wrong? That this whole thing is Adonna's fault, right?"

"Right," I say, but my voice is quieter because, now that he put it like that, it's kinda hard to convince him that the *whole thing* is Adonna's fault. I mean, the fight was definitely her fault and that was *definitely* wrong on her part, but everything else? I don't know. I mean, I know I made some mistakes. I can admit that. But does that give her the right to put her hands on me?

Renée is walking down the block just as we pull up to the curb in front of the brownstone. She looks beautiful in a tan summer dress with a short little jacket. Kenny shuts off the engine and watches her, and I know I should probably tell him about Gerard, just so he'll know.

But before I can figure out how to say it, Renée comes up to the truck and leans her head in on my side and says, "How much is an ice cream sandwich?"

Kenny looks at her and says, "For you, free."

"You're not going to make any money that way," she says.

"Don't remind me of how much money I already lost today."

236

I wanna open the door to get outta the truck before he tells her about the fight and she starts getting on my case, because I heard enough already. But Renée's standing right in front of my door and she's not moving.

"Okay, tell me what's going on," she says to me. "What happened?"

"Nothing," I say. "Excuse me, but I wanna get out."

"Answer my question."

I'm starting to feel trapped there between the two of them. "Can I please get out?"

Renée don't move, so I crawl between the two front seats and head for the back door, snatching a couple of Chick-O-Sticks on the way. Kenny gets outta the truck, too, and he stops me from walking past them into the brownstone. "Tell Renée what happened," he says.

I fold my arms in front of me. "I was leaving the school and minding my own business and Adonna tried to beat me up, and for some reason *he* thinks that's my fault."

Renée gets this crazy look on her face. "You're *fighting*?"

"I didn't do any —"

"What you gonna do about this?" Kenny asks Renée, pointing to me.

"What do you mean, what am *I* going to do?"

"Like I said."

For the first time, it actually looks like he's getting mad at Renée, which could be a good step for him if he wasn't getting mad at her over me.

"If you know what to do with her, you do it," Renée says, turning her back to him, and me, and stomping up the stairs of the brownstone like she's two.

He goes after her and catches up to her at the top of the stairs. "You know what? She wasn't having none of these problems before you came home. You wanna know what her problem is? It's you."

I swear, he's so mad I can see the spit flying outta his mouth when he talks. I stand at the bottom of the steps, wishing I had somewhere else to go.

Renée stares at him with her eyes all squinty. "Get out of my face, Kenny," she says all calm.

But Kenny's not done yet. "The other day — when was that? Saturday? — yeah, on Saturday. You know you had that girl crying her eyes out in my truck 'cause you was moving here without her. You know that? You know all this shit that's happening with her didn't start 'til you came back. You get that?"

Renée looks like she's all bored. "What do you want from me, Kenny? You know what her problems are, and you and her are so close, then why don't you figure out what to do with her? She's your daughter, too. When are you going to get off your ass, get a real grown-up job, move out of your mommy's apartment, and become a man? Because maybe your daughter wouldn't have to jump in bed with the first boy who pays her some attention if the father she loves so much were actually more mature than she is."

I look down at the ground. Just stand there, not looking at Kenny, because I can't stand to see the look that's probably on his face.

With my head down, I hear the front door of the brownstone open and slam closed. I hear Kenny walk down the stairs and, a few seconds later, the sound of the truck's engine start up again. When he's gone, the truck speeding down the street to the corner, it hits me for the first time, even though it's hard to believe I never thought of it before like this, but I now get it — *These are my parents.* And they have no idea what they're doing.

Upstairs I watch Renée, who is obviously pissed, take off her jacket, change from her shoes to her sandals, and put on a fresh coat of lipstick in the bathroom mirror. I wanna say, *Why did you have to do that to him? You have no right to speak for me, like I'm the one that feels that way about Kenny when I don't.* But I can tell she's not gonna wanna hear anything from me. Her face is set, and she looks exactly like Nana does when she's so mad she's about ready to boil over. I know enough not to turn up the heat.

So I go into the kitchen as quiet as I can and pour myself a glass of water. I'm waiting for her to say something about the fight, about how upset she is with me, but instead she picks up the phone and calls her friend Jennifer and makes plans to meet her somewhere. "I need to get out of this apartment," she tells her. "I can't even tell you what kind of day I've had."

When she hangs up, she grabs her bag and heads straight for the door, not even looking at me. She couldn't get outta the door any faster if she was flying.

If I was still with Nana, she would be breaking on me right now. She would tell me that just because I'm from the projects that don't mean the projects have to be in me. And that I have to remember my home training when I'm in situations like that and not let *that girl* lead me to do things I know are wrong.

I sit down at the kitchen table and drink my water. No matter what happens, I'm still here alone. Better get used to it.

The phone rings at about six, and as soon as I say hello, Nana is going off.

"Tell me what I'm hearing around here ain't true, because I know, *I know*, the child I raised isn't fighting in the street. And don't say shit — pardon my French — don't say shit about Adonna starting anything because —"

"I'm not getting into this with you," I say, trying to keep my voice calm even though I can't believe she had the nerve to call here.

Nana's still going, though. ". . . and that *other* grandmother of yours has the audacity to come up to me in the lobby and tell me that *you* got *her daughter* suspended, and half the building is standing there listening, and I have to hear that y'all are fighting like some kind of —"

"Nana."

"Don't you even think about talking back to me or I will come over there and —"

"Nana, I'm not listening to this. Not from you. Not anymore."

"Girl, don't you let your mouth get your ass in trouble."

It's getting harder and harder for me to keep calm. "You know what, Nana? You don't get to yell at me anymore. Because you're the one that threw me out, remember? So you don't get to be a mother to me anymore, because I have a mother now."

There's silence on the other end of the phone.

"Bye," I say, and hang up real fast.

My heart is racing. I can't believe I did that. I mean, I didn't actually hang up on her, but I might as well have. I didn't just stand and take it from her like I used to.

But still, I know there was probably a nasty scene between Nana and Grandma in the lobby, and I hate to think I was even a little bit of the cause of that, because the two of them barely get along as it is. And now Renée and Kenny are fighting, too. It's like all it took was for me and Adonna to fight for the whole family to fall apart.

And I'm alone.

Part of me, a big part, wishes I knew Nashawn's phone number, because I would call him and even go over to his house again and not sit here alone waiting for Renée, who probably won't even talk to me when she gets back. I mean, if I was with Nashawn for a little while, at least that would be something.

But I don't have his number so it don't even matter. And I know I told Renée I wouldn't do anything with him anymore, but I don't think she even cares one way or another. I mean, we had this whole long talk yesterday and I told her everything I was feeling and still, where is she right now?

I turn on the TV but don't actually watch anything. I just like having it on. Then I eat some cereal and leave the bowl in the sink. By eight thirty, when Renée's still not home, it's hard trying to tell myself that I'm not mad, because I am. I mean, I get into a fight, but she don't even ask me what happened and if I'm okay or anything. My whole life is messed up right now, and even though me and her are living in this tiny little apartment, it's still like she's far away from me. Nothing changed.

Renée is still not back when I'm ready for bed so I turn off the TV and all the lights and try to get comfortable on the

Aerobed. But it's hard. I can't sleep. My brain is like on rewind and fast forward at the same time and I can't stop it.

And in between thinking about the fight and Kenny and Renée and Nana, and how I have to go back to school tomorrow and face all those kids that were watching the fight and hoping I'd get my ass kicked, in between all of that, I'm thinking about Nashawn. I'm seeing his face in the doorway of the dean's office and how he begged me to come out. Just thinking about his face and remembering the way his body felt when we were together in his bed, it's enough to keep me awake and frustrated.

I slip my hands into my pajama shorts, close my eyes, and try to get myself back to that place, that feeling. It takes awhile, but soon my breathing gets a little heavier and my mind takes me back there. And it feels good, it does, but it's not 'til I'm done that I realize it's not enough. That's not all I want from him. I want *him*. All of him, not just what we been doing.

And that's what hurts, knowing that there's no chance for that. Because when it comes to me, all he wants is what he been getting already.

# THIRTY-SEVEN

I get to school even earlier than I did yesterday because today I really don't wanna see anybody. I couldn't hardly sleep last night thinking about everything that happened yesterday and all those kids that were out there watching the fight and not caring if Adonna ended up killing me. It's embarrassing that everybody saw that — me and her being family and fighting like that.

At least I don't have to worry about seeing *her* today. I wish she was suspended for the rest of the year. It's not fair that I'm gonna have to see her again next week when I'm already gonna be worried about passing my finals and stuff.

The school is just about empty except for the security guards and a couple of teachers and office people walking around on the first floor. Upstairs, the hall where my locker is at is completely empty, not even one person on the floor. I grab what I need from my locker and slam it shut real fast. Then as I head down the hall, I hear, "Kendra."

I know it's him, but I don't stop walking for a second. Matter of fact, I speed up a little bit.

"Kendra," he says again. "C'mon, let me talk to you for a second."

I turn the corner without looking back and see the bathroom down the hall. That's where I'm headed because I know he can't follow me in there.

Then I hear Nashawn call out, "Babe!"

And that gets me to stop. I put my hands on my hips and turn around. "Don't call me that!" I yell. "Who even told you about that?"

He keeps walking toward me, and his face has that smirk and he's so cute, but I'm trying not to notice that anymore.

"I was there on Saturday, remember?" he says. "I heard your father calling you that when you left his truck, but you were *gone*."

I put my head down. Man, I feel stupid. I mean, what was he thinking when he saw me just run into the building like that? And what did him and Adonna say to each other after I left, before she came upstairs and tried to make me feel bad because she got him and I didn't?

No matter what, I can't stop and talk to him now because I already know what he wants and now, with the school practically empty and everything, I know if I let him start talking to me here, we're gonna end up someplace together and I can't anymore. He made his decision already, and even though Adonna don't deserve for me to look out for her, not after what she did to me, still I'm not gonna go behind her back anymore. I'm not gonna be like that.

So I turn back around and keep walking and try not to

listen to Nashawn, who's following me, saying stuff like, "I just wanna talk to you. C'mon, all I need is, like, a minute."

I get to the bathroom, which is dirty even at this time of the morning. The toilets aren't flushed and there's toilet paper and stuff all over the floor. Like, don't they ever clean this place? Personally, I don't even know how girls could be so nasty.

And even though it's not the best place in the world to have to wait, I stay there for about fifteen minutes, 'til I hear more kids start to fill up the halls. When I go back out, I don't see Nashawn, so I go straight to homeroom, hoping he won't pop outta nowhere again. And he don't, thank God.

Mara's in homeroom, looking through her bio study guide, the one I never opened even once. I slide into my seat across from her.

"Studying?" I ask.

"Kendra!" She smiles at me all big. "You're here early."

"You, too."

"My mom was making me crazy this morning," she says, shaking her head. "All we ever do is argue."

"What about?"

She shrugs. "Nothing. Just everything, you know?"

I nod. "I moved in with, um, my mother on Saturday."

"That's what you wanted, right?"

"Yeah," I say, and can't help but sigh because it feels like there's a lot inside me that I don't know how to talk about. It's like everything is heavy and confusing. I mean, I feel bad that Mara and her mom are always fighting, but at least it's something. They're talking. Me and Renée don't really have a whole lot to say to each other at all. It's like we had that one talk for a few minutes and now that's it. We're done.

"Were you sick yesterday?" I ask her.

"Cramps," she says.

I make a face. "I know what that's like." Not that Nana would ever let me stay home for that. She would give me a whole lecture about how I'd better get used to it because when I get a job, no way is my boss gonna let me stay home every month.

Two girls come into the classroom and both of them stare at me, not even trying to hide it. One of them, Brenda, kinda shakes her head, and I can't tell if she feels sorry for me or thinks I was wrong to rip off Adonna's weave like that. Either way, I just hope the whole day isn't gonna be like this.

"What's going on?" Mara whispers to me when Brenda and Tyesha sit down in their seats on the other side of the room. "Did something happen that I don't know about?"

I nod. Mara missed a lot yesterday.

"Tell me," she says.

I turn back and see that they're both still looking at me. I shake my head and whisper back to Mara, "At lunch, okay? I'm gonna stay in Mr. Melendez's classroom because I can't deal with the cafeteria anymore."

"Alright," she says. "I'll stay with you, then."

I smile a little bit because I need to talk to somebody. And it looks like Mara's the only one I have left.


Mr. Melendez don't even seem surprised when both me and Mara ask him if we can stay in his classroom for lunch. "Okay," he says, looking at us, trying to figure out what's going on. "I'm sure there's a good reason why you don't want to go to the cafeteria — right, Kendra?"

I nod.

"Well, you know the rules. Lock the door if you decide to leave."

"Thanks, Mr. Melendez."

When he's gone, Mara takes two Snickers bars outta her backpack and hands one to me. "Here's lunch," she says.

"Thanks." I open the wrapper real slow, trying to think of a good way to start talking to her. It's not easy. And I know I'm gonna come off looking real bad even though I didn't want any of this to happen. Not this way, anyway.

So we eat for a little while without talking, and Mara's so sweet she don't even push me to talk. She waits for me. And I like that.

I'm about halfway done with my Snickers when I finally say, "You know that guy, Nashawn? He's a junior."

"Of course," she says. "He's *so* cute!" She giggles, then covers her face with her hands.

"He is," I say. "And his locker is right next to mine."

"Lucky."

I take a deep breath. "Me and him hooked up a few times."

Mara's eyes get wider, but I see her try to look like she's not surprised. "Yeah?"

"Yeah. It wasn't anything, really. Just, you know, sex. He really likes Adonna, and she's really into him, too."

"Then why did you . . . ? I mean —"

"I know," I say, looking down at the desk. "I just can't really explain, you know? I was going through a lot of stuff and it just happened the first time. Then, I don't know, it happened again,

247

and I didn't know how to stop it. Or if I really wanted to. Even though I knew it was wrong." I get tears in my eyes, but I try to blink them away. "Then he went out with Adonna and they looked all happy and everything. So I told Adonna, which was stupid, I know." The blinking isn't working and I have to wipe my eyes. "And then yesterday she started a fight with me in front of the whole school and —" I shake my head. "It was bad."

"I heard about the fight," Mara says. "These girls in English were talking about it. But they didn't know what it was about."

I pick my head up. "I know I did the wrong thing, but Adonna never should have started a fight. Especially at school. I mean, we're family and she's not supposed to bring family business to school."

Mara nods, but she kinda looks like she might not agree with what I'm saying. She's just trying to be a good friend.

"I feel so stupid," I say. "Nashawn was just using me and I should have known better, you know? And now the two of them are together and I don't have anybody."

Mara grabs ahold of one of my hands, and I keep trying not to cry. But all I can think about is Nashawn and Adonna being together and how she won. Not only did she get the guy she really wanted, she's always gonna know that he picked her over me. That I couldn't hold on to him. That she's better than me. Like she always knew she was. And it hurts to be this stupid.

Finally, Mara says, "You could have told me this before, you know. I wouldn't have said anything to anyone, and I could have helped you out. So you wouldn't feel so alone."

I nod and wipe my eyes again. "I know, but, you know, I

just didn't want you to think I was like that with guys, because I'm not. I mean, I never did anything like that before."

Mara nods and looks at me like she's really trying to understand me. "I know me and you aren't as close as you and Adonna are, or at least *were*, but to me, you're my friend, and you can tell me anything. Okay?"

"Okay," I say, trying to smile through my tears. It does feel kinda good to hear her say that, too. Mara's pretty cool. I don't know why me and her never got to be real close, like outside of school and everything. Probably because I always had Adonna for that. For everything.

Me and Mara change the subject and start talking about the volunteer thing Mr. Melendez told us about. Mara tells me her mother don't want her to do it. She wants to send her down south like she does every summer. "She doesn't want me and my little sister to stay home all day while she's at work. But I don't see why she can't send Nya without me. I'm in high school now."

"I think it would be fun working on the production," I say. "But I haven't asked Renée yet." Not that she's gonna mind. Most likely she wouldn't even care what I did. "Anyway, it's hard to think of summer when we still have to get through finals."

"Let's study together over the weekend," Mara says. "You can come over to my house. You can even spend the night if you want."

Renée would probably like that, I think. That way she'd get to have Gerard stay over.

"I'll ask Renée," I tell Mara. "That would be fun, though."

All of a sudden I'm feeling a whole lot better.

And that's when the door opens, and when I look over I see Nashawn standing there looking right at me. "I been searching all over the school for you," he said, "and I finally figured out where you were hiding."

Seeing him in the doorway looking at me like that, I can't help but feel a little nervous, a little weak. The way his eyes are just kinda focused on me the same way they did when we were alone together at his house, I can't help but feel like maybe that look actually means something this time. It's not smart — I know that — but if I was here alone and he was looking at me like that, I know I could get talked into anything in a second.

But I'm not alone. Mara's here. And when I look over at her, her arms are crossed in front of her and she's giving Nashawn the evil eye.

"Kendra doesn't have anything to say to you," she says, real blunt. "So keep stepping."

And all I'm thinking is, thank God Mara is here to protect me . . . from myself.

# THIRTY-EIGHT

But Nashawn don't listen to Mara, and he don't let her attitude stop him for a second. He comes right into the classroom, and when he turns around to close the door, me and Mara glance at each other and I try to tell her with my eyes how much I don't want him in here in with us. Mara nods like she understands, and that makes me feel a little more comfortable because I know she's not gonna leave my side. And no way am I gonna end up doing anything with him.

As Nashawn walks toward me, it's hard to look at him and not focus on his body, those muscular shoulders and his stomach and the way it felt to touch him without his shirt on. I shake my head and try not to think about any of that, but it's not easy. I mean, it's been like, what, two seconds? And look at me. I'm already all hot for him again.

Nashawn sits down at the desk right next to mine. "Are you finally gonna let me talk to you?" he asks, leaning even closer to me.

And the closer he gets, the more I feel my heart racing faster and faster.

I wanna tell him no, that there's nothing I wanna hear from him, but then I look in those deep brown eyes and I forget what I was gonna say.

Good thing Mara is there. She jumps right in with, "Well, she doesn't wanna talk to you. How many times does she have to say that? Huh?" And she has the right tone of voice, too, like she's not playing.

Nashawn sits back in his chair and even folds his hand like he's a good boy, but he still has that half smile on his face, and it's really making me crazy. I force myself to look away from him because, really, his lips look so good, if Mara wasn't there, I would be all over them right now.

So I go back to eating my Snickers bar, and Mara starts talking to me again, trying to pick up our conversation where we left off, like Nashawn isn't even there. "What kind of movies do you like?" she asks me. "Because when we're finished studying, we can watch some of my DVDs."

"I like funny movies," I say. "And romantic movies, with cute guys, of course!" I start laughing, maybe a little too much. But Nashawn needs to know that I have plans of my own this weekend. I'm not gonna be sitting at home thinking of him while he's probably out on another date with Adonna.

Mara giggles, too. "We're gonna have fun."

"Yeah," I said. "We might even do some studying!"

Me and Mara go on and on for a little while longer, but even without turning back to see Nashawn, I know he's still looking at me. Staring at me. It's making me feel kinda uncomfortable because I know he's probably thinking all kinda dirty things about me. But at the same time, it makes me feel kinda good, too, that he still wants me like that.

Finally, I can't take it anymore, and I do end up looking over at him again. And yes, he been staring right at me. "What do you want?" I ask him.

"To talk to you," he says, sitting up straight, with his hands still folded. "That's all I want."

"Fine," I say, wondering why he has to be so cute. It's not fair. "Talk, then."

"Alone," he says, glancing over to Mara. "Me and you. Alone. Talking."

I look over at Mara, who shakes her head and mouths, "No way."

When I turn back to Nashawn, I don't know if it's just what I want or if it's real, but he looks like he's telling the truth. Maybe he does just wanna talk to me. Maybe I owe it to him to at least listen.

For a few seconds I really don't know what to do. I know I wanna be with him, but no, I can't keep setting myself up to be hurt. But if he only wants to talk . . .

Finally, I turn to Mara. "Me and Nashawn are gonna go next door to the theater so we can talk. If I'm not back in five minutes, then come and get me."

Mara don't look all that happy about my decision, but she nods, anyway. Then she gives Nashawn a don't-try-anything-with-my-friend look and it's kinda scary, too. I really like that girl!

\* \* \*

I still have the key to the theater, and when me and Nashawn get inside, it's dark and seems even more empty now that the set is gone from the stage. Automatically, we both head straight for the dressing room, just like before. I'm not sure why, really, but I know we can talk in private there.

The second Nashawn closes the door behind us and we're in the dark, all I can think about is everything that happened here. And before I can even get a word out, Nashawn's lips are on mine and we're kissing up against the door. I'm surprised and not surprised at the same time. Because deep down I knew this was gonna happen. I knew this was what I wanted.

"I missed you," Nashawn says, kissing me on the neck and the side of my face.

I put my hands on both sides of his face and bring his lips back up to mine. *I missed you, too,* I wanna tell him. *You don't even know how much.*

Being here with him, it's hard to even think, much less keep time. I just let myself go, and without a doubt, I would do whatever he wants right now. But the thing is, something's different this time. Me and him are kissing, his tongue deep in my mouth, one of his hands on my waist, but he's not trying anything more. He's not trying to take off any of my clothes and he's not trying to get me on the couch.

And I'm confused. I pull away from him, and since my eyes are adjusting to the darkness, I can see the surprised look on his face. "What's wrong?" he asks.

"We're supposed to be talking, remember?"

"I think we wasted too much time," he says, kissing me on the cheek a couple of times. "Let's talk after school. Meet me at the lockers."

I feel myself getting kinda nervous about what could happen if we do get together after school. "I, um, I have to go straight home today," I tell him.

He's still kissing me. "I won't keep you too long."

*Just long enough.*

But Nashawn don't even let me really answer him. His lips are back on mine and right away my brain gets all cloudy again. I'm so weak and pathetic. It's like I can't even think straight anymore. I can't believe I'm with Nashawn again, especially after the way I felt just a couple of days ago, when I knew he was just using me. I'm stupid, I know it. But still, his lips feel good right now, and I'm tired of always thinking and thinking. Why can't I just have some fun?

So, in between kisses, I whisper, "Okay, I'll meet you."

"Good," he says, with his tongue now tickling the inside of my ear, making me giggle.

Me and Nashawn spend the next couple of minutes still pressed up against the door, kissing. And I can't help counting down the minutes in my mind, half expecting Mara to come barging into the dressing room any second. I don't want this to end. Because here, in this dark room, it's just me and Nashawn. There's no Adonna.

# THIRTY-NINE

It's a mistake and I know it. But still, after school I'm doing it, walking down the hall to my locker to get the books I need. *And* to meet Nashawn.

At first I don't see him, and my mind starts coming up with all kinda reasons, like maybe Adonna called his cell phone from home and they made plans of their own. Or maybe he just changed his mind about me.

I bend down and sort through the junk at the bottom of my locker. I take Adonna's shoes and umbrella and magazines and throw them out onto the floor. I don't care who takes them, either. Because I've had enough. I pull out my stupid algebra book and my bio study guide, and right before I close the locker, I get a tap on my shoulder. I look up and it's him, but I don't wanna look at him too long because the hall is crowded and I know everybody is probably looking at me after what happened yesterday. I definitely don't want them seeing me talking to Nashawn, thinking I'm going after him again now that Adonna been suspended.

"You running a flea market or something?" Nashawn asks.

"It's your girlfriend's stuff," I say, and my voice is definitely sharper than it was a couple of hours ago.

Nashawn bends down next to me and starts shoving all of Adonna's stuff in his locker. *Looking out for his woman.* And I don't know what happened to me between lunch and now, but I had second, third, and fourth thoughts about this whole "meet me after school" thing. I mean, it's one thing to spend a few minutes alone with him in the dressing room, but leaving school with him and doing I-don't-know-what, it just isn't sitting right with me anymore. Because I know I'm gonna be the one getting hurt here.

I stand up and start to walk away, and he slams his locker closed and follows me just like he did that first time when we ended up in the teachers' lounge. This girl Tracy is coming from the stairs and first she looks at me, then at Nashawn, and then at me again. Her face says it all. She's thinking I should be ashamed or something. And all I know is, I'm getting tired of this already.

I run-walk down the stairs, and when I get to the landing between the first and second floor, Nashawn catches up to me and reaches out to grab my arm, but I don't let him.

"What?" he asks.

"Nothing," I say and keep going down the steps.

On the first floor, I walk down the hall toward the front door — but, no, I don't wanna walk down the steps in front of the school after what happened out there yesterday. So I turn around and head toward the side door near the theater. Nashawn walks next to me and I know he's confused by the way I'm acting, but I'm confused by him, too. Like, he's supposed to be with Adonna and still he don't seem to care if half the school sees him trying to get with me.

In the little hallway near the door, Nashawn says, "Slow down, c'mon." And he finally grabs hold of my arm and stops me from moving. I try to pull myself away from him, but I can't. He's not letting me go.

So finally, after I give up, I turn to look at him and his eyes meet mine for a second. And even though I don't wanna feel it, that look is kinda like a kiss between us. It's quick and sweet and exciting.

"What about Adonna?" I ask.

"What about her?"

"Wrong answer," I say, pulling free from him and pushing the door open.

He lets me walk ahead of him for a little while. Then he's back at my side again. "Let me drive you home," he says. "I still wanna talk to you, remember?"

There are a lot of kids out there, walking down the street or hanging around talking. Not as many as in the front of the school, but enough to mind my business. And I just don't want them thinking I'm like this. "Nashawn," I start, but I don't know what to say next. I wanna tell him that I don't want him driving me home, that I don't even wanna talk to him anymore.

And I *would* say that, too, but there's something about being alone that's getting to me. If I let him go now, I'm gonna get on that train by myself, and when I get home I'm just gonna end up sitting there alone. Even when Renée comes home, *if* she don't go out with her friends, me and her aren't gonna talk, either. Not really.

We still haven't talked since Dunkin' Donuts. And

yesterday I know she was mad at me for fighting with Adonna, but she didn't even talk to me about what happened or anything. Even Nana would have done that. Well, *after* she finished yelling and telling me how I'm never gonna be allowed to leave the apartment again because obviously I don't know how to act in public.

Actually, I don't know which is better.

Nashawn grabs my hand and starts massaging my fingers through his. It don't take me long to give him an answer.

"Okay," I say. "You can drive me." And actually, I *do* wanna hear what he has to say to me.

As we're driving, I stare at the side of his face as he concentrates on the road. There's something about him, not just his cute face and perfect body. There's something else that makes him so hard to resist. Something in his eyes.

My mind is so caught up in thinking about him, it takes me a few minutes to notice that Nashawn's driving in the direction of Bronxwood. "Um, Nashawn," I say.

He glances over at me for a second. "Yeah?"

"I forgot to tell you. I moved on Saturday."

He slows the car down and pulls up against the curb in front of a grocery store. "You moved?"

"Yeah. In with my mother. To Harlem."

He shrugs. "Okay, no problem."

"You don't have to drive me home if it's too far. You can just tell me whatever you wanna say right here. I mea —"

Nashawn leans over and kisses me, stopping me from rambling on and on. The kiss is long and intense, and both of us are breathing hard and heavy. When it's over and his body moves away from mine a little, I can already feel the space between us now and I don't like it. "I wanna go to your house," I say, but my voice is really shaky. "Please."

Nashawn looks like he don't know what's going on with me. But he don't say anything. He just makes a U-turn and starts driving in the other direction while I look outta the window.

I really don't know why I'm so shaky, because I do wanna be alone with Nashawn again. I do. I definitely don't wanna go home. That's for sure.

"Where are we going?" I ask, seeing that we're heading toward the highway, which I know we didn't take last time I went to his house.

"I'm taking you home. But you're gonna have to tell me what street you live on or I'm just gonna keep driving around and around. And gas prices are —"

"I thought we were — I don't wanna go home."

"I know," he says. "But I don't wanna go home, neither."

I turn around, and the look on his face is sadder than I ever saw it. He's looking straight ahead, but now his eyes seem heavier or something. A second later he glances over at me real fast and asks, "You okay?"

"I don't know," I say, shrugging. "Are *you*?"

"Yeah, yeah," he says, but I'm not really believing him.

I reach out and touch his hand on the steering wheel. "What did you wanna talk to me about?"

"I wanna talk to you about Adonna," he says as we merge onto the highway.

# FORTY

*Adonna.*

Just hearing her name, it feels like I been punched again. Only not by her this time, by my own guilt or something. It's like all of a sudden she's in the car with us, because I can't stop thinking about her. About what I did to her.

Nashawn must be thinking about her, too, because for a while we drive without talking. I look outta the window thinking — *knowing* — I shouldn't be here with him. Not that it's really about him. Because it's not. It's about me. But no matter what I feel about him, it's not right.

*He should be with her.*

All the way to Convent Avenue, me and Nashawn hardly talk, except for me trying to help him find the right places to turn. Deep down I'm kinda hoping this trip will take longer than it is, because it's hard to think about not being with him anymore, even though we were hardly ever together. Not really. It's just hard to think that he'll be with Adonna instead of me.

We pull up in front of the brownstone and Nashawn turns

off the engine even though I just wanna get outta the car as fast as possible and not even have to listen to him talk. *About Adonna*. I mean, I already know what he's gonna say.

So I tell him, "Thanks for driving me," and reach for the door handle.

But Nashawn reaches over and grabs my hand, stopping me. "Wait."

I sigh. "I know what you wanna say and I —"

"Hey, why don't you let a man talk?"

I give him a look. "*Man?*"

"Okay, okay, let's not get into that again." He smiles, looking right into my eyes.

And that's all it takes to get me to stay where I am.

Nashawn now has my hand in between both of his. "What I wanted to say is, 'Sorry.' I feel bad 'cause you and Adonna's friendship is messed up, and it's a hundred percent my fault."

"It is not," I say. "It's my fault. Why do you think —?"

"Let me talk," he says, moving closer to me, as close as he can in that little tiny car. "That day, the Sunday when you were leaving the play and I was coming from the game, when me and you, you know, hooked up, I thought it was just, I don't know, like, fun. That's what I thought. And that's what I thought you wanted. Fun."

I can't look him in the eyes anymore, because what he's saying is killing me. It hurts so bad to know that I meant nothing to him except a good time. "You don't have to say this, Nashawn. I get that already."

He leans over to kiss me, just a quick one on the lips. "Every time you talk when I'm supposed to be talking, I'm gonna kiss you."

It's hard not to smile, but I don't. "Go on."

"Okay. What I was saying is this — I know you think I was using you, and in a way I was, but I didn't know I was using you 'til Friday."

I open my mouth to say something, but he's already kissing me. When he pulls away, I say, "I didn't say anything."

"You were gonna."

"That's not fair," I say.

"Okay, you get to talk one time with no kiss, but then after that, we go back to the kiss rule."

"Fine."

"*That* was your one time." He smirks, and it's so hard to keep my hands off of him. Really hard. "Now, as I was saying, when a girl like you lets a guy like me, you know . . ." He's looking for the right word and what he comes up with is, "hit it, of course I'm gonna do it. You're hot."

I roll my eyes because I know I'm not hot, but I don't say anything.

"I was just thinking it was . . ." He shakes his head. "Well, I wasn't thinking. Then on Friday, when you started crying and you left my house like that —"

"That wasn't your fault," I say, getting embarrassed. "I mean, when we were, *you know*, I thought it meant something to you and then when Adonna called, I knew you wanted to answer, and that's okay because I know you like her, but —"

"I don't like her," he says, and leans over to kiss me again, which I was kinda waiting for. "That's what I'm trying to tell you," he says. "I don't like Adonna. I like you." And he kisses me again.

But this isn't one of those you-interrupted-me-so-I'm-gonna-kiss-you-to-shut-you-up kinda kisses. This one is real. It's takes awhile for it to end, and I'm the one that pulls my lips away first, not because it's not good but because I don't understand. "What do you mean?" I wanna know for real if he likes me or if he just likes *hitting it*?

"I like you," he says again. "You."

I take my time looking at his face, his mouth and his eyes, checking to see if any part of him will give him away and let me know he's not telling me the truth. But what I see is straightforward and real. He means what he's saying. "But why didn't you tell me? Why did you go out with Adonna? And then yesterday I saw you and her in the hall together. I, I don't get it."

He shakes his head. "Me, neither. But all I can say is, it's hard being a guy sometimes. I mean, I'm gonna be honest with you. The only reason I went out with Adonna is because of how she looks."

I feel a sharp pain in my whole body when he says that. I don't know why. I mean, it's not like he's the first guy to notice Adonna in that way, but he just told me he likes me, yet and still, he's still thinking about the way Adonna looks.

"I went out with her for that, and because I knew she liked me. And when a girl likes you, a girl like that, as a guy it's hard to pass that kinda thing up. I'm just being honest."

I nod, like what he's saying isn't bothering me.

"But by Friday when you left my house, I could tell you had feelings for me and I didn't want you to go because I already knew I was starting to like you, too, so it was hard even going out with Adonna on Saturday. And that was the worst date I

264

ever had." He starts laughing. "Damn, that girl is hard to put up with, one on one. We went to Bay Plaza and we started walking around before the movie started and she was taking me past all the clothes stores and telling me what kinda clothes she likes on guys. And the stuff she was showing me was like eighty-dollar T-shirts and two-hundred-dollar jeans. And I'm not even gonna talk about the sneakers she likes." He's still laughing and shaking his head. "I would have to sell my car to afford them."

Even I have to laugh with him, because Adonna *is* kinda crazy about all that stuff.

"All through the movie I was thinking about you," Nashawn says. "And after, she wanted to go eat something and I was thinking, like, I can't take any more of this. So I told her I had to get home to feed my dog, you know, the one I don't have, and I took her home. And when I was walking her to her building, she was talking to me about what we could do together next week, and I was feeling bad because I couldn't figure out how to get outta this without hurting her, especially because I wanted to start going out with you, and you and her are family. You know?"

"Yeah," I say.

"So Monday I dodged her all day and she left me two messages on my cell after school, but I never called her back. Then on Tuesday she saw me in the hall and she was talking and talking and talking, so finally I told her right there that I like her but as a friend, but that I already like somebody else. And when she asked me who, I didn't wanna tell her, but she guessed it was you, and when I didn't say anything, she knew she was right. Then, after school, that's when she tried to jump you." He looks away from me. "I didn't know about it 'til it was over, but somebody came over to us at practice and told us what happened, and of course I felt like shit because I knew if I didn't tell her, she wouldn't have done that to you. You know, I messed up."

"It is a mess," I say, "but we're not your problem, me and Adonna. We're the ones that's gonna have to work it out, not you. And not now."

"C'mon," Nashawn says. "Let's walk around the block or something. All this talking is making me feel like I'm, I don't know, the emotional type." He laughs.

We get outta the car and right away he grabs my hand. And we walk down the block together holding hands and I really like this, being out in front of other people this way. We're at the corner when I say to him, "I think I was kinda using you, too."

He don't say anything, but when I look up at him I can tell he's listening.

"I had a lot going on at home. My mother and grandmother, and I thought both of them didn't really want me or anything. And I think I just wanted to be with somebody. But then it wasn't just somebody I wanted to be with." I take a deep breath, feeling kinda scared to say what I'm about to say, like I'm opening myself up too much or something. But I say it, anyway. "It was you. I only wanted to be with you."

Me and Nashawn kiss, and I think about what Nana would say if she saw the two of us standing here together, holding hands and kissing right here on the sidewalk. But to me, it feels like the right thing to do, and I'm glad we're doing it.

When we finish our walk around the block, we do it again and then again, walking and talking and kissing, in our own world or something. Finally, as we come around to my brownstone for, like, the fourth time, we see Renée sitting on the steps out front. And she's not dressed for work, so she must have changed already. "Are you two going to keep walking around in circles all afternoon?" she asks, smiling the whole time.

"The block is rectangular," I say, giggling a little bit. "And you weren't there before."

"I was watching y'all from the window."

We go up the steps and sit next to her, me in between the two of them. I introduce Nashawn to Renée and ask her why she's home so early. "I had a lot of reading to do, so I brought it all home," she says. She lifts her head so she can soak up some of the sun. "Isn't is beautiful today?"

Nashawn looks at me and says, "Yeah, it is."

I smile.

"Gerard's on his way over," Renée says, "and he's bringing pizza with him." She tells Nashawn, "You have to stay. This is the best pizza you'll ever eat." She looks really excited and I'm wondering if it has more to do with Gerard or the pizza.

Nashawn don't put up a fight and for a while we sit out there with her, talking about nothing, really, just killing time and enjoying the sun. Meanwhile, Nashawn hasn't let go of my hand and I can feel myself inside starting to relax because maybe everything will work out okay between us.

When Gerard arrives, he rushes up the stairs with a large pizza box in his hands. "C'mon, y'all. It's still hot." He gives Renée a kiss and says, "You playing hooky today?"

"I was working from home," she says.

"Yeah, right." He laughs.

We all go inside and up to our apartment. And it's not 'til

we get inside and get the paper plates out and the pizza box open that we see what it is, and to me it don't even look like pizza, because it has mashed potatoes and cheese and bacon and tomatoes and bits of green stuff all over it.

"What is *that*?" I ask, and me and Nashawn exchange looks.

Gerard takes a slice out and puts it on my plate, and it just sits there like a big mess. "Taste it," he says.

"Not 'til you tell me what it is!"

Renée elbows me outta the way and grabs a piece for herself. "It's called Loaded Potato Pizza. Gerard and I discovered it at this little hole-in-the-wall restaurant in Hoboken. And after one bite, oh, my God, we were in love!" She leans over her plate and takes a big bite, and even as she's chewing she's smiling so big I can't stop myself from trying it, and she is so right about it. I don't know if I'd really call it pizza, but whatever it is, it's good.

For the next twenty minutes, we don't talk. All we do it eat. Renée and Gerard sit at the table, and me and Nashawn sit on the futon with our pizza on the coffee tables. And I'm real happy being here with Nashawn and everybody, even though I still can't really believe it's happening.

Then, when we're all too full to eat any more, Gerard asks Nashawn to help him move the bookcase over to the other side of the room. And while they're doing that, Gerard starts asking him questions, and I'm wondering if this whole thing wasn't just an excuse to interrogate Nashawn, like he's someone Gerard just arrested or something. But at the same time, I kinda like that Gerard is looking out for me like this, making sure Nashawn is okay.

So while me and Renée clean up, which takes about thirty

seconds, I listen to what Nashawn is saying and again I see how much I don't know about him. Like, I find out about how Nashawn really wants to go to Morehouse College in Atlanta and play baseball for them, and how his grades are good, but he's not sure if they're good enough. And when Gerard asks him about his mom and dad, I find out that his mom works for an insurance company in the city, and his dad died when he was three.

Then Nashawn says something that really hits me. Just as they're finishing moving the bookcase, he says, "My mom's over in the Middle East right now, you know, with the Army Reserve. Her unit got deployed in March and she's gonna be there for a year. At least." And he gets that same sad look on his face that he got in the car. When he told me he didn't wanna go home.

"I didn't know that," I say, going over next to him and grabbing his hand. It's like I feel sorry for him and kinda guilty for never really asking about her.

"Yeah," he says. "I don't like to talk about it all the time? Not too much."

I nod, and I wanna hug him and kiss him, but I don't wanna do it in front of Renée and Gerard. Here I am living with my mother finally and he's away from his.

A little while later, Renée puts on some makeup and a pair of high heels and she tells me that her and Gerard are going out for a little while. "We're just going for a quick drink," she says. "I'm coming right back. *Right back*. Hint. Hint."

"Very funny," I say and try to look and sound real innocent. "You guys can take your time. Have fun. You don't have to rush back for us."

Anyway, I know what she's doing. She's testing me. Trying to see if I meant it when I said I wasn't gonna do anything anymore.

She probably thinks me and Nashawn are just like her and Kenny were when they were our age. But we're not.

I'm not gonna let us be.

# FORTY-ONE

"Your mom is cool," Nashawn says the second the door closes. "Leaving us here alone like this."

He comes closer to me and wraps his arms around me, but I'm still thinking that he called Renée my *mom* and how funny that sounds.

"You know, this never would have happened if I was still living with Nana," I tell him.

"Nana? She the one that was gonna have you checked?"

I laugh. "Yeah. That's her."

We kiss. And outta the corner of my eye I see the futon and my Aerobed, and I can't help but wonder how much time it takes for people to have a drink. I mean, I know I can drink a soda in, like, three minutes, but alcohol is different. It burns if you drink it too fast. At least that beer I drank at Nashawn's house did. But then I remember that I'm being tested and I better not even let my mind go there. I can't. "Let's make some popcorn," I say the second we come up for air.

271

"I'm stuffed from all that — what did they call it? Load of potatoes pizza?" He laughs.

"Something like that."

I'm stuffed, too, but I still want popcorn. I need a little time to cool myself off. In a way I'm glad I made Renée buy popcorn, because it'll give me and Nashawn something to do besides what we always do, to get to know each other with our clothes on. I mean, I'm not sure if that's what Nashawn wants, but I know it's what *I* need.

A few minutes later, with a big bowl of popcorn drowning in melted butter, we sit on the futon, turn on the TV, and try to find something good to watch. There's lots of news on and some reruns of sitcoms from, like, ten years ago but nothing good. So we leave it on but mute the sound, and we eat and talk. About everything.

He tells me about his mom and how much he misses her, even though they get to keep in touch by e-mail and even phone calls sometimes. And I find out that he has family in South Carolina and Texas, but he don't wanna go live with them, because he's gonna be playing in a New York baseball league this summer and he's hoping it can help him get a baseball scholarship to college.

I tell him about how Renée had me so young and how I had to grow up without her around most of the time. And how I went to two graduations before her last one and thought she was coming home both times, but she would just go back for another degree and leave me alone again.

We're doing that good kinda talking, sitting close and looking at each other in the eye and, yeah, whenever there's a little gap in the conversation, we're kissing like we're never gonna

272

see each other again. And these are sweet, buttery kisses, which are my favorite now.

"How'd you get a nickname like Babe?" Nashawn asks. He has an arm around me and I'm pressed up against him. "'Cause you *know* I'm gonna start calling you that, right?"

"You better not," I say, even though having him call me Babe would mean something different than when Nana or Kenny do it. Or even Renée. "The only reason I got that nickname was because, when I was born, Nana wouldn't let Renée give me Kenny's last name. I was gonna be, like, Erika Singleton."

"That's Adonna's last name, right?"

"Yeah. But Nana wasn't having it. She said no way was she gonna let me have the last name of some fifteen-year-old boy that wasn't ever gonna be any kinda father to me. So since I couldn't have his last name, Renée named me Kendra instead. But Nana still wasn't happy, so she just started calling me Babe. And unfortunately it stuck."

"I like it," he says, and kisses me on my neck. Then he whispers, "You are so beautiful, Babe."

I almost automatically say, *No, I'm not.* But I stop myself because I know what I'm doing. I'm comparing myself to Adonna, and I need to stop doing that.

Pretty soon me and him are practically laying together on the futon and we're still kissing, but now his hand is under my shirt. My body is on fire and my eyes are closed and I really, *really* don't wanna stop this. Really.

But I have to. I have to. And not just because of Renée is testing me, either.

So I pull myself away from him and sit up. It's not easy, but

I do it. And I'm still breathing kinda hard when I tell him, "I know we already hooked up and everything. But . . ." I can feel myself getting a little nervous. "I wanna go slow now. Okay?"

He flashes that little wicked grin. "Hey, okay. That's cool. I can probably wait, like, a week."

I grab some popcorn from the bowl, throw it at him, and laugh.

"Or two," he says, and nods. "Yeah, I can probably wait two weeks if that's what you need."

I scoop up a whole handful of popcorn this time and throw it, aiming right at his face. Then I scream as he reaches out and grabs me. And the next thing I know, he's tickling me and kissing me, and I'm real glad to get to see this side of him, because I like it. A lot.

Then, when we're both kinda exhausted, we're laying squished together on the futon again, and I ask him, "Do you mind waiting — I mean, really?"

"Nah, I'm okay." He slips his arm around me and he pulls me even closer to him than I already am.

"Good," I say. "Because I'm really not ready right now."

I love the way he's holding me like this. It's what I been missing in my life for a long time, this kinda closeness. It feels right coming from him. And it's enough for now.

"In the meantime," I say, my mind racing with ideas, "remember, I'm a very creative person."

"I like the way that sounds, Babe."

"Me, too," I say, flashing him my own kinda sneaky smile.

\*　　　\*　　　\*

274

Nashawn is long gone and I'm laying on my so-called bed wide awake when Renée gets home. I guess her quick drink turned into something more because she left, like, three hours ago. She comes in and says, "I brought back banana pudding." And she holds the paper bag up to show me.

"With the Nilla wafers?" I ask, sitting up.

"You know it!"

I hop up. "Where did you get it from?"

"This soul food place over on 138th Street." She's in the kitchen, getting the paper plates and plastic spoons out. And then I watch her scoop big hunks of the banana pudding out for us.

After she hands me my plate, Renée opens the futon into a bed. And when two pieces of popcorn fall out, she shakes her head and says, "I'm not even going to ask."

"Popcorn fight," I explain, picking up the pieces and throwing them away.

Renée makes herself comfortable, sitting up against her pillows. Then she pats the other side of the bed like she wants me to get in next to her. But I just stand there, not really sure that's what she means 'til she says, "Come here."

And that's when I smile and get in bed with her.

"Oh, this is sooo delicious," she says, as I make myself comfortable. "I'm going to get so fat living around here."

I heap a big glob of the pudding onto my spoon and eat it. And, man, it *is* good.

"So what time did your boyfriend leave?" Renée asks, then licks the back of her spoon.

"I don't know, maybe about an hour after you left. Or an

275

hour and a half. And I'm not sure if he's really my boyfriend yet." I can't help smiling, though, thinking of how good it felt to be with him like that, just together. "And I know why you left us here alone, don't think I don't."

"I don't know what you're talking about," she says, but there's a smile on her face. "Anyway you're going to have to make up your own mind about a lot of things now, Babe. Nana tried to micromanage everything you did and, look, you still ended up having sex, right? Well, I'm not her."

"Yeah, I know, but . . ." I start laughing because I can't believe what I'm about to say. "But, can you be *a little bit* like her?"

Renée laughs, too. "*What?*"

"I mean, you can't just leave me alone with the cutest guy in the tri-state area!"

"He *is* cute," she says. "I mean, for a little boy."

"Little boy? He's a *junior!*"

"Oh, well, excuse me," she says, shaking her head, smiling. "If I had known he was a junior, I would never have left you two here alone." Then she gets serious and says, "You know, I still have that prescription. When you're ready, just let me know and I'll get it filled. No lectures, no judgments. Okay?"

I nod, feeling relieved by what she's saying because, really, I don't know how long I'm gonna be able to wait. Like Renée told me the other day, once you start, it's real hard to stop. I mean, maybe you can, if that's what you really want. But *is* that what I really want?

While we're eating and quiet for a little while, Renée says, "On Saturday, when you got here, I didn't mean to —" She shakes her head real slow, thinking. "It just happened so fast and —"

"I know," I say, feeling my body tense up a little bit.

"I just want you to know, it's not about you," she says.

I nod and exhale. "I know. I mean, kinda."

Me and Renée finish our banana pudding and she tells me I better get to bed because she has to get ready for work. "I can't play hooky two days in a row," she says.

"I thought you said you were working from home."

"Complete bullshit," she says. "I was in that office and — you know when people say they can feel the walls closing in on them? Well, that's the way I felt. I was sitting at that desk, thinking, 'Is this going to be my whole life from now on? This office. This college? Teaching, grading papers, doing research, committee meetings?' You know, it's a lot all of a sudden, being out of school and working."

*And being a mother to me.*

"The pressure just got to me, so I told the head of the department I was going to the library to get some books and I practically ran out of there." She laughs. "It felt so good, like when Kenny and I used to cut school and sneak off to the movies in the middle of the day so we could be alone."

"Hmmm, that's a good idea," I say, laughing.

"Don't even try it. I know all the tricks."

"Not all," I say, because the thing with me and Nashawn is, we don't even have to leave the school, not as long as Mr. Melendez trusts me with the key to the theater. I mean, *if* we were ever gonna do any of that again, we always have our secret place. "It's gonna be hard," I tell Renée, "starting over with Nashawn. But he says he's okay with it."

"He likes you, that's why."

"I know," I say, even though I still can't believe it. "Just like Gerard loves you."

"I love him, too. And I'm trying really hard to accept him the way he is. Because he doesn't want to be a sergeant for anything!" She laughs, and she's so pretty when she laughs. "The only time he opens that book is when he's here, as if it's possible to learn the material just by holding the book in your hand."

I laugh, too. Then I tell her what Gerard said about liking his job now, and being a good role model to the kids in Newark.

"That's my Gerard," she says. "The cop." She gets outta bed to throw away our plates, and when she comes back, I'm still in her bed, all comfortable.

"You know, I need a real bed," I tell her just in case she don't already know. "And a room with, like, privacy."

"I need the same thing," she says. "And poor Gerard needs me to have privacy, too."

"*Ill.* Too much information," I tell her. "Way too much."

Renée looks around the apartment. "It's a cute little place, though, right?"

I look around and say, "Too little."

Renée nods and I know she gets it.

We can't stay here.

# FORTY-TWO

It's, like, a week a half later when I'm on my way back to Bronxwood for the first time, and the only reason I'm even going is because it's the Fourth of July and they always have a big block party there. And because it's the Friday that Renée and Gerard are going to Atlantic City for the weekend. So I'm back with Nana for a couple of days and having a hard time even figuring out what I'm feeling right now.

I mean, when Gerard's car gets close to Bronxwood, I start to get kinda excited, especially because we always throw the best block parties, even better than all the other projects around here, and I know I'm gonna have fun as soon as I get used to being back here. But, at the same time, coming back here reminds me of how I left, and it's kinda hard being here again.

It's only nine o'clock in the morning and the street is already blocked off by barricades, so Gerard stops his car at the corner to let me out. Renée turns around from the front seat and says, "Tell Nana I'll see her Sunday, okay?"

"Okay," I say. "Have *fun*, you guys." And I can't help but

giggle, because I know what they're gonna be doing in that hotel room.

Gerard puts his arm around Renée and says, "No doubt!" And he laughs, too, 'til Renée elbows him in the ribs. "Ow!"

I shake my head. *Men!*

When I get my bag from the backseat and close the door, I tell them bye and start walking toward my building. Well, my *old* building, anyway. Practically everybody's already outside. Some of the men are putting up decorations, standing on ladders to wrap streamers and stuff from the lampposts. This guy Tyrell from Building A is already setting up his DJ equipment on the sidewalk. And some of the women are unfolding their tables and covering them with those cheap plastic red, white, and blue tablecloths. They're gonna be selling food and raising money for the community center's trip to Rye Playland at the end of August, right before school starts again. I been going on that trip every year, and now I'm wondering if I'm ever gonna go again, now that I'm living with Renée.

"How you doing, Kendra?" Ms. Jenkins asks me as I walk by. She's taking paper plates and plastic forks outta a shopping bag and putting them on her table. "I heard you moved in with Renée," she says. "How's it going?"

I smile. "Everything's good." And it kinda is, too.

"Glad to hear that. Make sure you stop by my table, because I'm going to be selling my famous fried chicken. I got legs, wings, and thighs. And I'm gonna have potato salad, collard greens, and corn on the cob. And the peach cobblers are in the oven right now."

Ms. Jenkins's cooking is something everybody around here

knows about, and my mouth is already watering just thinking about it. "I'll be back," I say. "Definitely!"

We laugh and I keep walking, going even faster past Ms. Grier's table because I know she's gonna try to get me to eat some of the food from her nasty apartment. When I come around to Kenny's truck, he's setting up, too. He has crates of sodas and bottled water sitting on the street by the back door and he's bringing everything inside, trying to make room for all of it.

I haven't seen him since that day when he picked me up after the fight and Renée said all those terrible things to him. It took me awhile to even call him, because I know how disappointed he was with me, and how mad he was with Renée. I don't know, maybe I felt kinda embarrassed for him, too. But me and him been talking every day now and I told him I'll be his assistant in the truck today because he's hoping to make a lot of money from this block party, and I know he needs it.

"Kenny!" I say, standing outside the truck, waiting for him to come out and hug me. The smile he gives me through the truck's window is almost as good, but I want the whole thing. Two seconds later, he's grabbing me in one of his hugs and it feels so good.

I mean, me and Nashawn are officially together and his hugs are incredible — *he's* incredible — but I still need Kenny's hugs, too. Me and him stand on the sidewalk hugging and talking, and at the same time I'm kinda looking up and down the street and in front of the building to see if Adonna is around. Because me and her haven't seen each other since the fight. Well, I *saw* her at school during finals and Regents, but she stayed away from me and I did the same to her.

But I know there's no way I'm gonna be here today at the block party and not see her. It's impossible. Especially working in Kenny's Kandy, right in front of our building.

"Let me take my stuff upstairs," I tell Kenny. "I'll be right back, ready to work." Then, under my breath, I mumble, "Should be a law against this kinda child labor."

Kenny tries to grab me, but I'm too fast for him. "Wait 'til you get back," he says. "I'm gonna get you."

I laugh and walk down the path to my building. When I get upstairs I use my key to get in the apartment. I don't even think about it 'til I'm opening the door and remember that I don't really live there anymore and maybe I should have rung the doorbell. So, as I open the door, I call out, "Nana, I'm here!"

"No need to yell," she says from the kitchen. She's sitting there having breakfast with Clyde, and I'm wondering, hmmm, did he stay overnight or what? They're both dressed, it's nothing like that, but it's kinda early on a holiday and maybe the reason he's here is because he never left last night.

I mean, I always wanted Nana to get a life, but I still can't think of her actually *doing it* with anybody. My mind just can't go there. So I shake my head to clear out that kinda thinking. *Fast.*

Nana gets up and takes my bag from me. I haven't seen her since she threw me outta here, and it's really weird being back. But she did say she wanted me to come for the weekend. Now I'm wondering if we're gonna be able to talk or if Clyde's gonna be here the whole time.

Nana puts my bag on the floor in the living room and comes back to give me a hug. *Nana.* I mean, it's a real fast hug, so fast

I could blink and it would be over, but still. I have to take what I can get, right?

I follow her into the kitchen and say hi to Clyde. He's looking real comfortable sitting there in *my chair* having his coffee. Nana is back to the green tea, though.

"I bought that yogurt you like," Nana says. "And some cereal."

"Lucky Charms?"

"No, cornflakes."

"Oh, man," I say, and Nana actually laughs.

"You know I refuse to pay that kind of money for a box of sugar," she says. "Is Renée letting you eat that stuff?"

"Yeah," I say because Renée lets me eat whatever I want. Most of the time, she even lets me *do* whatever I want.

"Where *is* Renée and that boyfriend of hers?" Nana asks.

"They wanted to beat traffic," I say, opening the refrigerator and seeing that Nana did good. She bought two strawberry-banana, a peach, and a blueberry. "But they'll come upstairs when they pick me up on Sunday."

"They better," she says, and there's something about her that's kinda different. She looks more relaxed or something. Her face don't look so tight and even her voice is, like, a little softer. I don't know how much of it is because Clyde's there or because I'm not living with her anymore, but maybe she's just changing.

Breakfast with Nana and Clyde isn't all that weird, as long as I keep pushing the thought that Nana has a boyfriend outta my head. By the time I get back downstairs, more people are outside and a whole bunch of little kids are running around in the middle of the street acting crazy, like they can't believe they don't have to watch out for cars. And there are some young girls from my building out playing double dutch, which makes me think of Adonna because she used to be so good at that a couple of years ago. I glance up and down the block again, but I still don't see her, and I'm wondering if she's really not here. But no. I know her. She wouldn't miss the block party just because of me.

I walk toward the truck. It's a real nice day today, sunny but not all that hot. I just hope it gets a little hotter so Kenny can make money selling sodas and stuff. Because I want this truck to work out for him. I mean, I know I'm not supposed to be worried about him, it's supposed to be the other way around, but I can't help it. I see the way Renée has her own thing going on and how she thinks Kenny isn't going anywhere. And I want him to prove her wrong and start making at least a little more money. And if that means he's always gonna be right here at Bronxwood sitting in his truck, so what?

A couple hours later, the block party is really on. The music is pumping loud and the fathers are out there trying to organize some of the kids into races and stuff. And the rest of the kids are playing around in the fire hydrant sprinklers. Everyone else is just eating and having a good time.

And Kenny *is* making money. Not all that much, but he's getting a lot of people, and sometimes there's even a line outside. Me and him are working together good and he don't bring up anything that happened the week before last. He just asks me about school and if I passed all my classes, which I did. That kinda thing. And I tell him about the play I'm gonna be working on this summer with Mr. Melendez, but how Renée is

284

only letting me do it two days a week because she signed me up for some kinda summer leadership program for teenagers at City College and that's gonna take up the other three days.

"How *is* Renée?" he asks me about five minutes after I stop talking, letting me know he was thinking of her that whole time.

"She's fine," I say. "She's teaching a class that starts on Monday, so . . ." I don't know how to say this, but he needs to know. "So she went to Atlantic City for the weekend with, um, her boyfriend."

Kenny nods his head a few times before he says, "Oh. Oh, alright. Yeah, Atlantic City."

Lucky for him, this guy comes up to the window of the truck and asks for a loose cigarette, and Kenny has to go back to being Kenny, smiling and taking care of his customers like nothing ever bothers him.

I go back to taking some of the bottled waters outta the freezer and finding room for them in the refrigerator. Then I fill up the freezer with warm ones, just in case we need them.

When the guy leaves, Kenny starts laughing and moving to the beat of the music Tyrell is playing out there. It sounds alright, but it's definitely something old, because I never even heard it before. "That kid is good," Kenny says. "That's the kinda music me and Renée used to listen to back in high school. *Real* music." He's smiling all big and everything, and it looks like he's trying to go back in time or something.

Even after their fight, I don't think he's ever gonna get over Renée. He's always gonna think about the way they were back then. When he was happy.

Finally, when the music changes to something from *this*

decade, Kenny says, "So tell me what else is going on with you. And I wanna know everything."

"I'm doing good," I say. "Me and Renée are getting along okay. I mean, I still wish it was better than okay, but at least it's something. *And*," I go on, hoping I'm not smiling *too* much, "me and Nashawn are together now."

"That's the same boy that —?"

"Yeah," I say. And I know he's thinking about Adonna because so am I. I mean, I know for a fact she's gonna be hurt that me and Nashawn are going out. Me and him played it off pretty good at school. We didn't hang out together or anything, and we never said more than hi and bye at our lockers. But he did drive me home every day, and with all those nosy kids at that school, I wouldn't be surprised if someone told Adonna about it. That's the way they are.

"I don't know about this, Babe," Kenny says. "That boy is playing games with you and Adonna, and I don't want you . . . I know what he had you doing and —"

"Kenny." I sigh. "You don't have to worry about me, not when it comes to Nashawn. I mean, you're my father. I can't get into this with you anymore."

"Look, Babe," he says. "You know you can talk to me about anything."

"I know." But it's hard having this conversation with him. It's so embarrassing. "I know I *can* talk to you, Kenny, but I can't. I mean, I won't. Anyway, I talked to Renée already and she took me to the women's clinic, and Renée has a prescription for me when I need it, so —"

"*When* you need it?"

"Well, *if* I need it," I say, even though we both know I was right the first time. "Hey, when you were my age, you were doing it with Renée, right? So you have to let me figure out when I'm ready, and you can't expect me to tell you about it, because it's gonna be my personal business."

"I don't like this," Kenny says, grabbing me into a hug again.

"I know, I know," I tell him, trying to enjoy this hug as much as the first one even though this time it kinda feels like he's locking me in his arms and planning to never let me go.

But he does let go. Finally. I guess his stomach takes over, because he hands me twenty dollars and tells me to go get two plates from Ms. Jenkins before she sells out. "And don't let Ms. Grier try and talk you into buying nothing from her."

I make a face.

"And bring me back my change."

"Yeah, right," I say. I never gave him back change in my whole life.

Fifteen minutes later, we're sitting up front eating. He's in the driver's seat and I'm in the passenger's seat, and we been taking turns getting up and going to the window whenever somebody comes to buy something. But, really, the food is so good I'm hoping people would stop coming for a few minutes, at least 'til I'm finished the peach cobbler.

Finally, I work up the nerve to ask him, "Where's Adonna? I didn't see her once today." And I been looking, too.

Kenny shakes his head. "I don't want you girls fighting and messing up everybody's block party."

He knows where she is. "I didn't say I was gonna fight with her."

He's looking over at me, trying to figure me out. "I don't

287

know where she is, but she's probably over there behind Building C, watching them stupid boys play basketball."

I should have known that.

I stay with Kenny for most of the block party, but I go in and outta the truck and try to have some fun, too. Then, when the sun is going down and things are kinda wrapping up, I tell Kenny I'll see him tomorrow. But instead of going upstairs, I head straight for Building C before I can think too much about what I'm gonna do. Because the truth is, I don't really know what I'm doing.

And of course she's there, sitting on one of the benches next to Asia. The guys are on the basketball court, playing hard and sweating and looking good. Not that I'm checking them out or anything. It's just that I can see why she been back here all day.

I'm not sure if Adonna sees me or not. She's sitting there sharing a bag of sunflower seeds with Asia, but they're not talking. It's like they're together, but Adonna's alone at the same time. She looks nice, though. The weave is gone and her hair isn't all fancy. It's just combed back in a ponytail, kinda like mine. And yeah, she's wearing white shorts, but they're not all that short, at least not for her. The only thing sexy about her is her top, which is kinda tight and off the shoulders. But even that's more *cute* than anything else.

I walk real slow over to where she's sitting, and when I sit on the other side of her, she don't get up and move. And she don't punch me in the face again. So I'm taking this as a good sign. I just sit for a while, not saying anything because, really, what can I say to her?

It's Asia that talks first. She whispers to Adonna, "Oh, no, she *didn't*."

But all Adonna does is shrug her shoulders like she don't care. And she never looks away from the game.

Outta the corner of my eye, I watch her watching the guys, and I can see she's paying a lot more attention to one guy that's tall and cute but not Nashawn-cute. I never saw him before, so he must not be from Bronxwood. But he does kinda stand out from the other guys. Plus the fact that he's wearing probably, like, three-hundred-dollar sneakers don't hurt him none, at least when it comes to Adonna.

Then I look across from the basketball court to the playground that me and Adonna always used to play in when we were little. We weren't supposed to go across the street by ourselves, but the swings behind our building were always broken, and over here they had the biggest and best jungle gym in Bronxwood. So we used to sneak over here all the time and, for some reason, when we got here it always felt like we were far away from home. Like we were on our own or something.

Well, until Nana would come around here and bust us. She always had the worst timing, too. She would show up right when we were having the most fun and make me come home with her. It was so embarrassing, not so much in front of Adonna but in front of all the other kids that would be out here with us. Like everybody else could play all day, wherever they wanted, but not me.

The basketball bounces outta bounds a foot away from where we're sitting. Asia jumps up and grabs it before any of the guys can get it, and she runs away from the bench, laughing, trying to keep any of them from getting it back. She's teasing them, flirting like crazy, and I wonder which guy she has her eye on.

Next to me, Adonna calls out, "Don't give it to them, Asia!" And she's laughing, too.

Even I'm smiling.

The guys surround Asia and she looks like she's having the best time, with everybody's attention on her. I could never be that comfortable around guys like that. That's why I'm lucky to be with Nashawn. I don't have to go through all those games.

But since me and Adonna are sitting together, and we're by ourselves, I figure it's my chance to say something. So I take a deep breath, one loud enough for her to hear, and say, "I was looking for you all day."

Adonna don't even react. She sits there quiet, still watching Asia and the guys. And for a while I'm not sure she heard me, even though I'm sitting right next to her.

So I wait for her to say something, and really, it's kinda hard to breathe. I mean, she can't just *not* talk to me. She wouldn't be like that. At least I hope not.

Finally, she turns to look at me, and I can only stand to look in her eyes for a second because she's so hurt and so mad, and I'm the reason for it.

"What you did was fucked up, Kendra," she says, keeping her voice down. "I would never do something like that to you, and you know that."

"I know," I say. "You're right."

"And don't think you're gonna sit here and I'm gonna forgive you. Because you can forget that."

"I'm sorry," I say, looking her in the eye again. "I'm really sorry. But I didn't set out to —"

She shakes her head. "That's not enough."

"I know. But you can't be mad at me forever. I'm still your best friend. Right?"

Adonna looks away from me again, but under her breath she says, "Probably." And that's a big relief. "But," she adds, "I'm not ready to be friends again."

"Okay," I say, and I can understand that. I mean, this isn't like those fights we used to have when we were little. And we had some good ones, too. But no matter what, about an hour or two later, Kenny would make us say sorry and that's all we needed to go back to playing together.

So I sit there for a while longer. The guys get their ball back, but instead of going back to their game, they get into a slam-dunk contest, probably because they lost one of their players. He's over in the corner of the playground talking to Asia, who's leaning up against the fence trying to look cute.

"I'm gonna be here all weekend," I tell Adonna a couple of minutes later. "Okay?"

"Whatever," she says, and I know she's gonna make this as hard as possible for me. But, okay, I deserve it.

Just as I'm about to get up and leave, I see Nana coming across the playground and it's like I'm having a flashback or something because I know this can't be happening *now*. "Babe!" she calls out loud enough for all the guys to hear. "Babe, come out from behind this building. It's getting dark."

My mouth flies open, I'm so embarrassed. But next to me, Adonna busts out laughing, just like she always does, and me and her look at each other for a second. And I know what she's thinking because I'm thinking the same thing — that this is crazy. That nothing's ever gonna change.

I shake my head and give up without a fight. "Yes, Nana," I say, in that voice that always cracks Adonna up.

And it works. She's still laughing as I walk away. And, actually, so am I.

I mean, really, what else can I do?

Coe Booth started writing "novels" in second grade, then digressed, working with teens and families in crisis in the Bronx and as a writing consultant for the New York City Housing Department. After receiving an MFA in creative writing from The New School, she finished *Tyrell*. She was born in the Bronx and still lives there. For more, check out www.coebooth.com.